"A great storyteller."
—*Maine Sunday Telegram*

"Hard to put down . . . a deceptively simple jigsaw puzzle with seemingly unrelated pieces that fit beautifully together in the end."
—TheCelebrityCafe.com

"A well-written series [that] captures the spirit of the region perfectly."
—BookBitch.com

"Fascinating . . . wonderfully perceptive prose . . . highly recommended."
—HSMB.com

"Solid entertainment with a definite sense of setting and way of life."
—BlogCritics.org

"Lead a cheer for Archer Mayor and his ability not only to understand human relationships but to convey them to his readers."
—*Washington Sunday Times*

"Mayor's major strength is his ability to etch personalities in their settings so that they are as vivid as a video."
—*St. Petersburg Times*

Other books by Archer Mayor

PRAISE FOR
THE SECOND MOUSE
AND ARCHER MAYOR

more...

"Fascinating . . . a well-written mystery . . . Mayor uses words as one familiar with their power."
—**BookLoons.com**

"Mayor is a gifted writer with a straightforward, accessible style . . . From first to last, his novels are page-turners, and each page resonates with the author's authority . . . His storytelling talents and his sheer craftsmanship combine to make his Joe Gunther books hard to put down."
—*Tampa Tribune*

"Archer Mayor is one of today's most reliable—and most underappreciated—crime writers. His low-key police procedurals, which utilize their off-the-beaten-track setting to great advantage, are always entertaining, and his protagonist and iconoclastic supporting cast are unfailingly good company."
—*San Diego Union-Tribune*

"Mayor keeps getting better with age . . . Few writers deliver such well-rounded novels of such consistently high quality."
—*Arizona Daily Star*

"Mayor's strength lies in his dedication to the old-fashioned puzzle, brought to a reasonable conclusion."
—*San Jose Mercury News*

ARCHER MAYOR

• THE

SECOND MOUSE

GRAND CENTRAL
PUBLISHING

NEW YORK   BOSTON

Copyright © 2006 by Archer Mayor
Excerpt from *Chat* copyright © 2007 by Archer Mayor
All rights reserved. Except as permitted under the U.S. Copyright Act of 1976, no part of this publication may be reproduced, distributed, or transmitted in any form or by any means, or stored in a database or retrieval system, without the prior written permission of the publisher.

Grand Central Publishing is a division of Hachette Book Group USA, Inc.

The Grand Central Publishing name and logo is a trademark of Hachette Book Group USA, Inc.

Cover design and art by Robert Santora

Grand Central Publishing
Hachette Book Group USA
237 Park Avenue
New York, NY 10017
Visit our Web site at www.HachetteBookGroupUSA.com

Printed in the United States of America

Originally published in hardcover by Mysterious Press
First Paperback Printing: October 2007

10 9 8 7 6 5 4 3 2 1

To my mother, Ana Mayor,
with love and thanks for giving a
tough job the appearance of effortless joy.

Acknowledgments

As always in the writing of these books, I begin in utter ignorance, dependent upon the kindness and knowledge of others to guide me with their expertise. However, while the following book was written thanks to them, whatever faults there may be remain mine alone. My deepest gratitude, therefore (and perhaps apologies), to all the following individuals and organizations:

Butch Watters
John Martin
Steve Shapiro
Peter Barton
Miles Powers
Camillo Grande
Gary Forrest
Neal Boucher
Suzanne Webb
Richard Gauthier
Sally Mattson
Castle Freeman
Pam Tedesco

Paco Aumand
Mike Mayor
Steve Adams
Francis Morrissey
Joe Parks
John Leigh
Dave Stanton
Karen Mellinger
Jon Peters
Stu Hurd
Kathryn Tolbert
Julie Lavorgna

Dartmouth-Hitchcock Medical Center
Office of the Chief Medical Examiner–Vermont
Bennington Co., Vermont, Sheriff's Dept.
The Town of Bennington, Vermont
The Bennington, Vermont, Police Dept.

The early bird may get the worm,
but the second mouse gets the cheese.

—Anonymous

(As passed along to me by Elizabeth Scout Mayor)

Chapter 1

"Watch out for the cat."

Joe Gunther froze by the door, his hand on the knob, as if expecting the creature to materialize from thin air.

The young Vermont state trooper stationed on the porch looked apologetic. "I don't know if we're supposed to let it out."

Gunther pushed the door open a couple of inches, watching in vain for any movement by his feet.

Encouraged, he crossed the threshold quickly and shut himself in, immediately encircled by the room's strong odor of cat feces, wafting in the summer warmth.

"I vote for letting it out," he murmured softly.

He was standing in one corner of a cavernous multi-windowed room—almost the entire ground floor of a converted nineteenth-century schoolhouse located some five miles south of Wilmington. Contesting the smell, sunlight poured in through a bank of open windows, nurturing a solid ranking of potted and hanging plants. Old but well-loved furniture, none of it expensive and most of it bulky, did a convincing job of filling the expanse with a selection of oasislike islands—a grouping around the woodstove, another in a far corner flanked by floor-to-ceiling bookshelves, a third before a blank TV set. The most distant wall was dominated by an awkwardly linear kitchen—a parade of icebox, range, dishwasher, sink, and counter space. Gunther imagined any truly inspired cook here needing running shoes and patience, or a gift for organization. Giving the place a hint of old Africa—or what he knew of it from the movies—were several still ceiling fans with brass housings and long, dark wooden blades.

The pine floor was covered with a hodgepodge of worn, nondescript rugs, which in turn bore several small gifts from the missing feline. That detail aside, the entire space looked homey, rambling, a little threadbare, and quietly welcoming.

The house was also imbued with the silence that only death can visit on a place—a sense of suspended animation, striking and odd, as when a stadium full of people simultaneously holds its breath.

This stillness was why Joe was here.

At the far end of the row of windows, a shadow appeared in a narrow doorway.

"Joe?"

Gunther nodded. "Hey, Doug. Good to see you." Watching where he placed his feet, he approached his state police counterpart, Doug Matthews, the detective assigned to this region. Younger by several years, but a veteran like Joe, Matthews was experienced, low-key, and easygoing. Unlike many cops, he kept his opinions to himself, did the job, and maintained a low profile. To Joe, in a state with only a thousand full-time officers—an oversize family compared with some places—such self-effacement was highly valued.

Joe stuck his hand out as he drew near. "How've you been?"

"Pretty good," Doug replied, accepting the handshake with a smile, his eyes remaining watchful. "Better than some. Come on in. I'll introduce you."

They entered a much smaller room, tacked onto the building later in life and on the cheap. It didn't have the bearing of its mother ship—the windows were cramped and few, the plywood floor covered with thin wall-to-wall carpeting. Low-ceilinged and dim, it was paneled in fake oak, chipped and cracked.

But the furniture, also battered and old, was of the same ilk as its brethren, supplying a comforting familiarity. The dresser, the heavy desk, and the solid four-poster bed were of dark hardwood, and the dents and scars appearing on them spoke not of neglect but of simple domestic history, the passage of generations.

This feeling of simmering life was echoed by the postcards and photographs adorning the walls and horizontal surfaces. Some inexpensively framed, others merely attached by tape or thumbtack, these pictures displayed vacation spots or loved ones, sun-drenched or laughing, and gave to the room, along with its furnishings, a warmth and intimacy it lacked utterly in its bare bones.

Lying across the broad bed, as if she'd been sitting on its edge in a moment of contemplation before falling back in repose, was an attractive dead woman.

Matthews kept to his word about the promised formalities. "Joe Gunther," he said, "Michelle Fisher."

Joe nodded silently in her direction, and Matthews, knowing the older man's habits, kept quiet, letting him get his bearings.

Dead bodies don't usually present themselves as

they're portrayed in the movies or on TV. In the older shows, they look like live actors with their eyes shut; in the modern, forensically sensitive dramas, it's just the opposite—corpses are covered with enough wounds or artificial pallor to make Frankenstein swoon.

The truth is more elusive. And more poignant. In his decades as a police officer, Joe had gazed upon hundreds of bodies—the young, the old, the frail, and the strong. What he'd discovered, blandly enough, was that the only trait they shared was stillness. They displayed all the variety that they had in life, but in none of the same ways. In silent pantomime of their former selves, instead of quiet or talkative, gloomy or upbeat, they were now mottled or ghostly white, bloated or emaciated, transfixed into grimace or peaceful as if sleeping. Nevertheless, for those willing to watch and study, the dead, as if trying to slip free of their muted condition, still seemed capable of a kind of frozen, extraordinarily subtle form of sign language.

That limited communication worked both ways. Everyone Joe knew, including himself, began their interviews with the deceased by simply staring at them searchingly, awaiting a signal. He asked himself sometimes how many of the dead might have struggled fruitlessly to be heard in life, only to be scrutinized too late by total strangers anxious to see or hear even the slightest twitch or murmur.

So it was that Joe now watched Michelle Fisher, wondering who she'd been and what she might be able to tell him.

In fact, she was one of the rare ones who did look merely asleep, if unnaturally pale. She was dressed in a short, thin robe, untied at the middle and draped open to reveal her underwear. Her feet weren't quite touching the floor, and her hands, palms up, lay relaxed by her sides. There was a suggestive intimacy in the pose—she could just as easily have been awaiting the attentions of a lover as yielding to exhaustion at the end of a long day.

She was pretty, barely middle-aged, on the short side, with shoulder-length blond hair. Not thin, but in no way overweight, and from the little she was wearing, Joe imagined she was a woman who paid attention both to her appearance and to what she wanted her intimate companions to discover. Peeking out from the edges of her expensive bra and bikini underwear were two delicately rendered tattoos.

"She live alone?" he asked, not expecting what he then heard.

"Yup," Doug answered him. "She didn't used to, but from what I was told, her longtime boyfriend died seven months ago, and there's been nobody since."

Joe continued watching her. So it probably had been exhaustion, and the underwear a mere talisman of joys past.

"Who's your source?"

"Mom." Doug glanced at his pad. "Adele Redding. Lives in Massachusetts. Had a ritual of calling her daughter every morning over coffee, especially since the boyfriend's death. When Michelle didn't answer this morning, Mom called a nearby friend, who found her like this and called us."

"Door was unlocked?"

"Yeah. And all but one light out." He pointed to the night table lamp, still burning palely in the sunlight. "That one. The friend said the door was never locked."

Joe didn't respond at first, pondering the suggested

scenario that Michelle Fisher had died last night as she was getting ready for bed.

"What's the deal with the cat, then?"

Doug gave him a blank look.

"There's a litter box by the ki   oor, but the droppings are laid out as if shat on the   .. Doesn't seem like normal behavior."

"The friend might know," Doug offered. But there was a slight drop to his voice, as if Joe's last observation had been taken as a criticism.

Gunther pursed his lips, overlooking or ignoring the change for the moment. "You have cats?" he finally asked.

"Dogs."

Gunther nodded, wondering if fright might have caused the anomaly.

He took his eyes off the woman and looked around the room. "What've you got so far?"

"I haven't been here long," Doug told him cautiously. "There's an AA pamphlet on the desk in the corner, some recent bank statements that show she didn't have a hundred bucks."

"You find a lot of empties?"

Matthews shared his own surprise at that. "No. A couple of beer bottles in the kitchen, but they look old to me. They have dust on 'em and they're dry inside. I wondered about that."

Joe had begun circling the room, looking at the snapshots and postcards. He saw the same woman, animated, laughing, keeping company with pets, children, what were probably friends and family, and, time and again, a stocky man wearing a beard and friendly blue eyes.

"That the boyfriend?" he asked.

Doug shrugged. "I guess."

This time Joe acknowledged his colleague's affected coolness. He faced him squarely. "What's up?"

The other man looked slightly embarrassed. "Don't take this wrong, but I was wondering why you're here. This could be a natural, like a bad liver. Or even an overdose."

Gunther couldn't resist laughing softly, mostly at himself. They were both employees of the state, both cops, but from different outfits, and Doug's question ran straight to that divide.

Joe was VBI—Vermont Bureau of Investigation. Exclusively a major-crimes unit, it was made up of the best investigators culled from every agency in the state. A recent creation of the governor and the legislature, it had come into being both to give proven talent a place to go, regardless of departmental origin, and to provide the citizens with a truly elite team of skilled professionals.

Doug was VSP—Vermont State Police. Even more complicated, he was BCI, which, in this alphabet-happy environment, meant Bureau of Criminal Investigation. In the recent old days, *they* had been the state's major-crimes unit, made up solely of deserving troopers. Now, while still detectives, they'd been restricted in both duties and geographical reach, assigned to specific regions. On paper and on the street, despite the positive spin the politicians had given this change—and the logic it represented—it was still being seen as a huge black eye for the VSP.

Ironically and unsurprisingly, most of Joe's VBI— he was, in fact, its number two man, the field force commander—was made up of ex-BCI members. Nevertheless, a residual sense of loss and resentment lingered, if less among old-timers like Doug, who in his heart was actually grateful for the diminution of responsibility, if not the loss of prestige. Retirement was looming for him, and he was just as happy to go home on time every night, free of the drudgery and bureaucratic scrutiny that accompanied high-profile cases.

"I'm sorry, Doug," Joe apologized. "Dumb on my part. Not to worry. I'm relaxed either way. I knew you were tight on manpower, heard the call on the radio, and happened to be driving nearby. Consider me backup. But it's totally up to you, including throwing me out. No bones from me."

Doug took the statement at face value, as he'd learned he could from this man. Joe Gunther was a law enforcement legend in Vermont. A one-time Brattleboro cop, he'd cracked more big cases than any five other people combined, all without becoming an egomaniac. If anything, he was the opposite, ducking the limelight, quick to give credit to others, a major team player.

In fact, the only criticism Doug had ever heard about Gunther was that he was a bit of a Boy Scout. Not self-righteous in any way, but not one to kid around or carouse or hang out with other cops socially. A loner. And a bull-dog with a case.

Nice guy, though. Doug therefore hadn't really been bent out of shape—more just in need of clarification.

"No, no," he assured him. "Don't get me wrong. I was just wondering. You people don't usually show up until later, is all." He waved a hand at the messy desk and dresser and offered appeasingly, "Why don't we just go through all this stuff while we wait for the ME, and see what we find? Could be there's a smoking gun."

There wasn't. They pawed through every document and belonging they could find. After the ME came and had the body shipped to Burlington for autopsy, they expanded their search to the whole house, including the upstairs, which they found totally empty, as if the place were actually a movie set where only certain scenes were to be filmed.

They found no signs of violence, of disturbance, or of anything amiss. Just the home of a single woman who'd been found unexpectedly dead in her bedroom.

And they didn't find the cat. Despite all the open windows, every screen was tightly in place.

They did manage, however, to expand on Doug's limited biography of the dead woman. As so often in his career, Joe had been gratified and impressed by how much there was to learn from a person's possessions and surroundings. Especially one like this, who turned out to be quite a pack rat.

Michelle Fisher, born to an alcoholic, unwed mother and a father she'd never met, in Fall River, Massachusetts, forty-three years earlier, had once been married to an abusive man, with whom she'd had two children, a son and a daughter. The first of these had died of an overdose five years ago. The second had dealt with Mom by severing all ties and moving to California.

That had merely been Michelle's "productive" marriage—the only one resulting in offspring. She'd also been married to three other men, although not to the one who'd predeceased her earlier in the year. Tax forms, legal documents, medical records, financial statements, reams of correspondence, and no fewer than three volumes of old, no longer maintained diaries all told of a life of turmoil, rootlessness, and long stretches of unemployment, depression, and alcoholism.

They learned of a woman who loved hard and completely, who gave her heart unhesitatingly and without thought, who was the best friend y   ever have and clearly not much of a friend to herself. She loved kids, animals, men, and beer. She liked the wind in her face, shouting to be heard above a loud band, and eating with her fingers at roadside barbecues.

It turned out that the ex-schoolhouse was owned by Newell Morgan, father of Archie Morgan, the man of the beard and blue eyes, and Michelle's last companion, who'd died of a heart attack, no doubt brought on by sharing some of her enthusiasms.

Archie had been the local high school custodian and was not in a position to own a house like this. It seemed Newell had made a provisional gift of the place to his son, in exchange for Archie's functioning as a live-in caretaker who also did carpentry.

Clearly, however, that deal hadn't extended to Michelle. Joe found an eviction notice, signed by a judge five months earlier, bundled with a sheaf of increasingly angry letters, informing her that she had until two weeks from today to vacate the premises.

That notwithstanding, the one thing they hadn't found in all their poking about was packed bags, or empty cardboard boxes, or any other indicators that such a move was being contemplated.

A showdown had been brewing.

Three hours after his arrival, Joe settled on the living room couch—having made some effort to clean up the cat deposits, and therefore the air—and flipped open his notepad as Doug sat in an armchair opposite. Compared to some of the settings both men had worked in, this was unrivaled for serenity and comfort. What remained to be done in the short term was some follow-up digging while they awaited the autopsy results. For the ME, in large part, would dictate who got the case.

In the meantime, both men were treating it as a homicide.

"This is a funny one," Joe began vaguely, referring to the unattended death, and still sensitive to his unofficial presence.

"They all are a little bit," Doug only half agreed. "I haven't done one yet that didn't have a few questions we could never answer."

Joe didn't argue the point. "True, but this one will have a bunch of them if all the ME finds is liver failure."

Matthews pushed out his lips in contemplation. "I could still live with it. What's bugging you most?"

"How convenient it is. Newell Morgan loses his son and wants the house back; the girlfriend digs her heels in; the girlfriend dies. Pretty handy."

"She was no health nut," Doug countered.

Joe stared at the floor for a few moments. "True," he admitted.

Matthews waited patiently, expecting something more.

"What I would like to know," Joe finally said, "is what happened to the cat."

Doug laughed briefly, impressed by the older man's persistence. "Maybe it was an indoor-outdoor cat. Or maybe it found a way out."

"How?"

"I noticed a torn screen by the back door, near the garbage cans off the kitchen," Doug said patiently. "It wasn't much of a hole, but I've seen cats go through less. And we don't know how big it was. You gotta figure, with its owner dead, it must've freaked. That's why it shit all over the place, and why it's gone now. You know cats."

In fact, Joe doubted if many people truly knew cats. He supposed that was part of their appeal. But he'd recognized the tone in Doug's voice, and let the matter drop.

"You talk to the mother?"

"Yeah." Doug didn't sound too happy about it. "Kind of unavoidable, given that she raised the alarm, but I hate breaking the news to family members on the phone. She was pretty good, though. No hysterics."

"And the friend who discovered her?"

"Linda Rubinstein. She's an artist. I met her face-to-face, since she stuck around until I got here. Told me she didn't touch anything, that she could tell Michelle was dead right off."

"How? Most people can't."

"I wondered the same thing. She's only an artist nowadays. She used to be an ER nurse in the city. Gave it up to find her muse." He laughed.

"Is that you or her?" Joe asked.

Doug laughed. "The muse thing? Hey, I've got some artist in me. You should read my affidavits."

"Oh, great," Joe joined him. "I bet that goes over well. How did Rubinstein strike you?"

"Like, did she strangle the woman before calling us?"

"Stranger things have happened."

Matthews shook his head. "You should meet her. You wouldn't go there. Come to think of it, maybe you should—meet her, that is."

Joe raised his eyebrows. "Oh?"

The other man shrugged. "Purely in the interests of efficiency. If this case goes to you guys, you'll do it anyway. She's just down the road. Save you a step later; won't cost you anything now. Win-win either way."

Joe stared at him, the rationale being so unlikely, even

from a team player like Matthews. Doug eventually caved in and allowed an embarrassed smile. "All right, so word's out you and your girlfriend split up. Rubinstein's single and good-looking. You can shoot me now."

Joe couldn't not laugh, although there was little humor in him about the truth of all that. He *had* been linked to a woman named Gail Zigman for almost twenty years, and the relationship had ended, at least romantically, just lately. The laughter was real enough, though, because while he'd been on the receiving end of the bad news— Gail had been the one to call it off—that it was such common knowledge was pure Vermont. It reminded him of what a wizened uncle had once said about the whole place being the only family with its own state flag.

"All right," he said appeasingly. "I'll talk to her. You going to handle Newell?"

"Unless you object."

"This is your gig, Doug. I wouldn't have minded if you'd asked me to leave as soon as I walked in this morning."

"Never crossed my mind," Doug said candidly. "Okay, I'll take Newell; you take the neighbor. I'll give you the mom's contact information, too, in case you want to follow up with her. And that'll be that till Doc Hillstrom kicks in with her autopsy."

Both men rose to their feet. Matthews scribbled down what he had on the women and handed it over to Gunther.

"By the way," Joe asked, pocketing the slip of the paper, "where's Newell hang his hat?"

"Bennington."

Chapter 2

Nancy Martin ducked out of sight as the oncoming car's headlights swept across the windshield. She even cupped the cigarette in her hand, although she knew that the driver wouldn't see its red glow as he drove by. He was probably too plastered anyhow, she thought sourly. This time of night, only cops and drunks were traveling Bennington's streets.

And people like us.

"God almighty," she murmured, her nerves jumping. "What the hell'm I doing here?" She paused, leaned forward over the steering wheel, craning to see any sign of life in or near the gloomy hulk of a building outside. "And what the hell's taking them so long?"

Inside, Ellis Robbinson was wondering the same thing. Sweating in total darkness, brushed by cobwebs and smeared with dirt, he was breathing through his mouth, praying he wouldn't be heard by the watchman standing just on the other side of the utility alcove's thin panel door.

Footsteps shuffled a few yards down the corridor, and

Ellis heard the distinct snap of a cigarette lighter flaring to life. That was something he could do with right now— a cigarette would ease things a lot, if only temporarily. The pseudo door, a sheet of luan hinged in place by layers of duct tape, allowed the seductive aroma of burning tobacco to drift in.

The large, sweat-drenched man jammed tight against Ellis shifted slightly, as if he, too, were responding to the smoke. The sole of one of his shoes scraped on the floor ever so slightly.

Ellis froze, straining for a reaction from beyond their stuffy, unexpected, providential hiding place. God damn Mel. He felt like slamming him in the ribs, just to make the point. Except that even Ellis, so prone to careless impulse, knew that now would not be the time.

Still, Mel was why Ellis was stuck here, scared and pouring sweat, hiding in the middle of the night on the top floor of a National Guard armory. The one place in town, except maybe a bank or the frigging police department, where getting caught would put you in the worst hurt of a lifetime. And for what? Stealing something Mel had hidden years ago as a janitor and which he refused to identify, claiming that it would be one of their best "tricks" ever. Ellis already knew the surprise revelation wouldn't justify the risk they were taking—any more than it did with any of Mel's other crazy ideas.

He was such an asshole.

Ellis heard the watchman finally move on, oblivious to their presence.

"That was cool," Mel whispered.

Slowly, fearful of jarring the slightest object, Ellis raised his hand and wiped his glistening face with an open palm.

Jesus.

Mel eased the panel back on its flimsy hinges and stepped back into the corridor they'd been creeping along when first surprised by the watchman. The place smelled of Sheetrock dust and damp joint compound. The top floor of the armory was being remodeled, allowing, from appearances, for some updated wiring and new computer hookups. Which explained their hiding place: a triangular nook wedged under the staircase to the attic, otherwise jammed with metal racks, a spaghetti-like tangle of cables, and two servers with beady green glow lights that reminded Ellis of malevolent robots. Not that he hadn't been grateful for their company—the unfinished closet had afforded them their only harbor when the watchman had suddenly come clomping up the stairs.

"Fifteen minutes, tops, before he comes back," Mel whispered confidently, already moving up the last flight of steps to the attic. He added, "Assuming he doesn't have someplace to sack out."

Ellis rolled his eyes. With their luck, that would wind up being right under the window they'd used to break in.

There was a sealed metal door facing the top step. Mel pulled a thin, flexible putty knife from his pocket.

"Give me some light."

Ellis took out a small flashlight and held it steady on the door's lock.

"Move it over a little . . . so I can see into the gap."

Mel positioned the blade in between the jamb and the door and began working to push back the lock's spring bolt.

Minutes passed. Ellis kept thinking he could hear the watchman returning.

"Hurry up," he urged.

Mel straightened, momentarily abandoning his work. Ellis's heart sank at the all-too-familiar reaction.

"What did you say?" Mel asked, looking down at him from the top step.

Ellis closed his eyes briefly. "I'm nervous," he explained. "Give me a break."

"You give me a break, numbnuts. And don't tell me what to do."

"Okay, okay. I'm sorry."

"Don't do it again."

"I won't," Ellis pleaded. "I promise."

Mel seemed to consider that, weighing its value. "All right," he finally conceded, and bent back to his task.

But it wasn't going to work, not with one blade alone.

"You got a knife?" Mel finally asked.

Ellis felt as if he'd been standing there for hours. He fought back his initial one-word reaction, substituting instead "No."

Mel grunted. "Me neither."

"Maybe we should leave it. Come back another night," Ellis suggested.

Mel gave him that look again. "Look around, dipwad. What's it look like they're doing here?"

Clearly, he expected an answer.

"Remodeling," Ellis answered tiredly, unsure if being caught right now might not be preferable to this tiresome song and dance.

"Right. And what did I tell you might happen because of that?"

"They might find what you hid?"

"Very good. You still wanna come back later?"

Ellis almost answered truthfully, especially since he

had no idea what they were after, and was beginning to care less.

But he didn't—as usual. "No."

"Give me your belt," Mel said suddenly, looking down at Ellis's waist.

"What?"

"Your belt buckle. That'll probably work."

Suddenly hopeful himself, if for totally different reasons, Ellis went along, tucking the flashlight under his damp chin and struggling to free the belt.

Mel grabbed it and went back to jimmying the lock. In a couple of minutes, there was a click, just as—for real this time—Ellis heard the watchman returning.

Both men eased open the attic door and stepped inside, closing it behind them with a snap that seemed like a hammer blow.

Whereas the closet below had been hot, this place was a cauldron—a holding tank for the summer's daily heat. Ellis went back to breathing through his mouth, this time to keep from passing out. He barely heard the heavy footsteps pass below without pause.

"Okay," Mel said eventually. "It's over here, I think. Shine the light."

"You think?" Ellis asked, his eyes stinging with sweat.

Mel turned around, grabbed Ellis's right hand, and twisted it up painfully until Ellis was squinting into the glare of his own flashlight.

"What is it with you?" Mel demanded.

"Nothing. It just sounded like you weren't too sure."

"What the hell do you think? It's been years since I stashed this shit. Nobody missed it then and nobody's missed it since, but that doesn't mean it hasn't grown feet, right? I mean, what the fuck do I know?"

Ellis carefully didn't answer.

"You got a problem?" Mel persisted.

"No, no. It's cool. It was no big deal. I just . . . I guess the guard threw me off, is all."

Mel shook his head. "Damn. What a chickenshit." He took the light from Ellis's hand and headed off to a far corner of the immense attic, picking his way among piles of cardboard boxes, stacked crates, and assorted dust-covered debris. To give Mel some credit, there were signs of recent activity—holes drilled in the floor next to boxes of coiled computer cable and a scattering of tools.

Ellis wiped his face with his sleeve and followed as best he could, picking his way after the flashlight's erratic halo, hoping he wouldn't stumble over something or bang his head against the low, sloping roof trusses that period-ically leaped from the gloom like swinging baseball bats. As was so common in the midst of one of Mel's adven-tures, Ellis began wondering how and why he got into these messes.

Which was no mystery. It was Nancy. Had been ever since she'd joined them.

Suddenly, the light vanished altogether behind a half wall of junk. Ellis stopped to hear the sounds of some-thing like a heavy tarp being pulled away and Mel softly exclaiming, "I'll be damned."

"You got it?" Ellis asked, unable to hide his surprise. Despite his anxiety, he couldn't deny a growing curiosity about seeing whatever grail it was that had lured them this far.

"No shit, I got it. Right where I left it. These guys're a joke, for Christ's sake—fuckin' military. I can see why they mess up all the time—can't find their butts with both hands."

Slowly, gingerly, virtually blind, Ellis eased himself around until he saw the light again, this time dancing across the surface of a dark wooden box shaped like a miniature coffin, complete with rope handles at each end.

"What is it?"

The pale orb of Mel's face swung toward him, making Ellis instantly rue his own question. "You are such a dope. Can't you read?"

He flashed the light across the box once more. Ellis saw a bunch of words and numbers stenciled on its surface, "M-16" most noticeable among them.

"Holy shit," he said. "Guns?"

Mel laughed shortly. "Grab one end."

Ellis hesitated. "Why not just take 'em out?"

"Gee," Mel reacted caustically. "What a great idea. Why didn't I think of that? Hand me the crowbar and we'll get right to it."

There was a telling pause as Ellis filled in the blanks—that there was no crowbar for good reason, that had they brought one, the noise of using it might've woken up the neighbors, to say nothing of alerting any watchman. Without comment, he took hold of a rope handle, weighed down once again by the proof of his own plodding thought process.

Mel couldn't not drive it home. "That's it, Einstein. Do what you do best. Lift."

Clumsily, adjusting to the unbalanced load, they hung the box between them and began making their way as quietly as possible through the tangle they'd just traveled. For all the disagreements they shared, they worked well together, as they'd been doing for years, allowing for each other's timing and gait like a couple of old dancers.

At the attic door, Mel, in the lead, paused and listened for the watchman through a two-inch crack.

"Hear anything?" Ellis whispered.

Mel looked over his shoulder. "Yeah—you."

Ellis sighed. They went back more than ten years, from when he'd met Mel in an Albany drunk tank. There was nothing likeable about the man. He was a dismissive, belittling bully who routinely blamed his errors on others while taking credit for every success, deserved or not. But he had charisma, at least for Ellis, who wasn't in that holding cell because of a single bender. He was a full-time drunk back then, a down-and-out ex-biker, and Mel's offer of a place to stay in nearby Bennington had seemed like a hand up.

Which, in a perverse way, it had been. They didn't share the same trailer anymore, not since Nancy moved in four years ago, but Bennington had become home. Ellis had gotten his drinking under partial control, was renting a cheap place at the Willow Brook housing project, and worked legitimately, if part-time, more often than not.

Normalcy like that hadn't been his in a long time, and he owed it, initially at least, to Mel—even if his covert feelings for Nancy were the only reason now that he hadn't moved on.

Because that was the irony of his situation. While Mel had once been his salvation, Ellis knew that staying with him would eventually be his ruin. But he couldn't leave, because of his love for the other man's wife.

"Okay," Mel told him, tugging at the box. "Let's go."

The relative coolness outside the attic hit Ellis's damp body like a blast of air-conditioning. They were in Vermont, after all—not famous for hot weather—and the summer heat struck people here as snow does the average Houstonian.

They worked their way down to the hallway and silently approached the top of the main stairwell, both of them craning to hear the watchman's by-now-familiar tread.

But there was nothing.

Giving Ellis a sharp nod of the head, Mel started down the stairs. This was the point of no return, as Ellis saw it—if their nemesis appeared now, they'd have nowhere to hide, and not only would they be caught red-handed inside a government facility, but they'd be carrying stolen guns as well. Of all the various awkward positions Mel had put them in over the years, this had to be an award winner.

Outside, Nancy had run out of cigarettes, which meant she would soon run out of courage. She twisted around in the driver's seat, looking for Mel and Ellis, looking for the cops, looking for a way out that wouldn't get her in trouble with Mel later.

She hated this part—the waiting. She was always stuck here. The wheel man, Mel called her, as if he were Machine Gun Kelly. Except that most of the time, all he did was eventually saunter up to the car with Ellis in tow, after Nancy had gone almost nuts, with a bag of stolen goods or his pockets full of till money, and tell her to head home, as if he'd just gotten out of the movies.

He didn't need a wheel man. He needed a cab. And she needed to stop doing this. She was seriously beginning to lose her taste for it.

Mel and Ellis reached the second-floor landing, still to tomblike silence. Ellis noticed that even the sounds of the surrounding town were muted. It was too quiet, as if all the world had taken cover, knowing that something catastrophic was looming.

Still in the lead, Mel held up his hand and lowered the box in slow motion, with Ellis following suit. It touched the floor with a tiny bump. Ellis straightened, holding his breath, confused, watching his companion's back as Mel quietly positioned himself at the corner where the wall met the staircase leading down. Only then did Ellis hear the tired footfall he'd come to dread. As the watchman entered the stairwell below, the echo of his approach reverberated off the walls and ceiling. Ellis expected Mel to order a retreat again and began looking around for a place to hide.

Instead, Mel stayed put, waiting.

That wasn't good. Mel was no pacifist. He never shied from a brawl. But it had always been his rule to bring no violence to an operation. There was less resentment all around, he said, if all you did was steal the money.

On the other hand, he wasn't stealing money this time, and Ellis suddenly realized that all bets were off. The thought chilled him—was Mel about to expand how they appeared on the law enforcement radar scope? By association alone, was Ellis soon to become a serious felon? For a wild moment, quickly if regretfully overruled, Ellis was seized by the impulse to push the broad back before him, counting his losses before they became overwhelming, by sending Mel straight into the arms of their oblivious stalker.

Instead, he waited, rooted in place, and witnessed just the reverse. As the guard reached the top step, Mel swung his leg out, low and hard, and caught the man's left shin with his instep, causing him to pivot off balance and tumble headlong back down the stairs in a thunderous, rolling clatter.

Abandoning Ellis, Mel ran after his victim, jumping two steps at a time to keep up, and arrived at the bottom almost simultaneously. There, as Ellis watched, he crouched by the inert body, his fist raised to finish the job.

He needn't have worried. The body lay limp as a corpse. Slowly, Mel lowered his hand and rested his fingers against the watchman's carotid pulse. A few seconds later, clearly satisfied, he rose, rejoined Ellis at double time, and said in a normal voice, "Move it. We're wasting time."

Ellis didn't move. "You kill him?"

Mel had taken hold of the box's other end. "No, I didn't kill him. He's just out. C'mon. Grab on. We gotta go."

Reluctantly, Ellis obeyed, following Mel down the stairs and past the motionless guard, noticing the slight but regular movement of the latter's chest.

"Jesus, Mel," he murmured, so softly not even his intended listener overheard.

To the left of the ground-floor landing was a short hallway leading to an enormous two-story basketball court / meeting hall combination, complete with National Guard flags and banners, ghostly in its gloomy silence. If ever there was a moment for all the lights to come on and a phalanx of armed and angry soldiers to materialize from nowhere, this was it for Ellis.

But nothing happened. To cover their tracks, Mel paused to lock the window he'd jimmied earlier to get them in, and then gently pushed the panic bar on the metal door beside it to bring them out onto a small steel-mesh loading dock. There, a short flight of steps led to the parking lot that circled the armory like an asphalt doughnut.

Mel did this fluidly, without pause, leading Ellis in ten seconds to where they ended up crouching in the shadows beside a parked car.

"You okay?" Mel asked, surprising Ellis, who couldn't recall when or if he'd ever displayed such concern.

"Yeah," he stammered. "Good."

"Then move your butt. You're draggin'."

Mel rose, fast for a big man, and jogged across the lot, with Ellis doing his best to keep up. At the far end, parked under the trees and facing the street, were Nancy and the pickup.

They tossed the box into the truck and piled into the cab as Nancy keyed the ignition and began pulling out, waiting to turn on the lights until she had reached the road.

"Cool and easy, babe," Mel warned her. "Cool and easy."

Chapter 3

It wasn't until a few days later that Joe Gunther visited Linda Rubinstein. After he left Doug Matthews at the Michelle Fisher house outside Wilmington—or the house where Fisher had chosen to die, as her disgruntled landlord and pseudo father-in-law would probably have put it—it was late, and he hadn't seen any lights on at the address Matthews had given him.

He remained officially uninvolved—there was still no reason to think Fisher's death wasn't natural, especially since the ME's report remained pending. But he felt compelled by curiosity to pursue what angles he had available. Doug had left the metaphorical door open, after all. It could even be argued that by reinterviewing Rubinstein, Joe was merely acting on his colleague's veiled request.

Matthews had summed up Rubinstein as a transplanted urbanite and ex-RN who had given up the rat race to concentrate on her art, whatever that was. As a result, Joe had initially expected her address to be either a new house or a yuppified remodeling job, complete with slate roof and shingle siding. Thanks to his initial drive-by, however, he already knew to expect something far less predictable. The place where he now stopped was a true dump—sagging porch, iffy metal roof, peeling clapboards. There was even the "Vermont planter" of lore—a discarded car, half enveloped by the weedy front lawn.

It seemed that Rubinstein was either inattentive to her surroundings, flat broke, or both, unless this was the latest in negative chic.

He got out of his car, cautiously approached the porch steps and the front door beyond, and knocked, to an instant response of deep barks from within.

These were quelled by a short one-word command, just before the door swung back to reveal a tall, slim woman dressed in jeans and a soiled T-shirt, accompanied by a very large dog of confusing lineage.

"Hey," the woman said, with a wide smile.

The greeting alone set her up as an outsider.

"Hey, yourself," he answered, going along. The dog sat placidly by her side, waiting for direction. "I was wondering if I could talk to you about Michelle Fisher." He stuck his hand out. "My name's Joe Gunther. I'm with the police."

She shook his hand, her face more serious, if only slightly. Joe imagined that she had either gotten over the worst of her shock at Michelle's death or had only been a friendly acquaintance to begin with.

"You didn't talk with the other cop?"

Joe nodded. "He's the one who told me about you. Don't worry. I'm not here to make you go through the whole thing again. I just wanted to know if anything else had occurred to you."

She pointed to a dangerous-looking wicker armchair on the porch. "Sit?"

He chose the marginally more solid porch railing as she turned and addressed the dog. "You want in or out?"

The animal considered his options before turning around and vanishing into the darkness.

Rubinstein took the chair she'd offered Joe, looking at him carefully as she settled down.

"Does this mean you think something happened to Michelle?" she asked.

He shrugged. "Not necessarily, but it makes sense to ask."

"You get the ME report back yet?"

He laughed. "That's right. Doug said you used to be a nurse. Where was that?"

"New York," she told him. "Feels like a million years ago. We used to see a lot of you guys in the ER, poking around."

Her tone remained light, so he took her words at face value. "Yeah—always best to strike while the iron's hot. Is that the kind of work you did? ER?"

"Mostly," she admitted. "It finally got to me. Plus, it was time for a change."

Joe sensed volumes more hovering just beyond sight. Without thinking, but feeling the pain of a kindred spirit, he risked admitting, "Yeah—I know what that's like."

"You haven't always been a cop?" she asked reasonably.

His face colored slightly. In fact, he'd been a cop all his professional life, which was starting to mean something. But that wasn't what he'd meant. He thought back to how he'd laughed when Matthews mentioned his breakup with Gail, and how the woman before him might be worth visiting as a result.

The thought deepened his embarrassment. Was he here

because of that? He'd rationalized that he'd merely wanted to ask her about Michelle, but now he wasn't so sure.

"Oh, yeah," he said. "I guess I have at that."

Rubinstein looked at him quizzically. She was very attractive, wearing her years well. He guessed she might be close to fifty but had clearly stayed trim and fit. The New York connection was an interesting coincidence, since that was where Gail had come from originally, although the two women looked nothing alike. Their manner was similar, though—self-confident and assured. They both presented themselves as people who'd cut their own paths in life.

"Nothing new has occurred to me, by the way," she said, interrupting his daydreaming.

"What?"

"About Michelle."

He rubbed his face with his hand, pulling himself back on track. "Right. Sorry. You'd known her for how long?"

"A couple of years. We just kind of hit it off, and I really liked Archie. A truly sweet man. So after he died, it was pretty natural she and I got closer. She was a wreck."

"Took the loss hard?" he asked.

Her face hardened, throwing him off. He thought it might be because his question had sounded stupid. But her answer told otherwise.

"I guess everyone does that, don't they? Dance around certain questions without spitting them out. What do you want to know?"

Joe thought fast, wondering what nerve he'd struck. Falling back on the possible similarities between this woman and Gail, he decided to address her the same way. Directly.

"Michelle was an alcoholic," he said. "I was wondering if that's where she went for solace."

"You think she drank herself to death?" The tone bordered on accusatory.

"There weren't any signs of it. That's why I'm asking."

She was clearly surprised by his comeback. "I thought . . . How did you know, then?"

"We dug around," he said vaguely, just now sensing what might have set her off. "All part of the job." He paused and then took a stab at it. "I found an AA brochure on her desk. That come from you?"

There was no answer at first. On the face of it, his question could have been innocence itself. But by now they both were reading between the lines. And as it turned out, correctly.

"Yeah."

"That must've been hard on you, seeing her react that way."

She laughed bitterly. "Hard? Most natural thing in the world for some of us."

He didn't say anything, leaving an opening.

She sighed heavily and then metaphorically walked through, altering all his initial impressions. "It killed me. I've been sober five years. Fought my way back tooth and nail. Quit my job, left the city, got in shape. I don't have a dime left, which explains this place, but I've started to live again. The first day I met Michelle, I knew she was a drinker—she and Archie both. You just know. At first I was really scared. They weren't on the program. Hanging out with them might've been the end of me. But they'd figured something out. Somehow, they'd turned their love for each other into an antidote or a shield. I mean, they were clueless. They didn't know what they were doing, but it was working. I sometimes wished I could wrap up what they had and bring it back to AA."

She paused to shake her head mournfully. "And then he died. I couldn't believe it. It was the cruelest thing I'd ever seen, which is saying something."

She looked up at him suddenly. "They say drunks are the most narcissistic people you'll meet. You ever hear that?"

He couldn't say he had. "No."

"Well, there's something to it," she persisted. "In the middle of Michelle's crisis, as she was falling apart in front of my eyes, I thought maybe the whole thing was a test of me—that God was taunting me for my arrogance."

"How did you react?" Joe asked.

"Not well," she admitted. "Not initially. I let her hang. I saw what was happening and I ran. Like she was on fire and I was made of gasoline. It was one of the most shameful moments of my life."

"Were you all she had?" he asked, remembering not just the photographs on Michelle's bedroom wall, but how Rubinstein had been brought to his attention in the first place, through mention of Adele Redding.

The first touch of her old smile returned, albeit wistfully. "No, lucky for her. Her mother, Adele, helped us both get back on track. She called her every day after Archie's death, or called me if she didn't get an answer or didn't like what she heard." She laughed. "I hated that woman at first, forcing me to get involved, but she saved us both . . . Or at least I thought she had, until I found Michelle."

Joe returned to the impression he'd first had of Linda Rubinstein, of self-confidence personified.

"How are you doing now?"

"Better," she answered, nodding as if to double-check. "Maybe Michelle's death is kind of a relief for both of us. And then maybe it's because I've got Adele to think about now. Life just has a way of steaming on, reducing all our problems to size."

"Adele?" Joe asked, taken off guard.

Rubinstein laughed again, seemingly totally recovered. "Yeah. Now I'm the one who calls her every day. Isn't that screwy?"

Joe wasn't about to argue with her, not based on that evidence. Instead, he shifted the conversation slightly. "I hear relations between Michelle and Archie's father weren't as friendly."

That erased the smile quickly. "That son of a bitch. There's the guy who deserved what both of them got."

"The bad die last?" he queried.

"I don't know about that, but he's alive and they're not, and he did his level best to belittle his son when he was alive and make Michelle's life a living hell afterward."

"He must be a happy man now," Joe suggested.

"If there is a God," she answered bitterly, "he'll burn that house down just to teach the bastard a lesson."

"You ever meet him?"

"Newell?" She pursed her lips. "No, which is probably a good thing. As far as I know, he did all his torturing long-distance."

"We found eviction notices," Joe mentioned leadingly.

"Yeah." She dragged out the word. "Michelle said she'd force him to throw her out bodily. Sad part is, that's exactly what would have happened. She didn't have a leg to stand on."

"Did she have any plans? She sure hadn't packed her bags."

Linda Rubinstein tilted her head back and stared at the porch's ceiling. "God help me, I'd offered to move her in here."

"Really?"

"Yup. Adele was ready to help me by paying a little rent, from what resource, I don't know. She's on welfare as it is. We were going to give it a shot, anyhow."

Joe mulled that over, fully aware of how dynamics like what she'd just outlined could go horribly wrong.

"I know what you're thinking," she said. "A really bad idea. The way I looked at it, though, that's all the poor woman had done her whole life—make the wrong choices. And yet they'd worked out in the end, kind of. So maybe we'd get lucky. It was worth a try."

Joe looked at the floor for a moment, gathering his thoughts. "It's always worth that," he agreed. "Do you have any idea what Archie's father wants to do with the place?"

"Sell it, as far as I know," she answered. "It was only an asset to him, nothing sentimental."

"And yet he let his son use it."

Rubinstein made a face. "And charged him rent, and used him as a free Mister Fix-It, and whined about what a loss he was taking. Archie and Michelle always said there was no way they could've had such a nice place without the old man. Maybe, but I never thought it was worth it. Not with the baggage he threw in."

"How anxious was Newell to get Michelle out?"

She hesitated before answering, eyeing him carefully. "That's a loaded question, isn't it?"

He hitched a shoulder. "Not intentionally."

She laughed shortly, reminding him of the New Yorker

in her again. "Don't bullshit me. You're asking if he might've killed her."

He decided to deal with that straight on. "I'm asking if he was angry enough—and, from what you know of him, capable of it."

"You know something you're not telling me."

She was a good poker player, egging him on to show his cards. Sadly, he had nothing to hold back. "Don't I wish. I didn't bore you with the details, Ms. Rubinstein, but technically, I belong to a major-crimes unit, and this case is so low-profile I'm not even supposed to be connected to it. I happened to be in the neighborhood when the first cop you talked to caught the assignment, and I dropped by out of curiosity."

That didn't move her. "You're here now," she said knowingly.

Now it was his turn to play her. "I'm here now because the other guy thought you and I might hit it off. He's feeling sorry for me because my girlfriend and I broke up."

Her face went bright red. "Oh."

He laughed. "Sorry, but you walked into that. I'm not sorry he did it, by the way."

Happily, she joined him. "Thank you. Joe, right? I'll make sure to give you a call when I'm back in the market." She made a show of fanning her face, cooling it off. "Okay, you win. No, I didn't get the feeling that Newell was homicidal about wanting his house back. Just greedy, insensitive, and pissed off. And as for being capable of it, I have no idea. I never met the man and only heard about him through the two of them. But to me he sounded like a bitch-and-moaner—someone to make my own mother envious. Which also means, I guess," she added, raising her eyebrows, "that you can never tell when a guy like that finally gets enough and snaps—like in one of those road rage situations."

Joe nodded and rose to his feet. "True. Well, never hurts to ask." He moved toward the steps. "By the way, she had a cat, didn't she?"

"Yes. Georgia. She named her after Georgia O'Keeffe. You looking for a home for her?"

He shook his head. "I wish I was. She's gone missing."

Rubinstein frowned. "That's too bad. She was such a homebody, too. I'll keep an eye out for her."

Joe leaned in her direction and stuck out his hand again. She got out of her chair to take it in her own, smiling.

"It was nice meeting you, Joe. Tell the other guy he has a good eye," she said.

"Heard you went poaching the other day. Not nice, Saint Joe."

Gunther shot his colleague an inquisitive glance. He and Willy Kunkle, a member of his small regional VBI squad, were tucked away in their second-floor office in Brattleboro's creaky, drafty, eccentrically designed Municipal Building—a throwback to the 1800s—once a high school, and architecturally never more than an assemblage of forced-together puzzle pieces. The police department, the town offices, the historical society, and other odds and ends, including VBI and the low-watt community TV station, were all thrown together in a seemingly random pile.

"How do you mean?" Joe asked.

Willy leaned back in his chair and planted a foot against the edge of his desk. The desk was wedged into a corner, making access to the chair difficult—an elegant and loaded metaphor for its owner's personality.

Willy smiled. "Ooh, so coy. What's the VBI golden rule?" He dropped his voice to intone, " 'We will not serve where we're not invited'?" He laughed before revealing, "You went poking into that natural outside Wilmington on your own. Matthews called this morning."

"I was nearby when it came in," Joe told him, hearing how lame it sounded. "I told him to throw me out if I wasn't wanted. Was he complaining?"

Kunkle burst out laughing. "Right. Like some wannabe is going to bitch about Vermont's very own Dick Tracy. Not likely. No, he was sweetness and light personified."

As so often in these conversations, Gunther was struck by Kunkle's ability to spice up sarcasm with biting insight. In Matthews's place, per law enforcement's confusingly pseudomilitary self-image, Joe would also have been hard put to uninvite a senior officer. That said, there were times when he wished Willy would stop juggling extremes and either straighten out and play to his strengths, or screw up badly enough to defeat all protection and get fired.

And protection was something Joe knew a little about, for it was he, time and again, who had been Willy's sole guardian angel, arguing that he should be kept on the job when virtually everyone else wanted him gone—a paradox that even an otherwise pretty straitlaced Joe was hard put to explain. There was just something indefinably worthy about Willy, as both cop and human being, that Gunther missed whenever the man earned his occasional trips behind the woodshed.

They'd all almost lost him once. He received a sniper

bullet in the left shoulder years ago while on a case, a wound that had permanently disabled his arm. The winner of an Americans with Disabilities Act lawsuit—another Gunther suggestion—Willy had resumed his post, passing a modified police academy physical, and now used his withered limb as an intimidating prop to his already forceful personality.

Joe bypassed Kunkle's point and went to what had stimulated it in the first place. "What did Matthews say? He hear back from the ME?"

"He was sending you an e-mail. I love it when people phone to say stuff like that. Kind of defeats the purpose."

Joe was sitting before his computer, writing notes from his interview of Linda Rubinstein. He punched up his electronic mailbox. As promised, there was a message from Doug Matthews.

"Anything good?" Willy asked after a few minutes.

Gunther looked up over his reading glasses, his expression at once thoughtful and dour. "He's calling it a natural."

"Based on the ME?"

"Yeah." The word came out slowly.

"You got a problem with that?" Willy asked.

His boss was equivocal. "Not exactly. Questions."

This was pure music to Kunkle, who thrived on complications. "Like what?"

Joe referred to the preliminary autopsy report that Matthews had attached to his e-mail. "According to this," he reported, "we have a relatively young woman. She drinks; she smokes; she probably does some drugs now and then. She's had her kicks over the years. And now she's dead—no signs of violence, no recent romantic entanglements gone sour, and no lingering diseases. Her lungs are a little junky, her liver could stand a reprieve, and her body chemistry ain't what it used to be, but there's nothing lethal anywhere. She looks like she just keeled over. The ME's ruling undetermined, with nothing suspicious."

"Meaning she died of a little of this and a little of that," Willy restated. "We've had those before."

"Yeah. But not with a father-in-law/landlord standing in the wings who wanted her out after his son's recent death so he could get the property back."

Willy raised his eyebrows.

Joe continued, "The old man had served her eviction orders. As far as we know, she hadn't responded."

"So he knocked her off," his colleague concluded, as if finding that perfectly reasonable.

Joe thought back to Rubinstein's assessment. "That's the way the movies would have it."

"No," Willy countered. "That would be reality—you don't like somebody, you kill 'em. The movies would come up with a pile of crap that made no sense at all. You talk to the guy?"

Gunther shook his head and reached for the phone. "That was Doug's job. Like you said, the golden rule. I was playing support."

"That why you're dialing now?"

Joe laughed. "So it's pushy support. Sue me." He punched in Doug's extension after the state police answering machine came on.

"Detective Sergeant Matthews."

"Hey, Doug. It's Joe Gunther."

The other man's voice perked up. "Hi, you get that e-mail?"

"I'm looking right at it."

"Guess if it looks like a duck, it's a duck, right?"

"Well," Joe hedged, "it does look like a duck, true enough. I visited Linda Rubinstein today."

He could almost feel Matthews leaning into the phone, his pleasure obvious. "What did you think? Attractive, huh?"

"And interesting. She got me thinking about the father/son dynamics with Fisher's dead boyfriend. Did you ever get hold of Newell Morgan?"

Doug's voice dropped a notch. This was not the direction he'd anticipated. "I tried. Didn't get anywhere. I talked to somebody on the phone over there. His wife, I guess. He's supposedly out of town for a few days."

"You going to chase him down?"

"I suppose, just to get it done. It's not super high on my list anymore, not after that ME report. You have a problem with that?"

"More like a bug in my ear," Joe had to admit. "I'd love to get it gone."

"Be my guest."

Joe straightened in his chair, taken slightly off guard. Cops were traditionally more protective of their turf. "What do you mean?"

"That if you want to interview him, go ahead. Just copy me a report. I mean, I was going to do it. But if you're champing at the bit, feel free. Like I said from the get-go, if this does go somewhere, you'll end up with it anyhow, so it's a good deal for me if you want to poke into it early. You got a pen handy? I'll give you his phone number and address."

Joe took them both down, impressed by the man's affability and struck by his own ironic and miserly reaction to it: that Matthews was probably a slacker.

Maybe spending so much time with Kunkle wasn't such a good idea.

"You guys going to get together?" Matthews asked after he was done.

"What?" Joe asked, confused.

"You and Rubinstein. Remember, I get to be best man."

Gunther almost choked. "Right. I'll make sure you're the first to know."

He hung up just as another call came in. "Vermont Bureau of Investigation. Gunther."

A woman's voice let out a small laugh. "I still can't get used to that."

He laughed back, but recognizing the caller had stimulated a strong emotional jolt, especially on the heels of Matthews's parting line. "Hey, Gail. Yeah, you ought to try it from my end. I still feel like an impostor. How're you doing? This is a rare treat."

But not all that rare. If anyone had been keeping score, they'd have said Gail had ended their union, blaming the stresses generated by his job more than her own political ambitions. Of course, that was overly simplified. For one thing, the last "stressor" had involved a nutcase from out of state who'd tried to kill her to get at Joe. No small complaint. But whatever the causal agents, they had split up, and Joe had retreated to his work, to his woodshop at home, and into an unacknowledged emotional cocoon for which his farm-bred New England heritage had richly prepared him.

For that last reason, if for nothing else, all contacts between them since had originated from Gail.

"They gave us a break from a bunch of special hearings they're holding up here, so I thought I'd find out how you were doing."

She was a newly anointed state senator, and, as was typical with everything she took on, she was attacking it head-on. He knew for a fact that the meetings she mentioned were low-level affairs, usually skipped by the old-timers during the summer months, when most of Vermont's citizen legislators were scrambling to do the jobs they couldn't attend to during the half year the legislature was in session.

But, in addition to being hypermotivated by nature, Gail was also wealthy, not just by birth but via a long-abandoned, very successful career as a Realtor. She would make being a senator a year-round job, regardless of the low pay and other people's expectations.

"Not bad. Things are under control, if not exactly slow."

"Anything interesting?"

There was a time when he had regularly used her as a sounding board. "Not really. Crooks must be losing their creativity."

"How's your mom and Leo?"

Leo was his brother, who still lived with their mother on the farm they'd both been born on—a handy development for Joe, selfishly speaking, since the old lady now got around only in a wheelchair. "They're good. No colds or mishaps. She was asking after you a couple of weeks ago. You ought to give her a call. She'd love to hear from you."

There was a small hesitation at the other end. "I will. I hate to bother them."

"You don't, Gail. You never will."

Another pause. "Well, I can hear them getting restless behind me. I better get back. Take care of yourself, and give them my love."

"Will do. Take care."

The line died in his ear, and he slowly replaced the phone, reflecting on the irony of the two last calls coinciding—the ache of the past bumping into the giddiness of the future. But that giddiness belonged only to Matthews. Joe had enjoyed meeting Linda Rubinstein but had felt no urge to go further.

Across the room, Willy watched him over the top of a gun magazine he was pretending to read.

"Old ghosts?" he asked, not unsympathetically.

"Yeah," Joe answered, staring into middle space.

Chapter 4

It was stiflingly hot, the pickup had no air-conditioning, and they were moving slowly enough that the one thing circulating through the open windows was an ever-shifting cloud of bugs. As far as Ellis Robbinson was concerned, the only saving grace was that Nancy was sitting in the middle. He kept his eyes glued to the right, sightlessly watching the passing trees, but his mind was completely focused on the soft touch of her thigh and occasionally her breast as she jostled him every time her husband hit a root or pothole.

Nancy was clearly not as distracted. "Damn, Mel. Do we always have to drive so far out?" she asked, reaching to steady herself on the scarred and dented dashboard after one impressive lurch.

Mel would not be pushed out of the good mood he'd been in all morning. "Well," he answered, smiling broadly, "I considered asking the state police if their firing range was available, but then I figured, you know, if I do that, it would just be nag, nag, nag, all day long."

He laughed uproariously, and despite herself, so did Nancy. In truth, on days like today, he reminded her of the man she married—making love when they woke up, saying nice things about the breakfast she fixed, being civil to Ellis when they picked him up at his apartment, and generally keeping the abusive, hard-drinking bully she'd grown used to under wraps. These were the moments she wished she could bottle up and feed back to him when he turned dark again—even while she knew the remedy would always fall short.

They were driving through the steeply sloped woods northeast of Bennington, in the Green Mountain National Forest, along one of the barely visible roads used at various times of the year by poachers, game wardens, loggers, and recreational snowmobilers. These tracks wandered seemingly without purpose or direction, often ending after miles in a copse of trees or at the edge of a bog, or were sometimes simply reabsorbed by the wilderness if left too long without use. The one Mel had chosen, however, he traveled regularly to reach a rocky clearing in the middle of nowhere—his private retreat where he could shoot, drink, do drugs, or just get away from a world he didn't much like and did his best to combat.

The combativeness was a constant, and of late had acquired an additional edge, but as his wife had just been reflecting, the mood accompanying it was key, at least for anyone nearby. And on this occasion Mel's mood was up.

"There." He pointed through the bug-spattered windshield. "You can stop your whining. Now we'll have some fun."

The truck lumbered out of the woods and shuddered to a stop where, untold years ago, a rockslide had tumbled from the mountain above and settled in an oddly flat scattering of large boulders, prohibiting the growth of all but a few gnarly plants. With the forest all around and the blue sky above, these sparse green sprouts squeezing up through the rocks provided a view suggestive of the bottom of a dirty fish tank. In contrast to that wet and cooling image, though, this place was airless, hot, and dry.

Which enhanced Mel's sense of security, especially for what he now had in mind.

"All right," he said, throwing open the door and sliding out with a flourish, "let's hop to it. Nance, set up the targets. Ellis, get that shit out of the back."

Ellis, for his part, was also finding Mel's good humor infectious. In his element, in control, and in the company of those he considered his family—especially with a fun project in mind—Mel became the life of the party, one Ellis was happy to join.

Nancy took a garbage bag rattling with glass bottles and old cans—her husband's version of recycling—and lugged it across the broken field of rocks to a distant spot already littered with the shards of prior outings. Even wearing shorts and a tank top against the heat, she'd known to wear boots for the day, although they hurt and made her feet sweat. The shattered glass was already thick enough on the ground to make it slippery as well as blinding, reflecting the sun as it did in a thousand sparks. Slowly, squinting, as the men set up the guns, the ammo, and of course the beer, she placed her targets across the scarred, burning surface of the tumbled granite.

After Nancy returned, Mel gave her a kiss and a beer, pressing a can on Ellis also, which the latter didn't resist, and then broke out the two M-16s they'd stolen the night before and had spent the intervening hours cleaning and oiling. None of them had slept more than two hours, and that only because Mel had wanted to get his wife into bed.

There was laughter and an exchange of bad jokes, body checks, and false punches. Finally, Mel took first honors, looking, with his beard, large stomach, and bandy legs, like an oversize G.I. Joe doll constructed of rejected parts. He fired off the first air-splitting rounds, the shiny flickerings of spent brass shells flashing in the bright sun.

None of them wore ear protection, and the fully automatic gunfire filled the air, pierced their skulls, and stung their noses with its acrid smell. Nancy covered her ears with her hands until Mel handed her one of the rifles and insisted she give it a try. She did, tentatively at first, then with more comfort, and finally with abandon as she yielded to the gun's steady thud against her shoulder, and the fascination of watching the continuous spray of rock dust leaping from around the cluster of punctured and smashed targets. The pure power of the moment and its attendant destructiveness hit her like a tonic, and it was only reluctantly that she yielded the gun to Ellis while her husband kept firing with the other one.

But Ellis saw the look on her face, now glowing with sweat, and rather than take the weapon, he instructed her on how to hold it down by her hip, the butt tucked against her, so that she could spray the field in a cross burst, keeping the barrel steady with her left arm extended down forty-five degrees. As he gently positioned her hands, his back to Mel, he admired the tank top clinging to her body, took in the smell of her, and couldn't help but notice how her nipples reflected her excitement. It took all he had to merely step back and give her a nod rather than put his hands where his eyes had just been.

Again, she began, a few shots at a time, getting a feel for the recoil and the new stance. But then she settled in, becoming one with the gun's staccato rhythm, enjoying how it vibrated against her ribs and spread across her hips. Her husband's lovemaking this morning, even though desired, had been brutal and perfunctory, as usual. And, as usual, it had served mostly only to whet her appetite for more. She had no idea what effect shooting guns had on men—glancing over at Mel, she saw nothing like what she was experiencing—but she now knew its appeal for her, at least in this one instance.

They continued shooting for several hours, taking turns with the M-16s and firing a couple of pistols as well, until the beer and the ammunition were spent, the guns almost too hot to handle, and their ears numb and throbbing with the abuse. When silence finally fell, none of them had any appreciation of it. They lay on the rocks, soaked through, their hands tired and darkened with gunpowder, and themselves as dazed and glistening as fish brought to the surface by a grenade.

Mel was the worst off. He'd fired the most and consumed the most alcohol, ending the session by chasing the beer with whiskey. He'd acted out the day as he typically did, at full bore, without restraint, talking nonstop, laughing and swearing, his body language balanced on a perpetual knife edge between camaraderie and hostility. Even in this place of his own choosing, his humor always approached anger, his jabs and pokes falling just shy of punches. But now he was unconscious, deeply asleep in the sun, his mouth open and his eyes closed. For Ellis and Nancy, this was the moment they'd come to anticipate—when Mel's self-indulgence would once more do its near daily job of reducing him to a genuine nonthreat.

As slowly as dogs left too long in the sun, the two of them finally stirred, peeling themselves off the rocks and staggering toward the pickup parked under the trees.

There, their backs against the relative coolness of its metal side, they shared a bottle of lukewarm water from the toolbox behind the cab. Then Ellis, still holding the bottle and with a careful glance at the distant, audibly snoring Mel, said softly to Nancy, "Put your head back."

She, too, followed his gaze, intrigued, and smiled up at him, oddly stirred by how his tone of voice fed into the sensual mood that had been percolating within her all day. "What're you going to do?"

"You want to find out?"

In response she tilted her face up, her shoulder blades flat against the side of the truck's bed, her damp hair hanging loose over its edge. Her breasts rose and fell under the thin fabric of her tank top.

Slowly, Ellis upended the bottle, letting the water dribble onto her forehead. She shut her eyes and laughed softly as the liquid began trickling down her face and neck. Ellis increased the flow slightly, and the water spread to her upper chest and slipped under the tank top. Nancy blew some air through her mouth, causing a line of small bubbles to form at her lips.

Without a word, he stopped pouring the water and brushed those lips with his own, barely touching her. She smiled. They had kissed before, in a perfunctory social way, either following a congratulation or in celebration of a birthday. Not that it had been completely innocent, either. Separately, each had harbored the memory of such contacts and wondered what any kind of follow-up might be like.

But those exchanges had been either in public or before Mel. The two of them hadn't been slippery with sweat, half drunk, and in Nancy's case, thoroughly worked up by both her earlier sexual encounter with

Mel and the odd experience she'd just been through with that vibrating machine gun.

Ellis pulled back slightly, poured more water on her, and watched as it soaked her top.

At that, they reacted simultaneously. As she lifted her head off the truck's gunwale to kiss him fully and passionately, he slipped his free hand up inside her tank top and took her bare breast in his palm. She gasped at his touch and reached out for him, pulling him close and grinding up against him, her leg sliding up the outside of his thigh, and her foot hooking behind the back of his knee to bring him closer. Their hands skimmed across each other as if seeking cover, exploring, learning the topography. It was as if the only time they had available would be gone in a moment.

Which was exactly right.

Ellis broke off first, being the more cautious. Nancy had just slipped her hand down the front of his pants when he straightened and pulled back, his hand on her wrist, stunned and pleased by her eagerness but terrified of its consequences.

"Wait, wait," he panted, nervously looking over the hood of the truck at Mel's recumbent shape. "Not here."

"Where?" she asked, breathing like a runner. "I want to do this."

Though gratified, he wasn't surprised by her comment, even if he was by its timing. He knew of her background, after all, and of her particular appetites. That was in part what had fueled his own desire. He was already Mel's sidekick when they'd first met Nancy at a biker bar outside Albany. Both men had Harleys, criminal records, and generally poor attitudes, although only Mel really worked at the bad-boy stereotype. Mel would engage in the male

rituals that some of his brighter companions were beginning to see as old news, while Ellis headed straight into
the anesthesia of cheap beer, loud noise, and a fog of cigarette smoke.

Nancy took to Mel right away that night, responding to
his challenge of her date like a doe might to a dominant
stag. Ellis had almost laughed at the lack of subtlety, except that he, too, had been captivated by her youth, looks,
and open sexuality. It was with mixed emotions that he'd
seen his friend eventually translate this particular mating
encounter into a walk up to the altar.

Nancy followed Ellis's glance toward her husband,
who'd rolled slightly onto his side to face the other way.

"He might as well be dead. We could do it right here."
She rubbed the front of his fly with her open hand, kiss-
ing his neck as he averted his face, trying to think clearly.
"Shit, you're so big."

She suddenly unsnapped her shorts and tried unzip-
ping them before he stopped her.

"Wait, wait," he said. "He sleeps like that for hours,
right?"

She kissed him again. "Like a dead man."

"Then we can take him home and you can drive me to
my place. We've done that before."

Which they had, with him longing for exactly what
was about to unfold. In fact, it had been at such a recent
drop-off that she'd first told him of her unhappiness with
Mel, much to his private delight. Not that Ellis had been
surprised. The marriage's troubles had been clear for
quite a while.

It was all she needed to hear. She rebuttoned her
shorts. "Let's get him in the truck."

The whole trip back, Ellis worked to maintain the

mental fog he trusted to cloud his better judgment. He had practice at this—even considered himself an expert. The countless bars he could no longer recall, the times in Mel's company, as at the armory, when he'd known he should be elsewhere.

And Nancy did her best to undermine his failing self-preservation. As he drove toward Bennington on ever-improving roads, she undulated against him, slipped her hand up under his shirt, and kept trying either to kiss his neck or bite his ear as he halfheartedly fended her off.

Mel, in the meantime, stayed jammed into the cab's far corner, snoring, his legs sprawled.

Ellis had to admit that the presence of a man he knew would kill him for what he was thinking, much less what he hoped to be doing in thirty minutes, heightened the excitement to a nearly uncontainable intensity.

But it was a long trip, and it was harder getting Mel into the trailer than it had been hefting him into the truck. Inevitably, he woke up, at least enough to demand what the hell was going on; the enhanced meaning of his question wasn't lost on his companions. By the time they finally reached their goal, and Nancy, now at the wheel, pulled up beside Ellis's motorcycle at his apartment across town, they were sitting at opposite ends of the cab, each waiting for the other to pick up the pieces of their passion and see what was left.

Nancy killed the engine, put her hands between her thighs, and let out a deep breath, staring straight out the windshield.

"Fuck."

He laughed softly. "Right."

"What do you think?"

"Probably a bad idea."

She made a face but didn't turn her head. "Yeah." It was a sigh, tired and sad, and it touched him in the middle of his chest.

"It's not for lack of interest."

She looked at him. "You mean that?"

He caught her meaning. "Ever since me and Mel both met you in that bar, way back when."

She twisted in her seat, her face bright with a surprised smile. "You're shitting me."

"Nope. From the start. That can't be news. Every guy I know thinks of you like that."

She waved her hand dismissively, looking disappointed. "Oh, that stuff. I thought you meant something else."

But they both knew he did. He confirmed it a long pause later by admitting, "I was the unhappiest man there at your wedding."

She reached out and touched his hand briefly. "That's really sweet, Ellis. I don't guess I was too happy, either."

"You're just saying that now," he told her. "You were in seventh heaven."

She gazed down at her hands. He barely heard her say, "Yeah. I was."

There was silence as they thought back across the intervening years from different perspectives—Ellis reflecting how the lusty joy between new husband and wife had eroded to where Mel regularly dismissed it by word and deed, picking up women at bars almost every weekend; and Nancy ruing the death of her dream of kids, a house, and a life of security, paradoxically and illogically hinged on the wild man who'd won her heart.

Each was left wondering at the implications of such thoughts.

"You want to ask me in anyway?" she finally asked. "If only for a cup of coffee?"

He nodded and got out of the truck, digging for his front door keys as he approached one half of a gray, slightly worn building that represented his small part of a ninety-unit affordable-housing complex—a scattering of two-story wooden boxes.

He opened the door and stood back to let her in. In the few years that he'd lived here, after moving out of the trailer to make room for her, he'd never asked her in.

Glancing about in the twilight afforded by the drawn curtains, he was now embarrassed that he had.

"I'm sorry," he said as she entered. "It's a mess."

He closed the door and turned to find her not surveying the shabby view, but standing in the miniature entry hall, staring at him.

There, without another word, they moved into each other's arms.

The frenzy of an hour ago was gone, its explosiveness replaced by a deeper appreciation for what they'd enjoyed in one another for years but had never openly acknowledged—his tenderness and quiet consideration, her openness and honesty.

This time their hands moved slowly, their earlier eagerness for pure inventory yielding to the pleasure of time and temporary safety.

Stumbling slightly, they moved from the foyer to the small living room and then to the couch facing the blank-faced television, their clothes dropping along the way. By the time he helped her fall back naked against the cushions and nestled between her legs, he felt all his burdens slip free and believed himself to be the luckiest man he knew.

Chapter 5

Joe Gunther left Brattleboro with Sammie Martens by his side around midmorning, heading west on Route 9 over the southern tail of the Green Mountains, toward Bennington. By map it didn't come to much, maybe forty miles, but it did bridge the state from border to border and included some of Vermont's least heralded yet most tumultuous scenery, including a cluster of eleven wind turbines stabbed onto the top of Searsburg Mountain like a sampling of supersize whirligigs.

"This is near where your undetermined turned up, isn't it?" Sam asked, reflecting on a passing road sign near Wilmington, the journey's midpoint.

"Five miles down that road," he agreed.

Route 9's geography had long been of interest to Joe. It marked the upper east-west edge of a roughly ten-mile-wide corridor whose lower line of demarcation was the border with Massachusetts. Just north of them, deep in the Greens, were the ski resorts of Haystack and Mount Snow, and a string of tourist-centric towns sporting an often frail veneer of seductive, economy-impervious Vermont quaintness.

To the south, however, throughout that far less traveled swath where Michelle Fisher had lived, the area had a more curious and telling identity. Mountainous, weather whipped, thickly forested, and crisscrossed with twisting paths, trails, and roads—many unmarked—this dramatic and secluded section of the state kept aloof from its neighbors. Thinly populated and not easy to access, it was a hunter's heaven, a Realtor's dread, and a cop's nightmare. Emergency responses to the region took forever, to the point where routine law enforcement fell largely to a few marginally trained, locally elected constables.

Sam was evidently thinking along similar lines as they skirted the region's boundary. "God, I'm glad we didn't have to cover all this when we worked for the PD. I never envied the troopers this territory."

It was a salient point. She, Willy, and Joe had all once worked for the Brattleboro police, and half their turf had extended in this direction and had involved some remote stretches, although thankfully not quite this far.

The region resembled Vermont's famously quirky and isolationist Northeast Kingdom, in the corner where Canada meets New Hampshire. Unlike that area, however, it had no title or identity, no picturesque, flinty reputation. Aside from the Harriman Reservoir, attractive to fishermen and boaters, for the most part it remained a large and unknown place to contemplate from a moving car.

And therein was the telling symbolism that had triggered Gunther's musings to begin with. Given their target destination, it was less this particular countryside that he was considering, and more how it served as a no-man's-land between the rest of the state and that much overlooked town.

"You go to Bennington much?" he asked her, almost as a test.

She shook her head. "Never have much reason to. I don't know anyone who does," she added after a moment's reflection.

He smiled and nodded as if in confirmation. "Right."

Bennington was in Vermont's southwest pocket, shoved up against New York and Massachusetts, and while it did connect to its mother state via the Route 7 umbilicus heading north to Manchester and Rutland and finally Burlington far away—as well as Route 9 going east—it was, and always had been, isolated by the very Green Mountains that Joe was presently enjoying. It had forever been Bennington's burden to be considered, geographically and thus psychologically, more a part of its neighbors than of Vermont.

From the air, this became even clearer. Bennington's sprawl didn't loom into view until the last of the Greens gave way to the relatively flat farmlands of New York beyond. Only the token Mount Anthony in the town's southwest quadrant presented one last upheaval, and it remained largely undeveloped. By contrast, Brattleboro was so scattered across hilly ground that it could barely lay claim to a single flat acre.

Those weren't the only important differences between Vermont's two southern corner towns. Unintentionally, Sam had revealed an instinctive and time-honored common prejudice that had favored her home over Bennington for hundreds of years.

Brattleboro, after all, had the interstate and the Connecticut River—commercial conduits, new and old, that had all but guaranteed its label as the Gateway to Vermont— along with a solidly anchored middle-class population, while Bennington remained merely another ex–mill town to the west, host to several small industrial plants and a large medical center, forever regretting the erosion of its own middle class and the fates that had spurned it when Interstate 91 had been drawn elsewhere on the map in the 1950s.

Bennington County regarded itself as Vermont's black hole, and its populace instinctively looked inward to solve most of its own problems. This was an area of practical-minded, largely working-class people who didn't pay much heed to what was going on in a state they figured didn't have much time for them in the first place.

Sam suddenly laughed. "I heard somewhere that in the old days the Indians wouldn't bury their dead in Bennington because of the ill winds. Guess the place has always kind of sucked hind tit."

His mind having wandered already, Joe reacted only halfheartedly. "I like it. It stands on its own two feet."

She snorted. "Stands more in Mass and New York, from what I hear. And what's the deal with that weird bypass? Their politicians live and die by whether they support an interstate traffic circle that's supposed to go completely around the town? That is really bizarre."

Joe glanced at her. He wasn't about to argue the point one way or the other. For years almost uncountable, Bennington had, in fact, had a huge bypass on the books that would ease the pressure from the all-important intersection of Routes 9 and 7 in the heart of downtown. One side of the debate called it financial suicide; the other touted it as economic salvation. Only one leg of it had been completed thus far—a beautiful quarter circle running from New York State to Route 7 due north of Bennington, complete with sweeping panoramas of the valley and bordering mountains. But since it didn't accomplish the overall goal, most outsiders—and a few locals—were still hard pressed to figure out what it foretold.

Joe only knew, as apparently did Sam, that unless you held an opinion on the matter, you were clearly overlooking one of the area's touchstone topics.

Without comment, he returned his attention to the road, although he found his thoughts focusing neither on the scenery nor on the condition of Bennington's battered self-image.

It didn't take long for Sam to notice the change. "You all right, boss?" she eventually asked him. "You're kinda quiet."

He turned briefly to glance at her. "Sorry. A little distracted. Something about this case has gotten under my skin. Don't know why."

"She didn't seem old enough to die of natural causes," Sam ventured.

Joe burst out laughing. Sam was the youngest of his squad, and an interesting clash of boldness and hesitation, ambition and self-doubt, experience and naïveté, which her taste in men helped exemplify. Currently, and for the past couple of years, she'd been discreetly but determinedly involved with Willy Kunkle, a hookup that boggled Joe's mind, although he tried to show his support.

"Very diplomatically put, Sam. Nicely done," he finally said.

Sam was looking flustered. "I didn't mean *you* were at death's door . . ."

He waved her off. "I know, I know. I'm just pulling your leg—an old man's prerogative. That is part of it, actually—she *was* young in my book—so you're right.

But there's a whole element of pathos around this, plus a hint of something darker."

"Newell Morgan?" she asked, having already read the file.

Joe pursed his lips before responding. "The ME sees nothing wrong, Matthews is happy to move on, and nothing jumped out at me at the scene, so I'm hardly planting a flag in the ground here. But Morgan is definitely a man I want to look at eye to eye."

Gunther began the miles-long curving descent off the western slope of the mountains, his softly playing car radio losing contact with all signals to the east and picking up instead the latest news from around Albany. They passed through a couple of vague hamlets, mostly made of nondescript one-story homes and winterized trailers, before he finally made one last gentle turn—down on the flats at last—and abruptly entered Bennington's Main Street.

"You got that address?"

True to form, Sam didn't need to check. She rattled it off without hesitation.

Newell Morgan lived nearby, off Gage Street, somewhere shy of the historic red-brick downtown—a street referenced by local politicians when invoking the area's blue-collar bulwark. Joe, who knew Bennington well, took the first available right in pursuit of Gage.

It was an unremarkable neighborhood, neither old nor new, and not given to any style beyond functional. For all that, it was pleasantly shaded by trees, and each house seemed reasonably cared for. It was the sort of street that Gunther, long ago in his patrol beat days in Brattleboro, had traveled only to get from one part of town to another.

Not that everyone living in such a neighborhood was necessarily squeaky clean—such as, perhaps, Mr. Morgan. Unfortunately, the emphasis right now was on the "perhaps," since Joe's digging hadn't revealed much about the man.

Armed with a name and a birth date, most cops in Vermont could search a single widely shared database called Spillman and find out if the individual sought had been even peripherally involved in any shenanigans. It was an advantage most other states lacked, since the majority of departments nationwide, although computerized, worked with closed systems. There were so-called national data banks, like the famous NCIC, but your information had to qualify in order to be inserted, and Newell Morgan didn't reach that standard.

Which was the bad news, in terms of research—in Vermont, Morgan had surfaced in connection only with a few traffic stops, a check fraud case, and two neighbor disputes. He'd also been the complainant a half-dozen times in situations ranging from someone not cleaning up after their dog to a neighborhood teenager playing the radio too loudly. A pain in the ass, in other words, but not a Dillinger. As to what he might have done outside the state, nobody knew—and nobody would unless they could build a bigger case against him.

Gunther pulled up opposite the address Sam had recited, and waited while she radioed their arrival to dispatch. Over the few short years of the Bureau's existence, niceties such as office space, basic equipment, and communications had been slow and cumbersome in coming, if they came at all. A smoothly working radio system had been a recent arrival only, obviating the need to rely on either the state police or a cell phone system that both Vermont's topography and its cranky antitower regulations made spotty at best.

Not that Joe minded the deprivations as much as some. He got a perverse kick out of being considered among the profession's elite while simultaneously being underfunded and ignored. There was a puritanical element lurking there that helped him feel he could keep pridefulness at a safe arm's length.

"You want company?" Sam asked as he unlatched his door.

"Oh, you bet," he said, smiling to himself at her predictable politesse. "That's why you're here."

He had wanted her along as a witness and a possible sounding board later, but as their feet touched the lawn, he thought the additional role of backup might also come in handy. They hadn't advanced two yards before the house's front door banged open and a large man in a bulging T-shirt stepped out onto the porch with a querulous expression on his face.

"Who're you?" he asked.

Not for the first time in such situations, Joe was instantly grateful he hadn't asked Willy along. He pulled out his identification as he continued toward the porch steps.

"Joe Gunther. Vermont Bureau of Investigation. This is Agent Martens."

The man sneered. "Big surprise. You guys all drive the same cars."

Joe paused with his hand on the railing. "You Newell Morgan?"

"Yeah. What d'you want?"

"Talk about Michelle Fisher a bit."

"She's dead."

It was Joe's turn to smile. "Yeah." He dragged out the

word tellingly, allowing the ensuing silence between them to speak for him.

Morgan got the point. He scowled. "Oh, for Christ sake. Fucking woman'll never let me go." He turned on his heel and added wearily, "Come on in."

Joe climbed the steps and opened the screen door that Morgan had let slam behind him. He and Sam entered a freezing air-conditioned living room clearly decorated by a woman. Only a single La-Z-Boy planted before a flat-screen TV set of Olympian proportions and brilliant clarity had escaped her touch. Running soundlessly across its surface, pumping the air with one fist, was an overweight baseball player trailing a mane of greasy hair. The TV and chair made the scene appear farcically lopsided, the former's robotic sleekness and size making the room's array of 1950s china figurines crowding every flat surface look like refugees seeking a way out.

That wasn't the only contrast. The chair and the rug immediately surrounding it, unlike the rest of the truly pristine room, were borderline disgusting, stained and soiled by its occupant's haphazard eating habits. It seemed clear that a truce of sorts had been made in this house—she could rule, and clean, the roost, in exchange for his living like an old dog in one restricted corner.

Morgan half fell into his reclining throne and reached down to retrieve an opened beer can placed on the embattled rug, spilling part of its contents in the process. He stared at the muted screen without expression and took a noisy gulp from the can. He did not offer either of them a seat.

"I guess you two didn't get along," Joe suggested as Sam began walking slowly around the room, quietly taking inventory.

The fat man swiveled his head to look at him. "Fucking right we didn't. That little whore may've turned my idiot son's head, but she didn't fool me."

"How so?" Joe asked when nothing further was added.

"She was a leech. A freeloader. She saw him as a soft touch, and she milked him till he died."

"There didn't seem to be much to milk," Joe said mildly, sitting in a ladder-back chair near the wall.

"That's because I wouldn't let it happen," Morgan muttered, and went back to watching the game.

"Oh?"

He kept his eyes where they were. "I controlled the purse strings. Archie didn't know anything about money. She would've cleaned him out."

"I thought you said she did."

Morgan angrily hunched forward in his chair, fixing Joe with a glare. "I said she would have. I didn't let her. I can smell someone like her a mile off—a conniving little cock teaser. And my son was the perfect mark."

"How did they meet?" Joe asked, hoping to move him along.

"What do I know? She probably got him drunk and spread her legs. Archie was no rocket scientist. He went where you pointed him."

Joe scratched his head. "From what I've learned, they seemed pretty happy."

Morgan looked as if he were addressing a moron. "Well, of *course* they were happy. They had me to mooch off of, all the booze they could drink, and no responsibilities. What's not to be happy about?"

"They mooched how? The house?"

"Well, *yeah*."

Joe pretended to be confused. "But they paid you rent and made and paid for any renovations. I saw the bills."

Morgan was clearly stumped by that, if only for a couple of seconds. "That was nothing," he finally blurted. "It was the least they could do for my giving them a place to live. I could've sold that house for a small fortune instead of letting them run it down."

"What do you do for a living, Mr. Morgan?" Joe asked out of the blue.

"I'm on disability," Morgan said quickly. "The battery plant fucked me up and I can't work no more. How's that matter?"

"Just wondered," Joe said. "Does your wife still work?"

Morgan's face reddened. "Yeah, she works. Look, what're you busting my balls for? Why're you even here? Am I supposed to get a lawyer or somethin'?"

Joe's eyes widened. "A lawyer? What for? You feel like you need one?"

"No. That's not what I'm saying. It's just, all these stupid questions. I mean, who cares? The bitch is dead. There's nothing to talk about."

Except maybe how she got that way, Joe thought. "It must have been tough on you, after Archie died, having to deal with Michelle directly," he said instead.

"Trying to deal is more like it," he grumbled. "She just pretended I didn't exist." He suddenly put the beer down, as if to clear his mind. "Look. I tried being nice. I'm no shit bag. Whatever she was after at first, I knew she was up a creek after Archie died. So I told her she could stay an extra month before I threw her out. She ended up totally abusing that generosity, like I was some landlord she could fleece or something. I mean, damn"—here he pounded his fleshy knee with his fist—"I gave that woman the roof over her head. You'd think she could show some consideration."

Joe nodded. "You'd think. What reason did she give for staying put?"

"Oh, Christ. You know, 'I can't find a place,' 'I have no money,' 'I'm looking for a job.' All the usuals. She was just trying to see if she could ride me as easy as Archie."

All these allusions suddenly prompted Joe to ask, "Did she try anything sexual to convince you?"

Newell looked stunned for a moment. "Me? She's not my type. I'm a married man, besides. She would've known what I'd say."

But he hadn't actually answered, Joe thought, and the question still remained whether Newell had ever propositioned her. "She was a good-looking woman," he pressed.

The fat man allowed for half a concession. "If you like that type."

"When did you last see her?"

"I didn't. I mean, not lately. I'd call on the phone. Later I communicated through my lawyer."

"But when was the last time?"

Morgan put on a show of thinking hard. "Well, there was the funeral. I tried being nice then, like I said, dropping by to see how she was doin'. God, I don't know . . . maybe about four months ago."

"That would be after you served eviction papers on her, right?" Joe pretended to be scribbling something in his pad, unconcerned and purely conversational.

Morgan's face reddened, but he said nothing.

Joe looked up. "Isn't that right?"

"Yeah, I guess. That was just a legal thing, to show her I was serious."

"I heard you've been out of town for a few days."

"So?"

"Where'd you go?"

Joe expected some resistance, but Morgan immediately said, "New York—Frankfort. It's outside Utica. It was like a reunion with some buddies."

"You were there the whole time?"

The big man's eyes narrowed, and he stood up, looking down at Joe. "Yeah. What's that to you?"

Joe's response was mild, although he noticed that Sam had casually taken up a good place from which to throw a tackle if necessary. "This is a death investigation, Mr. Morgan. Pretty routine question."

"Bullshit, it is. You're thinking I had something to do with her dying. I heard she did herself in. You saying she was murdered?"

Joe put on a show of bewilderment. "Jeez Louise. You're starting to make me think this is something it's not. What's got you so worked up?"

"*You do,*" Morgan blustered. "I know who you are. The VBI is like major crimes. They only do murders and rapes and bank robberies and stuff like that. If Michelle drank herself to death, there'd be some deputy dog here, not you."

He was perfectly correct, which made Joe long for the recent past, when he'd routinely had to explain that the Bureau wasn't an enforcement arm of something like the restaurant sanitation division.

"The FBI does banks," he explained disingenuously. "And I'm just here covering for the state police."

Morgan rose and moved toward the window, as if giving himself room to escape. "Right. Real likely. That's why there're two of you."

Joe stood up at last, his face set and his voice harder. "Think what you will, Mr. Morgan. Can you prove you were in Frankfort?"

"You bet. I got six buddies to vouch for me, and if you think they're all in the bag, then I got a bunch of credit card receipts and shit like that to back me up. I wouldn't stick my neck out killing that fucking whore. No way she was worth it. What happened to her was just a matter of time anyhow. It wouldn't have been long before I got my house back. Besides, even if she hadn't died, she would've found some other sorry loser like my son to move in with."

Gunther took the pad he was holding, flipped to a fresh page, and handed it over. "Write the names, addresses, and phone numbers of the people you were with, as well as the names of any motels or restaurants you might have used."

Morgan held the pad in his hand, motionless. "Why do I have to jump through a bunch of hoops for you?"

Joe tilted his head slightly to one side. "You don't, which'll really start me wondering why you've gotten so cranked up over this. Do yourself a favor, Mr. Morgan. Cooperate."

Morgan did just that, moving over to a couch and hunching over the coffee table to laboriously scratch out his information. As Gunther glanced around the room, trying to gauge from its contents the lives it contained, his reluctant host chanted a muttered, half-intelligible but clearly vituperative recitation in frustrated protest.

Finally, he put his pen down, lunged to his feet, and thrust the pad back at Joe. "There, have fun wasting your time and pissing off my friends."

"Thanks," Joe said, pocketing it and moving toward the door, Sam silently in tow. He put his hand on its knob and then asked, "By the way, what's going to happen to the house now?"

"I'm going to sell it. See if I can at least break even."

Gunther laughed and headed out onto the porch. He knew how long Morgan had owned the place, how much he'd charged his son in the interim, and what the market would probably deliver in an upscale area like greater Wilmington. Morgan was going to make a killing—assuming he hadn't already done so.

"You have a good day, Newell. Enjoy what's left of the game."

They got back into the car, and Joe continued driving west into the center of town, rejoining Route 9, passing through the infamous intersection with Route 7, and going up the hill past the old Hemmings News gas station, the elaborate Catholic church, and the art museum, into what was called Old Bennington—the fancy historic part of town that had also once been its center before industry decreed that the mills and their workers gather on the banks of the river below.

"What was your take?" he asked Sam as he drove.

"I disagreed when he said he was no shit bag, but looking around, I didn't see anything that suggested he was another Ted Bundy. Just a slob. I hope his wife isn't there much."

"How 'bout his story?"

"I think you got him when you said he'd been to see her after filing the eviction papers. You have anything behind the theory that he put the moves on her and got turned down?"

"Not a shred."

He left Route 9 at the top of the hill and drove along a block suitably named Monument Avenue, lined with a series of old-time New England mansions, classic enough to have appeared in a daguerreotype. Just beyond it, opening up onto a gently rounded hilltop, was the site of the famous Bennington Battle monument, a three-hundred-foot-tall obelisk built in the 1880s and more an homage to local jingoism than to historical accuracy. In fact, the Revolutionary War battle so celebrated took place five miles away in New York State—Bennington and its alluring supply depot had been merely the goal of an ambitious British army.

Nevertheless, the area had become a graceful, peaceful, oddly sylvan spot from which to enjoy the low, rolling countryside around it, and Joe parked by the monument's side to give them a suitable setting for contemplation and, a little subversively, to enhance Sam's impression of the town.

"Still," he resumed, "assuming we ever get enough to officially take this case, I wouldn't mind canvassing Michelle's neighborhood with a picture of Newell and whatever vehicle he drives. I have a hard time believing that a guy like him could leave a woman like Michelle alone in her time of grief."

Sam groaned. "You're probably right. Gross. Maybe she did commit suicide."

Joe nodded wordlessly. Newell Morgan's personality hadn't come as a surprise. His findings at Michelle's house and his chat with Linda Rubinstein had prepared him for it. What did keep tugging at his mind were less obvious loose ends—details of pattern and cadence, of inflection and body language. From Michelle's posture on her bed to the recent bluster of her landlord, there had been subtle discordances. Not any of them alarming or even unusual, but all together forming a picture of incomplete parts. Joe was feeling like the only man on board a ship surrounded by calm water and fine weather, who was fighting the strong urge to seek cover.

"It does always end up going back there, doesn't it?" he asked almost rhetorically.

"Where?" Sam asked.

"The body," he said. "What, exactly, did her in?"

He reached for his cell phone and dialed Beverly Hillstrom, the chief medical examiner. They had long used each other as sounding boards over the years, forming a bond he was pretty sure she shared with no other cop, most of whom were stymied by her aloof and rigorous personality. He knew that side of her—he'd all but smacked into it on their very first meeting—but he'd soon discovered that couched behind it was a woman who merely demanded higher standards than the norm and showed her impatience with all who fell short. On that level alone, she'd quickly seen Gunther as a kindred spirit, even if his style was far from her own. In fact, to this day, in observance of her sense of propriety, they still referred to each other by title and always kept strictly to business.

"Doctor Hillstrom," he therefore started out once she answered the phone, "it's Joe Gunther."

"Agent Gunther," she said shortly.

Even given her normal manner, this was unusually brusque, and generally unheard of once she knew he was on the line. He made a note to stay strictly on the straight and narrow this time. She was clearly preoccupied.

"I'm sorry to interrupt," he continued, "but I'm wondering once again if you might indulge me for just a couple of minutes on a case."

"I wasn't aware VBI had sent us anyone recently."

He pursed his lips slightly. Her tone was bordering on

hostile. "We didn't. It came through the state police. Technically, in fact, it's still theirs, but it's got some questions attached that'll probably—"

He didn't get to finish.

"If it's still theirs, then you better have them make the contact. And make sure," she added pointedly, "that they follow proper protocol. This office does have a full-time police liaison. Things have begun to slip along those lines."

"Right, I promise I'll—"

But the phone had gone dead.

Gunther closed the cell and slipped it back onto his belt, feeling the warm breeze on his slightly reddened face through the car's open window.

The view he'd driven here to enjoy remained unappreciated. Fighting his own immediate disappointment and embarrassment, he stared sightlessly into the distance, struggling instead to see a connection, if any, between his last two conversations. Both of them had certainly been straightforward enough—Newell Morgan had clearly stated his dislike of Michelle, his lack of regret at her passing, and what seemed to be the makings of a solid alibi. And Beverly Hillstrom had responded to his request for a special favor with an official thumbs-down. Yet each exchange had contained undertones that made him wonder if what he'd heard had in fact been the whole truth. The trick was to discover if the timing and tone of both were coincidental, or if they were tied to the evolving mystery that had made Joe initiate them in the first place.

"That didn't sound good," Sam suggested, watching him closely.

He started the car. Morgan's background and alibi would take some footwork to check out. Hillstrom was a friend. For that reason alone, she merited his attention first. But he wasn't kidding himself, either—he now had frankly ulterior motives beyond mere friendship.

"It wasn't," he told Sam. "Looks like I better drop you off back in Bratt, pack a bag, and head up to Burlington. Something's up with Hillstrom, and it's gotten her all prickly. If I don't smooth it out somehow, we may never discover what else poor ol' Michelle Fisher has to tell us. And that, I'm starting to think," he added after a pause, "would be a real shame."

Chapter 6

"Under the B, twelve. That's B-twelve."

Nancy Martin scanned the eight paper cards spread before her, saw three spots numbered 12 under her assortment of B's, and hit them quickly with her bright pink dauber.

Mel glanced up at her from his place across the table, having perused his own four cards without success. He muttered, "Shit—wish I could figure a way to cheat at this." The woman beside him, with fifteen cards and a daubing hand as quick as a hummingbird, shot him a scandalized glance.

The caller at the head of the stuffy room held up another ball, extracted from the hopper by his side. "Under the I, twenty. That's I-twenty."

Nancy kept her eyes on her cards, hitting only one spot this time. She wasn't having much luck tonight, and she sure wasn't having any fun.

"*Bingo,*" Ellis shouted in a loud and startled voice, causing the quick-handed woman to groan under her breath. Nancy had to sympathize, despite her happiness at Ellis's success. He had but a single card centered before him.

"Hold your cards, ladies and gentlemen. Hold your cards," the caller droned, as one of the bingo hall attendants wormed her way through the crowd toward Ellis, who was now waving his paper card in the air so she could more easily reach it.

While the attendant read the winning numbers to the caller for confirmation, there was a muted chorus of rustled paper as everyone else in the hall ignored the caller's instructions by crumpling up their cards to make room for new ones.

Ellis kept laughing at his moment of victory. "I can't believe it. I never win at things like this. I'm the reason slot machines were invented."

"Why'm I not surprised?" Mel said in a low voice, clearly irritated, dropping his wadded-up paper ball onto the floor beside him, avoiding the trash bag in the aisle.

The attendant finished confirming the numbers, extracted a twenty-dollar bill from the pouch around her waist, and handed it to Ellis.

"Congratulations, sir."

Mel reached over and snatched the bill from between Ellis's fingers. "You loser—you owe me at least that much for beer," he said, and shoved it into his shirt pocket.

The smile crystallized on Ellis's face for a split second, and then it widened paradoxically as he cut a quick look at Nancy and said, "When you're right, you're right, Mel. Happy to share."

Nancy covered her smile with a hand.

"What're you laughing at?" Mel growled at her.

She lowered her hand and pointed to a fictitious spot over his shoulder. "Just a kid acting funny over there."

She knew he wouldn't look, and he didn't. "You and

damned kids. Give it a rest." He turned to the woman next to him and demanded, "When do things wrap up here?"

"Last round's at ten," she said, not bothering to look at him, her lips pursing afterward.

"Christ," he muttered, and began spreading out a new set of cards.

They were at a rural bingo hall outside Bennington, owned and operated by a volunteer fire department as a weekly fund-raiser. Mel had actually come up with the idea, based on information he'd been given but wasn't sharing. His companions knew they were "on a raid," as he called these outings, but not its nature. The amount of cash being handled around the hall, however, pretty much spoke for itself. Someone, somehow, was going to have their stash lifted.

Nancy didn't much care. Ever since that afternoon with Ellis, when he'd made sure she'd had three orgasms before he let her go—a gift her husband hadn't attended to in living memory—she hadn't been able to think of much else. She'd always liked Ellis. He'd always been polite to her, and she appreciated his quietness. But she'd also always seen him just a bit as her husband did—a loser. In a world of loud men with demonstrative habits— from her abusive father to a string of violent boyfriends, and now Mel—Nancy had formed a habit of pegging such behavior to manhood. Anyone not fitting the mold was probably either weak-willed or gay. In any case, not worth her attention.

Ellis had opened her eyes. Never before had she been so catered to. He'd not only worked hard to build her excitement and bring her to climax, but when he'd finally joined her, he'd made his own enjoyment enthusiastically clear, bringing her own satisfaction to a new height. Sex had always been something she'd assumed she was there to provide—not a feast two people could share.

The very thought of their time together made her squirm slightly in her chair. Now that they'd done this once, nervously and spontaneously, she couldn't wait to try it again with more forethought and planning. She was going to make sure Ellis had never had anyone better.

The last game wrapped up close to when their neighbor had said it would. The three of them stood in line along with the hundred-plus other people in the hall and began shuffling toward the door. Ellis made sure he was last in line behind Nancy and Mel so he could occasionally brush her butt with his hand, pretending he was being jostled. Mel couldn't figure out why his wife was so cheerful.

In the back of her mind, however, was still the question about what they were doing here. Playing bingo was hardly one of Mel's enthusiasms, and his manner during the event notwithstanding, he'd even made an effort to change his appearance, if only slightly, by wearing a collared shirt and tying his long hair back with a rubber band. He was up to something. The question was, now that they were filing out into the parking lot, what?

The answer wasn't forthcoming as they fit into the pickup but remained parked. Mel stayed quiet, his hands on the steering wheel and his eyes on the crowd still streaming from the firehouse doors. His mood had improved, however, and there was a gleam to his eye that he got as every raid began gathering steam.

Ellis had noticed the same thing. He sat motionless beside Nancy, attuned to her presence but with his fingers interlaced in his lap, working to keep his focus on Mel's lead. He knew from long experience that anything could happen from this point on, and probably would, and that his own survival would depend on thinking clearly. Because one thing was consistent with Mel—he never had your safety in mind when he acted.

The parking lot was thinning out. Mel lit a cigarette and watched meditatively as car after car slowly filed onto the road. His companions knew better than to ask questions. There was a balancing act to observe here, after all. Something between showing trust and getting enough information to stay alive.

Ellis made a small reconnaissance into this minefield. "Lot of money changes hands at these things."

Mel nodded, his eyes on the string of flaring taillights. "That it does."

"Kinda makes the mind work."

Mel let out a short, quiet laugh. "Can't talk for you, Ellis, but it did get me going."

The subject now seemed officially open for discussion. Nancy spoke softly. "That is something you know how to do."

Mel reached out and patted her knee. "Well, somebody's got to keep us fed. Christ knows, you two can't. What did you see tonight?"

Neither of them could go too far wrong at this point. "A bingo game," Nancy said.

"Money," Ellis contributed. "Like I said."

"Yeah," Mel drawled, leaning forward slightly to turn the ignition key, bringing the truck noisily alive. "Money coming in from a whole bunch of pockets and ending up in one."

He pulled the truck forward and slipped into the line of departing vehicles.

"Right," Ellis said appreciatively. "Kind of like a bank."

Mel cut him a look and a quick smile. "For a dumb drunk, you do get lucky every once in a while." He pointed at the building they were passing on their way out of the lot. "Exactly like a bank, without all the inconveniences."

Nancy was staring straight ahead, feeling the tingle of apprehension she'd last experienced outside the armory, during the theft of the two guns. Thus far, she didn't know what to do with it. Was Mel speaking philosophically and therefore still in the planning stages, or had that been a tactical comment? Were they about to go active? The military words and phrases clattered in her head, put there by constant repetition. Mel used them constantly— the frustrated combatant who'd been dishonorably discharged from the very Guard unit they'd just ripped off.

She found she was clenching her hands together and willed them apart, placing them flat on the tops of her thighs.

Mel swung out onto the road and picked up speed, leaving the firehouse behind. Nancy was just thinking about relaxing when he slowed again a few hundred yards later, pulled into a dirt road, made a tight U-turn, and parked just shy of the intersection. He switched off the lights, helping the black truck blend into the dark stand of trees beside them.

"Field glasses," he ordered, his eyes fixed in the direction they'd just traveled.

Ellis extracted the binoculars from the glove box as Nancy shut her eyes, feeling her heart rate double. Whatever it was, it was happening tonight.

"Gotta do a little recon," Mel murmured, fitting the glasses to his eyes and adjusting the focus. Ellis could still make out the firehouse lights through the intervening stretch of undergrowth, glimmering like a distant campfire. Traffic was almost nil by this point, and only rarely did a pair of headlights come sweeping down the road to flash briefly through their windows. Every time that happened, though, Mel lowered the binoculars.

Twenty minutes later he returned them to Ellis, put the truck into gear, hit his own lights, and resumed driving down the paved road. "We're good" was all he said.

The village the fire department served lay less than a mile farther on. It was getting late by now; it wasn't too large a place to begin with, and the few stores lining the square had all closed long ago. As they drove quietly into the downtown's embrace, Ellis thought of the fake equivalents he'd seen in cheaply made movies, where there were no people, few lights, and an artificial cleanliness that had made him think that every wall was an inch thick. Even the brick bank building seemed made of Styrofoam, under the glow of the one sodium streetlamp standing guard over the sidewalk.

Mel backed into an alley between two dark stores and killed the engine. Opposite them, through the grimy windshield, the front of the bank was clearly in view.

Breaking the unwritten rules, Nancy blurted, "The bank? What're you *thinking*?"

Mel scowled as he twisted toward her, making Ellis tense up. He'd seen Mel hit her before. He knew he wouldn't be able to allow that again without acting in her defense, just as he knew he wouldn't stand a chance. He was big enough but lacked the instinct to win that Mel had acquired through long practice.

"More than you are, you stupid cow. You think I'm going to drive through the front door? God almighty, girl.

You couldn't make money lying on your back. You are that dumb."

He opened the door angrily and stuck one leg out. "Just do what you know how to do, okay? Put your hands on the wheel and get ready to go. Leave the thinking to somebody who knows how." He glared at Ellis. "Move it."

Ellis slid out the far door, exchanging one last hapless glance with Nancy, and joined Mel in front of the silent truck. The latter's face was still brooding, but he was evidently back on track. He pointed across the street. "Night deposit box, right of the door. See it?"

Ellis nodded, the plan finally coming clear in his head.

"We got cover from the bush to the left, and that wood garbage can box with the lid on it to the right. The target should be here in five minutes, tops. You take the box and be the diversion."

That was it. Mel jogged across the darkened street, barely a shadow even by the dull streetlamp. Ellis didn't think twice before following suit. This was the flip side of Mel's managerial style—in exchange for his survival-of-the-fittest dismissiveness, he inadvertently injected in those who did stay with him a certain quick-witted autonomy. Through an intuition born of years of association, Ellis knew not only what the plan was, but its goal and how to carry it out.

The garbage can box, about the size of three stacked steamer trunks, was painted dark green to blend in better with the shrubs it fronted. It had been planted parallel to the sidewalk and thus afforded the ideal hiding place for Ellis's purpose. Settling in behind it, he half wondered why some preceding mugger hadn't thought to leave a garden chair for convenience's sake.

Not that he would have used it for long. Barely two

minutes after taking cover, he heard a slow-moving car approaching from the direction of the firehouse and poked his head out to see an ancient rusty Toyota come to a stop at the curb before the bank. From it emerged an older man with a well-cared-for belly and a scraggly beard who took his time becoming upright. After casting glances up and down the street, apparently having considered what was just about to happen, the man extracted a swollen, zippered bank bag from the dashboard, circled the front of the car, his blue-jeaned knees flashing briefly in the headlights, and trudged toward the granite steps leading up to the bank's front door and the night deposit box mounted into the wall beside it.

This was Ellis's moment. Mel had told him he was the diversion, which could have meant merely stepping out into the open and asking for a light or the time of day. But one of Mel's trademarks was to leave no witnesses, or at least none who could later identify any member of the raiding party—a lesson Ellis had taken pains to remember. It was also why he had made sure to leave no footprints behind in the soft earth of his hiding place, choosing only hard surfaces to step on.

So rather than show himself, he merely groaned loudly from where he was.

He heard the man's heavy tread stop.

"Help," Ellis moaned.

"Who's there?" His voice was clearly frightened.

"I'm hurt . . . can't move."

Ellis could feel the older man's fear like a cold fog filling the air. "They really hurt me," he added for good measure, hoping to appeal to what he thought was a fireman's natural credo.

It worked. He peeked around the lower edge of his hiding place to see not only his prey yielding to temptation but Mel's shadow detaching itself from the bush behind him and approaching like a spirit.

Without word or warning, Mel smacked the old man across the nape of the neck with a weighted sap. His victim had barely crumpled to the ground before Mel quickly pulled a slipknotted pillowcase over his head to blind him.

Ellis was momentarily stunned. The man lay facedown on the sidewalk like a dropped walrus. Never before had Mel hit one of their targets like that. That was the whole point of the pillowcase—to render all violence unnecessary and lessen the penalty if they were ever caught. Admittedly, they'd never attempted a haul like this before, having just mugged people for wallets or stashes of dope—and then only lowlifes who wouldn't go to the cops. But the trick with the bag was key. It made the theft almost comical, leaving their victims twirling around like errant adult partygoers, trying to snatch their blindfolds away. This brought back his earlier apprehension about Mel's handling of the armory guard.

Ellis bolted from cover and checked for a pulse as Mel collected the money bag.

"He alive?" Mel didn't sound particularly concerned.

Ellis nodded. Both men quickly checked for any movement up and down the block, then ran across the street to the sound of the darkened truck starting up.

Ellis hadn't quite closed the passenger door before Nancy began rolling just slowly enough not to burn rubber.

"You didn't kill him, did you?" she asked, echoing Ellis's alarm. "You hit him awful hard."

Mel was laughing, already working on the money

bag's flimsy lock with a pair of pliers. "Nah. Piece of cake. The old fuck's had hangovers worse than that—I guarantee."

Ellis's eyes were on Mel's progress with the lock, his curiosity about their haul tempering his anxiety—they *hadn't* killed the guy, after all. And much as he hated to admit it, he did love these moments, brief though they were, when all was harmony in the flush of success.

Not so Nancy. She drove on, obeying the speed limit, her hands tight on the wheel, all but convinced that blue lights would appear suddenly in the rearview mirror. She was as apprehensive now as she'd been adrenalized by similar events a careless year or two earlier.

She had no idea how much longer she could keep denying the change in herself.

Chapter 7

In isolation, the Office of the Chief Medical Examiner in Burlington was a relative jewel—clean, modern, well laid out—especially considering that when Joe Gunther first visited it years ago, he'd used a dentist's parking lot off Colchester Avenue and climbed an exterior staircase to what had once been an apartment. Needless to say, no autopsies were conducted on site in those days.

In fact, the only drawback for the denizens of these new digs was that they were no longer housed in isolation, but in the middle of the totally revamped Fletcher Allen Medical Center—just like Jonah's erstwhile home inside the whale. This construction project was taking years to build, costing a bundle over original estimates, and had already resulted in the jailing of some of the honchos involved. An example of thrifty, practical, hard-bargaining Vermont this new hospital was not.

Every time Joe came to visit, he resigned himself to negotiating a whole new labyrinth of garages, hallways, and elevator banks that appeared to be in perpetual re-design, aided in his journey only by an ever-shifting Scotch-taped trail of paper signs discreetly labeled

OCME. Stepping inside the Office of the Chief Medical Examiner had become like surviving a miniature odyssey.

Suzanne Webb, the unit's medical records specialist, rose from her desk as Joe closed the door behind him, and crossed over to give him a hug. She had been there for years and knew the workings of the office inside and out. She was always the first person Joe contacted when checking the psychological temperature of the waters.

He kissed her cheek as she said, "A miracle of timing. Five more minutes and the place would've been empty. To what do we owe the pleasure, Joe? Haven't seen you in forever."

"You probably know more than I do about why I'm here, Suzanne," he said, stepping back. "I'm hoping to see the chief—I figured this would be saner than earlier in the day. My last phone conversation with her was downright weird."

She looked over her shoulder to make sure they were alone in what functioned as a catchall central office. When she turned back, her expression was glum. "It's Freeman, our boss of bosses. It's like he's found religion or something. All of a sudden, out of nowhere, he's been hassling us for every last thing, from procedures and tox panels to how many paper clips we order."

Joe knew of Floyd Freeman, who oversaw Hillstrom in the arcane bureaucratic structure that supposedly sheltered her office. The man was a political appointee of the governor's but, more tellingly, had been a candidate a few years back for that office himself. He and Hillstrom had never been friendly, but there seemed to have been at least some unwritten agreement between them to stay clear of each other. The OCME, after all, was the smallest of his responsibilities and by its nature not an entity that attracted much attention.

"Where is she?" Joe asked Suzanne.

She gestured with her thumb through the nearest wall. "In her home away from home."

He knew what that meant, since it marked another trait he and Hillstrom both shared. When they were under the gun, they didn't reach for the bottle or take vacation time. They went to work.

"It's late for that, isn't it? Don't you guys usually do procedures in the morning?"

Suzanne merely smiled and rolled her eyes.

It was enough. He'd been right. He squeezed her hand. "Thanks. Wish me luck."

He left the office, turned the corner, and walked down a short, wide hallway, skirting a large floor-embedded scale of the kind he'd seen in fancy veterinary clinics, used here to weigh bodies as they arrived at the facility. The door at the end of the corridor was unmarked but by its very width and location had an air of importance.

He paused at its threshold, prepared himself mentally, and pushed it open.

The autopsy room was spacious and well lit, with two bays and room for two more, as well as an array of storage units, body coolers, a vault for saved samples, and even a skylight, which had been Hillstrom's pride and joy when the design of the place had been finalized. Floyd Freeman hadn't been on board in those days, but his predecessor had clearly been confused by the need for natural light in such an area, believing, like most everyone else, that medical examiners and their activities were best kept in basements, under sixty-watt bulbs. He, at least, had been persuaded to amend his prejudice.

Beverly Hillstrom was standing before a naked male of about fifty years, flat on his back with his torso opened wide as if it had been unzipped from throat to groin. As Joe entered, she extracted the man's small intestine and ran it through her gloved fingers, studying it as she went.

"Doctor," he said quietly, approaching the table slowly.

She glanced up just enough to recognize him. "Agent Gunther. You happen to be in the neighborhood?"

"Hardly."

She didn't respond at first, and he didn't add anything.

"I was wondering if you might drop by," she said at last.

"I was concerned."

She kept to her study. "I apologize for my tone. It was very unprofessional."

He laughed gently. "If anything, it was a little *too* professional."

She looked up again, and he could see the hint of a smile in her eyes. "Right. Point taken."

He let her continue, watching her deftly disassemble her patient, organ by organ, cataloguing in her mind the map of his demise.

"Heart?" Joe ventured after a while.

"Very good," she said. "That and pulmonary disease. A lifelong smoker."

Joe nodded without comment. He'd attended many autopsies, especially before the state police had assigned a full-time liaison to report back to interested departments. But he still found them fascinating, not the least repellent, and continued to fit them in whenever he had the opportunity.

Hillstrom finally straightened and gazed down at her

work. "An unattended from Ludlow. Hardly a mystery, but he hadn't seen a physician in years, and the family was anxious to know."

Joe had already guessed at the scenario, if not the specifics. He was curious, however, at her having detailed them the way she had. He took a stab at the reason.

"Meaning that as a case, he straddles a very fine line, at least in Freeman's eyes."

She stepped back from the table and removed her gloves. An assistant had appeared, ghostlike, from another quarter and now moved into her place to finish things up.

"Lately," Hillstrom said, addressing his comment, "I'd say Freeman would be calling this one a total waste of money. The line is no longer so fine."

She stripped off her outer gown and shoved it into a hamper, replacing it with a lab coat that she wore over her scrubs as a semipermanent uniform.

She headed for the main door. "Let me park you in my office while I change. I'd just as soon not have this conversation here."

He followed her quietly down the corridor, past Suzanne's now empty enclave and to the back, where she kept a small corner office. He'd been here before, too, and was always struck by how it invoked the work of a very good if self-effacing interior decorator. Even the papers on the desk looked positioned for a photo shoot. During less charitable moments, he'd entertained the notion that the photographs on the shelf behind her chair weren't actually her kids but some family cut out of the pages of a magazine.

Hillstrom motioned him to one of her visitor chairs. "Have a seat, Joe. I'll be right back."

He froze for a split second, as startled as if she had screamed at him. In all the years they'd known each other, she had never—not once—referred to him by his first name.

"Take your time," he muttered, nonplussed, and settled down to wait, surveying the room as he did. The art was tasteful, muted, and neutrally appealing, the framed awards and degrees plentiful and impressive, the plants in perfect health. The pictures of the kids he recognized from years ago—two striking blue-eyed blondes like their mother, but both probably in college by now. He'd always wondered what their father looked like. He had heard he was a high-priced Burlington corporate lawyer. There was no picture of him.

He turned at the sound of the door opening quietly and did his best to hide his surprise once more. Hillstrom had changed from her green scrubs into a light, flowered spring dress, buttoned down the front, nipped in at the waist, and free-flowing below. It had short sleeves and a V-neck that revealed a beaded necklace and an attractive cleavage. Her legs were bare, she wore low-heeled sandals, and she'd loosened her long hair so that it hung about her shoulders. She was stunning.

She laughed at his expression. "Like seeing your teacher out of school?"

He rose, smiling broadly. No teacher I ever had, he thought to himself. She looked beautiful.

She blushed slightly at his obvious if silent appreciation and turned back toward the hallway. "Let's get out of here. Where are you parked?"

"I wish I knew," he said, following her lead, still adjusting to the view before him. "I think it was level three."

She glanced back at him. "That's where I am. Let's go

in separate cars. We can eat at a steak house I've tried just down the street. It'll be virtually deserted this time of night."

They followed her suggestion, plunging into the building's entrails until emerging from the underground parking lot's embrace ten minutes later like escapees from a penal colony.

She led him to a bland if well-appointed motel on the other side of the nearby interstate, where the first floor was dominated by a combination bar and restaurant. As she'd predicted, the place was nearly empty. They got a booth along the back wall.

He waited until the waiter had taken their drink order before finally asking, "What's going on?"

Hillstrom leaned back against the fake leather cushion and passed her hand across her forehead wearily. "Before I begin," she said, "I'd like you to know how grateful I am you're here. I never would have asked, but after we spoke, and despite my treating you so poorly, I did hope you'd come. That you did confirms what I've always thought of you." She suddenly stretched out her hand and laid it briefly on his. "I consider you one of the most decent human beings I've ever known."

He thought to take up her fingers in his own, but she'd already withdrawn her hand. Instead, he watched her for a moment, astonished at how her troubles had transformed her. "Beverly, I didn't have to think twice about it. The respect is mutual."

She gave him a weak smile. "Thank you. That means more than you can imagine right now."

"What exactly is Freeman up to?" he asked.

"The *what* is probably less telling than the *why*," she said, pausing to sip from her wine as it was placed before her. "But what he's doing," she resumed, "is niggling my entire staff half to death about every item he can think of, including stationery supplies, no doubt hoping to push me into the one act of insubordination that will allow him to fire me. And trust me," she added, "there are days like today when he almost succeeds."

"I noticed," Joe told her. "But how can he get away with it, and why now?"

"In a nutshell, because he's come into some information he's using to blackmail me."

Joe stared at her, his mouth half open. "Beverly. For Christ's sake."

She held up her hand to stop him. "That's what it boils down to, Joe. In truth, it's not quite that dramatic. I'm a little at wit's end. You'll have to forgive me."

"Of course, but what's it all about?"

"God knows how many years ago, I was working in Connecticut for a man named Howard Medwed. You might have heard of him, even not being in the business."

"I have," Joe interjected. "He's like Helpern or Noguchi, right? One of the legends?"

"Correct. Very good. A wonderful man and a mentor in the truest sense of the word. If I were to claim just one person as being the single biggest influence in my life, it would be Howard. He gave me my first job, straight out of school, back when women were as rare as hen's teeth in this profession, and he set about making me the best I could possibly be, just as he did with many others. He was an inspiration."

Joe smelled a too-good-to-be-true setup. "Except for . . . ," he suggested.

She gave him a sad smile. "One single mistake, not a character flaw, and one he had good reasons for making."

He shook his head slightly.

She understood. "I know, I know. I'll explain." She paused to take another large sip of wine and motioned to the waiter for a second glass, even though hers was still partly full. Joe, drinking Coke, merely took note.

"Howard Medwed was near the end of his life when this happened," Hillstrom continued. "He was seventy-three years old, his wife had died six months earlier, and he was being pressured as never before from a group of political opponents. Also, unbeknownst to everyone except me and his son, he'd just been diagnosed with terminal cancer. So, in purely practical terms, politics notwithstanding, he felt he needed to maintain his medical benefits."

Joe frowned. "Couldn't he have retired and kept the coverage?"

She held up a finger. "That gets complicated, but more to the point, it misses the bigger problem—the same people who wanted him gone were also backing a candidate he knew would be a disaster. It was only Dr. Medwed staying in place that was stopping them. I won't bore you with ancient history, but in a nutshell, if he retired too soon, this idiot was a shoo-in; if he held on for just a few months, then the idiot went away and Medwed got to name his own successor. It was thornier than that, but that's what it came down to: timing."

The second wine arrived. Hillstrom drained her first glass and pushed it toward the waiter, who lingered with it in his hand.

"Would you like to order?"

"I'm not hungry," Hillstrom said shortly.

"You have any soup?" Joe asked.

The waiter recited the options, and Joe chose a bowl of

split pea, causing his companion to capitulate and join him with a French onion soup and a side order of bread to share.

Joe waited for the young man to leave before asking, "What happened?"

"There was a high-level case," Hillstrom went on. "A reported dog in the road being hit multiple times turned out to be the remains of a woman. It became front-page news when she was finally identified as the wife of a prominent local politician, who, as luck would have it, was also a major backer of Medwed's."

She paused again for another sip before resuming. "It was a real mess. What was she doing in the middle of the night far from home? Why had she been on a busy road, on foot, where there were no businesses or residences she might have been visiting? Had she been murdered or did she die of natural causes? It went on and on. Howard did the autopsy himself, it being a high-level case, but later I assisted him with the follow-through because of its complexity and his poor health. That much was acceptable procedure. The hitch cropped up when he discovered the woman was pregnant. That, he kept private. He told me much later that he felt it wasn't relevant, would only hurt his friend, and that no harm would result from withholding it."

"Was he nuts?" Joe exclaimed. "After all those years on the job, he should've known better."

"I grant you that," she agreed. "But he was sentimental, having just lost his own wife. The woman in question was fifty years old. She and her husband had always wanted kids but never could. And finally, once the cause of death was ruled a natural, he didn't see the point. The problem was, it got out anyhow and caused a whole secondary ruckus."

"Hold it, hold it," Joe interrupted. "I know you don't want to get bogged down in details, but how did it end up a natural?"

"She was a jogger," Hillstrom said simply, "named Judy Morgenthau. She was on a new route she'd never tried before, running a little later than usual and thus in the dark, and she suffered a heart attack. We hypothesized that as she reacted to the cardiac event, she stumbled into the road and was hit. After that, she became just a lump in the road, struck again and again and again, eventually becoming unrecognizable. Believe it or not, they actually found the first car that hit her—a man who thought he'd struck a dog and just kept driving. They matched the blood on his bumper to the decedent. The whole thing was very sad."

"What happened when news of the pregnancy got out?" Joe asked as the soup arrived.

"The opposition went wild. They screamed cover-up; they claimed that if this was withheld, then other more important information might well have been, too. They demanded retests and spread rumors that the woman had been on drugs or drunk or had a bullet in her somewhere." She shook her head, smiling. "It's all so ridiculous in retrospect. A true tempest in a teapot. It didn't make the national news; it didn't change the course of anything. But at the time, it was all anyone could talk about, and it damn near cost Howard Medwed his job."

"Why didn't it?" Joe asked, starting in on his meal.

"Because I took the heat," she explained. "I told everyone that I'd been the one who'd both discovered the pregnancy and covered it up. I took a drubbing for it and was properly pilloried behind closed doors, but I wasn't fired outright, and Dr. Medwed gave me a glowing recommendation for my next job. The opposition didn't get their man in, Medwed stayed put for another six months, and the office's reputation was safely handed off to the next generation."

Joe thought about all this while Hillstrom halfheartedly poked at her French onion soup.

"And that's what Floyd Freeman is holding over you?" he asked eventually. "How did he find out about it?"

She shrugged. "Who knows? Things like that eventually get out. The price of living in a small world. The point is, he did."

"Why don't you just tell him to drop dead?" Joe suggested.

"Normally, I would, but therein lies part of the problem. I've told him to drop dead ever since he became my boss a few years ago. He doesn't know what the OCME does, except in the crudest sense, and he doesn't care. It's all about the bottom line with him. Initially, before the new governor came in and the whole power structure shifted, I could pretty much dismiss him. I had my allies to protect me. Now I no longer do. Freeman's never forgotten my early treatment of him, and at last, along with the power, he now has the ammunition he's always craved. He's dangling it over me, making it his life's work to force me through his hoops."

Gunther scowled. "That's ridiculous, Beverly. He doesn't have enough to fire you—"

But she reached out and stopped him in midsentence by taking his hand, her expression deadly serious. "Joe, don't. I'm on the receiving end here. I know what I'm facing. Don't tell me what can or can't happen."

This time he did grab hold of her fingers. "I wouldn't dream of it. That's not where I was going. I don't doubt your assessment. It's just that legally speaking, what he's got on you doesn't seem that dangerous. Maybe you're too close to it to see that clearly."

Hillstrom smiled and squeezed his hand supportively. "Or maybe you're not close enough."

"What do you mean?"

She let go and sat back in the booth, looking unusually vulnerable and frail. Dressed as she was and with her hair loose, weighed down by her recent troubles, she displayed none of her typical self-confidence, seeming instead like a normal human being running low on options.

"Daniel's left me," she blurted out. "I have a huge house and two daughters in college. If there's a divorce ahead and a major financial readjustment, I cannot afford to lose my job. This is it for me, in any case. I'm too old to qualify for another office. I'd have to do consulting work, and while that can be lucrative, there are no guarantees. Plus, Freeman would still be out there, more than willing to smear my name and ruin my prospects. It's too big a risk. For my girls' sake and my own sanity, I don't feel I have a choice but to play his game for as long as he likes." She let out a short laugh. "I guess I've ended up right where my mentor was all those years ago: between a rock and a hard place. At least I'm not terminally ill, and I've only got four years to go before I can retire with no loss of benefits."

Joe was stunned by this last admission. He'd known next to nothing about Beverly's private life but had made the unwarranted assumption that she had it under as tight control as she did her office. He felt like a fool for having thought so conveniently.

"I know this sounds trite, Beverly, but I am truly sorry."

She made a small face, pressing her lips together. He could see the pain in her eyes as she said, "Thank you, Joe. People say it makes you feel better to talk about it, but I don't think I agree."

She suddenly leaned forward again and grabbed his hand for the third time. "Oh, Lord. And I just remembered hearing that you've just gone through the same thing. What was I thinking?"

He shook his head emphatically. "No, no. Not the same. I mean, Gail and I are no longer together, but we were never married and have no kids. Anyhow, don't worry. We're fine. We still talk all the time. She just needed the space to make a grab for the rest of her life. How're you doing with it? No, that's stupid. I mean, how long ago did this happen?"

This time, she left her hand in his, rubbing his fingers between her own as she stared at the table between them. For the first time ever, he saw her as other than just the medical examiner, even if a very attractive one. With the subject of both their relationships before them, he found himself looking at her as a woman, and even wondering what she might be like in that context.

"About a month ago," she was saying. "I received information that there was possibly another woman. Daniel claims there isn't, and I don't want to know, but he is certainly attractive enough. I'm not sure I'd even blame him, given the little time I have for him."

Joe shook her hand to make her look up. "You know what that sounds like, right? That's no excuse."

"I know, I know. I do get angry sometimes. It all seems so pointless, after everything we've gone through. We should be nearing our very best years together. Not this."

"What is he actually saying?" Joe asked, hoping to steer her back to more solid footing.

She sighed and finally broke their contact, sitting back again. "All the usual midlife crisis one-liners. I need to be alone. I need time to think. It's not you, it's me. I still love you." She tilted her head back and stared at the ceiling for a moment. "God almighty. Never in a thousand years . . ." She looked at him again. "I'm not saying he doesn't mean what he's saying. Maybe this will be the one time it will actually work out." She paused to touch her cheek briefly. "It all sounds so trite . . ."

Joe had been struck by that very thought, harking back to his own conversations with Gail, where she'd said many of the same things. He, too, had never suspected another man, and still didn't, but the language had been the same, along with the end result.

Was every one of us so unoriginal that in the end we all relied on the same script to set ourselves free? Given the supposedly unique effort that was put into these love affairs, the possibility of such commonality was downright depressing.

Perhaps to spare them both, Joe went back to an earlier topic, though not without an ironic smile. "Beverly, since we're on the subject of irrational behavior, do you have any idea why Floyd Freeman has it in for you?"

She shifted to place her elbow on the table and her chin in her hand. "Jesus, I guess I do have a way with men, don't I?"

"That's not what I meant."

She laughed then. "I was kidding. Well, kind of kidding. No, actually, my troubles with Freeman go back quite a ways. Remember when he made a run for governor?"

"Yeah. That's when I first heard of him."

"Same for most of us. Self-made millionaire, ready to inject even more ego into himself. He stepped out of the drab gray line of businessmen and took a stab at the headlines. Unfortunately, that's exactly what I gave him."

Joe was already laughing at her phrasing. "You? How's that?"

She became more serious. "It was actually a sad case—a young woman found alone, dead at the wheel in a single-car accident. The police investigated from their end, I did the procedure from mine, and we agreed on a finding of accidental mishap. She'd clearly been driving too fast, there was some alcohol involved, and the roads were slippery. That was that, as far as everyone thought, even though the woman happened to be an au pair working for our aspiring politician and his wife."

Joe began nodding, gradually recalling the case from what he'd read in the papers at the time.

"Freeman," Hillstrom resumed, "was suitably distraught, having his picture taken at the airport, where the coffin was being flown back to Europe for interment, and issuing the right comments to the press. Unfortunately for him, several days later, a friend of the dead girl discreetly contacted the police after returning to Europe herself and told them that the au pair had actually committed suicide over a sexual liaison she'd been having with Freeman. The friend had a letter and photos that the girl had given her to prove it, but she'd waited to share them for fear of being arrested or detained while she was still over here."

"I remember all that now," Joe said. "The dead girl was named Ellen Turnley. She was a Brit. But how's that fall back onto you?"

"I had to change the death certificate," she explained.

"At first, that was no big deal. The way the news came to the police, and given Vermont's discreet and old-fashioned press corps, no one heard of this development. There was no effort to cover it up, but no one advertised it, either. Still, I was suddenly faced with a change in the facts—palpable evidence of suicidal intent—and felt it my duty to write an amendment. I made no more fuss about it than anyone else, but someone in the media finally woke up, and it was my amendment that tipped them off. One thing led to another, the whole thing blew up—along with Freeman's marriage and his political ambitions, and guess who he blamed forever after for his downfall?"

"My God," Joe said. "Just like the proverbial messenger."

"That's it," she agreed. "You can imagine my feelings when the new governor made Freeman my boss. I knew there'd be trouble sooner or later."

Joe thought back to something she'd mentioned earlier. "And yet you said that you've been telling him to drop dead from the get-go."

She looked at him ruefully. "Suggesting a lack of diplomatic skills? More like an excess of arrogance. Joe, you may not realize it, but you're about the only man I know besides Daniel who puts up with me, and now I'm not so sure about that."

Joe didn't press his point. Instead, he tried to dull its impact. "You're not that difficult. You set a high bar, but you set it higher for yourself. I have always enjoyed working with you, Beverly, and I will for years to come. Let me help out with Freeman."

Her eyes widened as a smile played on her lips. "How will you do that?"

"Let me think about it a bit. For that matter, maybe the less you know, the better for right now."

She was laughing. "Ah, my knight. You will rue this decision. We'll both end up unemployed." The smile died quickly as she added, "Seriously, that's very sweet of you, but potentially self-destructive. Freeman's in the catbird seat right now. He's powerful and dangerous, and to be honest, you and the VBI are not so firmly anchored in the harbor, either. Politics created you, and politics can make an end of you." She gave him a look of utter sincerity. "I could not live with myself, Joe—not the way things are going for me right now—if I were the cause of any harm to you. You may be the last friend I have on earth."

Impulsively, he took up her hand and this time gave it a chivalric kiss. "Not to worry, madam. We'll see this through together."

She flushed slightly as she pulled her hand back and stared at her unfinished meal. "Well, whatever happens, I guess we're done here. I'll understand if you're thinking more clearly in the morning."

Joe laid a generous amount on the table as he slid free of the booth. "Don't count on it, Beverly. That's not what friends do."

He reached out and helped her to her feet, which gesture brought them close together by the edge of the booth, a position neither of them moved quickly to remedy.

"Thank you," she said softly, her face inches from his.

Her clean smell of soap with just a hint of perfume drifted by him, and his awareness of her proximity suddenly sharpened. Without thinking, he slipped his hand around her waist and stepped back a pace, ushering her toward the far entrance with his other hand. "Shall we?"

She kissed his cheek, laughing. "We shall."

They walked arm in arm across the nearly deserted restaurant and out into the balmy air of the parking lot to their cars. There he paused and admitted an earlier concern. "Beverly, I don't want to sound mother-hennish, but I'd be happy to drive you home. I'm not saying you drank too much tonight, but I—"

She interrupted him by kissing him gently before saying, "I'm as sober as a judge, Joe Gunther."

Both his hands were on her waist by now, and he slowly brought them up the sides of her rib cage and to her shoulder blades, feeling the heat of her skin and the outline of her bra through the thin cotton fabric of her dress. "I guess you are," he murmured.

They kissed again, their bodies coming together. He dropped his right hand down below her waist and pressed her closer to him.

Between kisses she said, "I have a much better idea than your driving me home. This is a motel, after all."

He managed to say only, "True," before she covered his lips once more.

They proceeded slowly after reaching the room, removing each piece of clothing with the erotic attention it deserved, commingling experience and exploration in their motions. The bathroom light was left on so they could relish what they saw.

There was an unspoken understanding in all of this, which made it doubly precious, for they each knew that what they were doing was as much an homage to their pasts as it was a yielding to the moment. This was a watershed, a marking of passage, but by no means the beginning of anything new. For Joe, he had to accept the finality of Gail's decision. In Beverly's case, she needed to feel she was desirable and capable of spontaneity. Both of them knew they were with someone they could trust.

And so, without a word, this fragment of time was to be prized in private, and in all likelihood, never repeated.

Finally, the last garment slid loose and they stretched out naked. Limbs intertwining, they each shed their ghosts and obligations and made love without constraint.

Chapter 8

Nancy Martin opened her eyes briefly and then shut them again with a wince, the light through the trailer's window hitting her like twin lightning bolts. She had a headache so painful it made her nauseous.

She rolled over toward the dark closet and tried again, this time managing to see something. Her bedroom. That much made sense. The bed was empty except for her. That was good news. She'd had enough of Mel for the time being.

Slowly, she propped herself up on one elbow and dragged herself along until her shoulders were resting against the bare wooden headboard. She looked down the length of her body to measure the damage. Her torn underwear circled one knee, there were red marks high on the inside of her left thigh from where Mel had bitten her, her breasts were swollen and very tender, and she could feel the tightness of a bruise building on her cheek where he'd butted her with his head. Having sex with her husband had become a hazardous experience.

She tentatively touched a welt along the outside of her hip. And whoever said that ripping underpants off a woman was sexy—even thongs—had clearly never been in them when it happened.

Nancy closed her eyes again and sighed. Drinking wasn't the anesthesia it was cracked up to be, either, at least not in the aftermath.

She'd had worse; there was that to cling to. And in the throes of it, she couldn't even say it was so terrible. To be hungered for that much was actually kind of flattering. She'd heard the other side, of course. The times she'd gone to Planned Parenthood for exams or the ER for the occasional repair work, she'd been lectured to by earnest types with plain hair, big butts, and sensible shoes about abusive relationships and sexual dominance and a bunch of other crap she ignored. Those women were college grads from regular homes, taking pity on the less advantaged, with no clue about her crowd or how to actually enjoy life a little. To them, it was all victim and carnivore. They had no idea how you could play the angles, even turn things around now and then.

Nancy thought back to Mel, who'd come home shit-faced and amorous the night before, smelling of stale beer and body odor. She'd held him off at first, thinking of Ellis, but it was clear how things were going to end up. A practical woman, a survivor, she had started matching him shot for shot, hoping either to drink him into unconsciousness or to numb herself enough not to notice what followed.

It hadn't been that bad, anyhow. He was no Ellis—gentle, attentive, respectful. But then, a little of the rough stuff had never killed anyone.

Until maybe the next morning.

Groaning, she worked her way over to the edge of the bed and dropped her feet to the floor, breathing deeply in order not to throw up.

She surveyed the room through narrowed eyes, trying to separate last night's detritus from the everyday chaos, wondering what to wear that might be halfway clean.

The phone began ringing from somewhere under the bed.

"Christ," she murmured and dropped to her knees, ignoring the lurch in her stomach. Thankfully, the portable phone was under the first pillow she moved.

"What?" she asked.

"Wow," said Ellis, clearly taken aback by her greeting. "Tough night?"

"You know it."

His laugh sounded forced, and she imagined him putting on a brave face to mask his disappointment. "I do. He left me to go to you. I saw the shape he was in. You gonna live?"

"I don't know yet."

"He still there?" His voice had dropped a confidential notch.

She stood up, the remnants of her underwear slipping down her leg to the floor. She felt dizzy and no less ill, but catching sight of herself naked in the closet mirror also came as a pleasant surprise. She paused and turned slightly, looking. The face wasn't much—that she knew. It was becoming hard, and the jaw was wrong somehow, and the nose a little out of whack. But the body looked pretty good. Compact but athletic. Wouldn't be too long before her butt began to go, but so far, so good. And her breasts were damn near perfect—a point of some vanity with her.

"I don't know," she said. "Let me check."

Buoyed by her self-appraisal, she left the bedroom naked and entered the narrow hallway to the living room.

The place was quiet, and Mel's truck was gone from its usual parking space.

"We're alone."

"Don't I wish," he said leadingly.

Not that attractive a notion right now, Nancy thought, brushing her throbbing forehead with her fingertips. But she understood his need to voice the desire, especially with Mel's success in that department still lingering between them.

"You up for a trip?" he asked, surprising her.

She was more up for six aspirin, but the softness of his voice stirred a nascent interest. "Where to?" she asked.

"I'd like you to meet my mom."

That made her laugh. "God, Ellis. I don't guess I ever heard that one before. Where's she live?"

"Well, it's not a house or anything. She's in the hospital. Dying of cancer."

"Oh," Nancy said, caught off guard, the smile still on her lips. Her nakedness now felt merely embarrassing, and she returned to the bedroom for a robe.

"I'm sorry," he said quickly. "I didn't mean for it to come out that way. I've gotten too used to it. But she's good people and I wanted you to meet her at least once. Sort of stupid, I know—"

"No, no," she interrupted. "It's not stupid. I just wasn't expecting it. I didn't even know you had a mother." She held her aching head in frustration. "I mean, I figured you did, but . . ."

"That's okay. I don't know anything about your family, either."

She laughed again, but without humor this time. "Yeah, well, let's keep it that way if it's okay with you. Not a place I want to go back to." Standing again in her bedroom, the robe forgotten in her hand, she surveyed the mess around her, feeling the meaning of it seeping in. Her new boyfriend was asking her out on a date while she was staring at her husband's underwear on the floor.

"Hey, why not?" she finally said. "Mel'll be gone for the rest of the day, probably cooking up new ways to get us killed. Can you give me a couple of hours to put myself together?"

"I'll pick you up at eleven," he said.

The hospital was at the edge of Bennington. They rode on Ellis's Harley, barely talking because of the wind and the noise, the bike having a muffler in name only. But despite her slowly ebbing headache and fragile stomach, Nancy discovered it was all curiously soothing. She found herself holding on to Ellis's waist, enveloped by the summer warmth, her eyes closed, breathing in the smell of him and thinking of next to nothing. Times like these, she could almost believe that life had a future worth anticipating. There was no Mel, no madcap schemes, no vigilance about whose headlights might be lurching over the trailer park's uneven road late at night.

Ellis had given her a glimpse of something better than the ever more slippery slope she occupied with Mel.

When they arrived, Ellis stowed the helmets in the bike's travel bags and led the way into the hospital's lobby, bypassing the receptionist with the ease of familiarity.

"You come here a lot?" Nancy asked, getting used to the antiseptic smell she found that all such places shared.

"As much as I can," he said, slowing down to fall in beside her down the wide hallway.

"I gotta tell you, too," he added in a low voice. "It's been a little rough lately. Mom's got thyroid cancer.

Maybe it's all the smoking. I don't know—it's not what they say, but you gotta wonder. Anyway, they've been trying stuff on her and they just got through something that pretty much cut her off from everybody for a few days, so she might be kind of emotional."

Nancy looked alarmed. "What did they do?"

His eyes widened with the memory. "It was like *Star Wars*. Two guys in white suits. I was in a gown with gloves and booties and a hat. She's in a lead-lined room where everything's covered in plastic. All so they can give her a single pill. But it's radiated, like nuclear or something, so it has rays. They took it out of a box inside another box, and as soon as she took it, her whole body lit up the Geiger counter one of them had. It was really creepy. And then we all had to leave—for days."

"Oh, my God," Nancy said. "Why?"

"The thyroid eats up iodine like it's going out of style—or in her case, what's left of the thyroid. Why, I don't know. But that's what the pill was—loaded with radioactive iodine. So the iodine goes straight to the remaining thyroid tissue, and the radiation kills the cancer there. At least that's the theory."

Nancy pondered that for a moment before saying hesitantly, "But you said she was dying."

Ellis stopped to look at her. "She is. I'm sorry. I'm not doing this right. They took the thyroid out with surgery. That was before. This was just to catch what bits and pieces they might've missed. But no one's kidding anybody. Her chances are basically nothing. This thing's a killer. It isn't always. In fact, with younger people it's usually not that big a thing, but for people her age, it's a done deal."

She reached out and put her hand on his arm. "Ellis, I'm so sorry."

He smiled back sadly. "It's really not that bad. We've all accepted it. There've been counselors and everything. Most of the time we joke about it. It's just that this time might be a little worse, only because she's been alone so much. I did wave at her through the window a couple of times," he added brightly. "I think that helped some."

Nancy frowned, trying to absorb it all. "What're we about to do here?" she finally asked.

He resumed walking and laughed at her, understanding her reservations. "It's over now, Nance. It's safe now. That's why we came. Because they're done and she can see people again. This is sort of a welcome-back visit."

"She in really bad shape?" she asked, her voice small.

He remained upbeat, totally at ease with the patient, the disease, and the routine. "She might be a little shaky after this round. She's just a skinny little thing, so it sort of takes it out of her, but you'll like her. I wouldn't have brought you otherwise."

Nancy kept silent.

He tried to make her feel better. "It bummed me out at first, but she's really been a trouper. Made me realize that if she's okay with it, I should be, too. Here we are."

He held open a door leading into another hallway, this one clearly not shared by a lot of people—narrower, quieter, and with more ominous-looking signs on the walls warning against contamination. Nancy got the distinct sensation of being swallowed deeper inside a building containing dangers she didn't want to know about. There had been a time when not much had given her pause, from barroom brawls to men better suited to post office walls. And though she was tiring of that life now and becoming more vulnerable to its downside, she still had an instinctive kinship with it.

But this was very different. Places like hospitals were all about the lack of knowledge, coded information, and the maintenance of a hard, placid sheen over the human business of wasting, dying, and despair. It was very far from what she knew, and it made her anxious.

"Okay," Ellis finally said, stopping before a door with a movable wardrobe beside it. "Here we are." He opened the wardrobe and handed her a white jumpsuit. "Gotta get into one of these. Just this time, since it's so soon after. And you can't get closer than six feet today. Doctor's orders," he added with a laugh.

Dreading what she was about to see, Nancy covered up and stepped over the threshold.

The room was spare, larger than she thought it would be, and dazzling white, the outside sun reflecting oddly off a sculpture on the lawn and shooting straight at the door. Nancy stopped dead in her tracks and shielded her aching eyes. Her headache, almost gone, got a sudden jump start.

"Come in, come in," said a small, frail, distant voice. "It's nice to see people, even space walkers."

Squinting, Nancy identified the problem and side-stepped the shaft of light.

"Wow," Ellis said, coming in behind her. "Like walking into a spotlight."

"Here," said the voice. "I can fix that."

With a mechanical snapping sound, the room suddenly went so dark, both visitors were left walking with outstretched arms in a twilight brought about by a striped line of vertical venetian blinds.

A thin, reedy laughter greeted their reactions. "God, this isn't working out at all."

"No, no, Mom," Ellis said, stepping farther into the room, with only one hand out now. "It's okay. It's getting better already. How're you doin'?"

Nancy came up behind him, using his bulk to stay half hidden, the jarring entrance having undermined her attempt at self-confidence.

"I'm fine, Ellis. A little beaten up, but fine. Introduce me to your friend. Don't be rude."

Her eyesight recovered, Nancy was ushered forward and saw a small, emaciated woman dressed in a hospital gown and sitting in a fake-leather armchair by the side of the window.

"How do you do?" she asked, not daring to approach for fear of breaking a rule. All around her, as Ellis had described, everything was wrapped in plastic, from the furniture to the phone to the TV on the wall. She felt as if she were surrounded by invisible killer rays, all watching for a chink in her rustling white armor.

The old woman's face broke into a wide smile. "Dangerous question to ask around here. But I'm fine. I'm Doris Doyle, by the way, since my son has totally forgotten his manners."

"I'm sorry," Nancy said, remembering her own. "Nancy Martin."

"The thing with the sunlight threw me off," Ellis tried to explain.

Doris Doyle gave her son an approving look. "I don't care about that. You've done well. She's a very pretty girl. Complicated, but very pretty."

Both younger people were at a loss for words. Doris nodded toward Nancy's left hand. "The wedding ring."

Nancy's face turned bright red, making Doris laugh again. "It's all right, dear. Lives are led all sorts of ways. I'm no one to judge, God knows."

She leaned over slightly to fetch something by the side of her chair, clearly fumbling.

"Can I help?" Nancy offered.

"No. You better not. There's some candy they gave me. I keep it in a cup. The treatment swells up your throat a bit."

She finally located a plastic cup and poured a lemon drop into her thin hand.

"Was it pretty uncomfortable?" Nancy asked.

They were a little farther than six feet apart by now, and she could almost see the pain pulsing at the back of Doris's eyes.

"It's nothing much," the older woman said quietly. "There is one thing, though."

"What's that?"

She looked at her son. "Do you remember that pendant your aunt Rose gave me years ago? The heart-shaped one?"

"Sure," he said, pulling two chairs over and proffering one to Nancy.

"It disappeared. I think I threw it out by mistake when I was cleaning up around here. They had me tying off garbage bags like there was no tomorrow, even for a couple of tissues."

Ellis shrugged. "Too bad."

His mother leaned forward slightly. "But that's not it. I think I can get it back. When they do all this radiation stuff, they keep everything you throw away—all your trash, your clothes, your laundry. It's contaminated and they have to lock it up for a long time before they can throw it out for real, or they get in trouble with the land-fills for pollution. One of the nurses was telling me all about it. It's very regulated."

"Did you ask them about it, then?"

"No. I just barely noticed it was gone. I'd taken it off, and I was looking for it this morning because I knew you were coming. Ellis, sweetie, could you see if you could find it? I hate to ask, but . . ."

Ellis held up his hand, already half out of his seat. "Don't worry, Mom. I'm on it."

He hesitated halfway across the room. Doris knew why. "You can leave Nancy here," she told him. "I'll fill her ears about what a problem child you were."

Ellis wandered down the hallway toward the nurses' station, unsure of how to proceed.

"May I help you?"

He turned to a woman in her mid-forties wearing a friendly expression. "Are you a friend of Doris's?" she continued. "I saw you come out of her room."

"I'm her son."

She smiled broadly. "You have a terrific mom. She really lights the place up. Can I help you with something? I'm Ann Coleman."

He touched his throat. "She lost a pendant. She's afraid she threw it out in one of the garbage bags. It's a real sentimental favorite."

Coleman made a face. "Ooh, that's not good. Does she remember when?"

"Maybe just this morning. Somebody told her you keep all that stuff until it's safe."

Coleman nodded. "That's true. We do." She seemed to mull something over in her mind for a few moments before finally saying, "Okay, tell you what. This is totally against the rules, but I really love your mom. You have to keep it under your hat, though, okay?"

Ellis held up his hand, pleasantly surprised. "You bet. I promise."

Coleman led him over to the empty nurses' station, looked around guiltily, and then opened a drawer under the counter. "I'm actually the floor supervisor here, so it's not like it's a criminal act or anything, but it's hot-water territory for sure." She extracted a key from the drawer. "I'm not even supposed to *have* one of these, for example, but it just makes life so much easier. Follow me."

They went down the hallway to a door marked Stairs and descended a flight to the basement as Coleman continued chatting. "Between you and me, most of the security around the low-level nuclear medicine stuff is a little much. In the old days, they had no idea and I don't think it killed anyone, but everybody's so hypersensitive nowadays that they've almost started analyzing pencil shavings. Did Doris wear that pendant all the time?"

"No—mostly just to dress up."

"Meaning she probably just had it in her nightstand drawer while she was undergoing treatment. I bet if they ran a Geiger counter by it, it wouldn't even register. The more I hear, the less worried I am about returning it— assuming we find it," she added, looking over her shoulder at him.

Upstairs, Nancy sat awkwardly in her chair, her hands between her thighs, wondering where to look. She didn't want to stare at Doris but didn't want to be rude by looking out the window.

"It's okay, honey," the older woman said. "I used to

hate going to hospitals, and the sick people were only part of it. These places smell bad, and they give you the willies, and half the time you don't know what anybody's saying." She laughed. "And then you throw us old folks on top of it. *We* smell bad, *we* give you the willies, and you can't understand *us* half the time, either."

Nancy was already shaking her head. "No, no . . ."

"Don't kid a kidder, girl. I wasn't always a fossil at death's door. And don't you believe for a second that Ellis's old man was Father Knows Best."

Nancy stared at her, unsure how to react. Doris raised what was left of her eyebrows. "There you go. Fact is, Ellis doesn't even know who his father was, and to be honest, I don't, either. Could've been one of several friends I had at the time."

Nancy smiled nervously.

"You shocked?" Doris asked, still upbeat and cheerful. "You're cheating on your husband."

The headache returned with new fierceness. Nancy was torn between defending her ground and simply leaving the room. Had her companion taken another tone of voice, she would have left, but all this was being said almost as if Doris considered her the best of pals and was just pulling her leg.

Nancy took a breath and, more for Ellis's sake than hers, decided to trust to this last notion. She forced a small smile. "Not to be mean to Ellis, but you should see his competition."

Doris put her head back and laughed. "Oh, that's good," she finally said, wiping her eyes. "Poor Ellis. He's a nice boy, but my God, I do wonder sometimes." She reached out and waved at Nancy in lieu of tapping her on the knee. "I like you. Did the second you walked into the room. You'll probably end up dumping my son. Most people do. But while he's got you, I hope you can do him some good."

Nancy was struggling for her footing. She understood that she'd passed a test of some kind, and she appreciated Doris's candor, but she was still left wondering about how mother and son were connected emotionally. The simplicity of the images Ellis had evoked in Nancy when he'd invited her on this supposedly sentimental trip had been muddled and warped by how Doris really was. The older woman might have looked the role of a nursery rhyme mother, but her attitude made Nancy doubt how great she'd been performing it.

"What was Ellis like as a kid?" she asked, hoping for both a place to start and a way to duck the spotlight.

Doris shook her head and for the first time looked a little thoughtful. "You're probably asking the wrong person. I'm not going to pull your chain here . . . What did you say your name was?"

"Nancy."

"You have kids?"

"Not yet. I'm hoping to someday."

Doris waved her hand in the air dismissively. "Yeah, well . . . Somebody told me once that having a kid changes your life, moves your priorities around, makes you realize stuff you hadn't thought about before. I think all that's a bunch of bull. I had a kid because I had sex with somebody. I probably could have had an abortion, so I won't deny I was curious about being a mother, but once he was out and I figured out the lay of the land, I couldn't get rid of him fast enough. I'll always owe my sister for that. She took him off my hands almost from the start.

She may not have been any big shakes as a mother, but Christ knows what I would've done to him."

Nancy was disappointed, if not startled. She wished better for Ellis, and perhaps herself by proxy, but given her own knowledge of the world, she didn't find Doris's admission shocking. In fact, she appreciated her honesty. She'd known her share of parents who only paid lip service to what Doris had been smart enough to heed. Doris might have been careless getting pregnant and selfish afterward, but who was Nancy to say that she hadn't best understood her own limitations and, in fact, acted in the child's best interest? Despite her own yearning to become a mother eventually, Nancy was the first to admit that many humans had nothing on bugs when it came to child rearing.

For that matter, maybe Doris should be complimented.

She went at her next question obliquely. "Ellis has never mentioned your sister. Is that the aunt Rose who gave you the pendant?"

Doris's expression was rueful. "Good sister, not so good at life. That's what threw Ellis and me back together—they fell out once he got to be a teenager. No surprise there. She's gone now, so I'm all he has left, and as adults we're pretty good. But bad as I would've been, I wonder if I couldn't've done better than Rosie, now that it's all said and done."

She glanced out the window and sighed. "God, what a life it's been. I'm not really sure why I'm bothering to hang on. Scared, I guess."

She looked back at Nancy. "Rosie drank herself to death. She took Ellis in, but she never treated him as her own, and he was real sensitive to that as he got older. He had to pretty much figure out growing up by himself, and he didn't have very good examples to go by. I give him credit for still being alive."

"He's better than that," Nancy said, finally seeing a place for her own insight. "He's gentle and kind and thoughtful."

Doris smiled at her. "That's nice to hear. I think so, too. He learned it all the hard way, that's for sure, and it cost him a lot, but he's a good man. I realize now how smart I might have been not having that abortion."

Nancy nodded, but the words kept rattling around inside her, taking on more complex and contradictory meaning with each lap. Maybe it was better enjoying how Ellis and his mother had finally ended up than analyzing how they'd gotten there.

In the hospital's basement, Ellis and Ann Coleman walked down a sterile, windowless hallway clearly designed for employees only, with all the doors labeled with numbers and letters, until they came to one with nothing on it whatsoever.

Coleman slipped in her key and turned the door's lock. "Discreet, huh? You'd never know what this one led to."

She swung it back, and they entered a small corridor. There were three more doors leading off from it.

"That's the dangerous one," she said, pointing to the end. "Even I'll admit that. The stuff they keep in there'll kill you before you reach the lobby. They lock it in a huge lead safe called a pig."

She stopped at the first door. "But that's not for us, so we don't need to worry. The iodine treatment trash is all in here."

As she put the key in again, he stepped back a foot.

"Don't worry," she told him, laughing. "I wouldn't do

this if it was dangerous. Like I said, they've overreacted a little. Occasional exposures like this one amount to less than if you stepped out into the sunshine. Radiation is all around us, after all."

She opened the door to reveal a small room filled with a towering pile of thrown-together semitransparent plastic garbage bags. It looked like the very clean interior of a rental moving truck.

"Jesus," he said softly. "How're we gonna find it in there?"

"Simple," Coleman answered, stepping in amid the pile and looking around. "Each bag is labeled with a date and a room number. All we have to do is find your mom's room number and the latest date, which"—she laughed as she reached out—"should be right on top." She turned with the small bag in her hand. "Voilà."

"Cool," he complimented her.

She held the bag up to the light. "If it looks like what I think it does, and it's loose, it should have settled to the bottom. There. What's that? What do you think?"

Ellis squinted through the cloudy density of the plastic. He could dimly make out a hint of gold sliding around, a little bigger than a dime. "That looks about right."

Coleman slipped on a pair of latex gloves from her pocket and opened the bag. She reached deep inside, fished around for a second, and came back out with the prize in hand, glittering from her fingers in the light.

Ellis impulsively kissed her on the cheek. "You are great. I really appreciate it."

Ann Coleman patted him on the shoulder, resealed the bag, and threw it back onto the pile. "Happy to help. Any son of Doris's is a friend of mine. Remember, though . . ."

He held up his hand as if swearing on the Bible. "I know. Not a word. Not even to Mom."

Back upstairs, Ellis found Nancy and Doris laughing together and chatting as he walked into the room, dangling the pendant from his outthrust hand. His mother's eyes widened with pleasure.

"You got it back. I don't believe it."

He walked over to the bed, hung it on the bedpost, and then, laughing, pushed the bed in her direction, thereby maintaining the six-foot proximity rule.

"How did you do it?" Doris asked, smiling and slipping the pendant over her head.

"I'd tell you," he said, "but then I'd have to ki—" He stood before her, frozen, his expression stunned.

She laughed at him. "Kill me? Too little, too late, Ellis." She looked meaningfully at Nancy and added, "And I thought we were getting along so good."

Ellis stammered. "Jesus, Mom . . ."

She shook her head. "I'm kidding, sweetie. It was a good line. I guess you had some help out there."

He sat down, his embarrassment still evident. "I sure did, but they swore me not to tell."

She touched the pendant at her throat. "Well, I'm grateful. I always thought this pendant kind of holds us together, considering where it came from—puts a little Rosie in the room."

Ellis ducked his head and stared at the floor for a few moments before saying, "Yeah."

"She tried, Ellis," his mother said. "In her own messed-up way, she made this possible, you and me, after all these years."

He looked back up at her. "I'm happy for that."

"And," Doris continued, "maybe that made it possible for the two of you to meet up, huh?"

Ellis reached out to his side and took Nancy's hand in his own, a gesture she wasn't sure she could ever remember coming from anyone else.

"If it did, then I guess I can live with it," he said.

Nancy looked at his profile, already weather-beaten in his late thirties, a mix of maturity and childishness. His was like the heart of a boy beating inside a tired bear of a man, and she felt, then and there, that maybe she could be the one to help influence which extreme won out.

Taking her along in the process.

Chapter 9

Several days following his visit to his mother, Ellis woke up and turned his head. Nancy was sleeping beside him, her breathing deep and regular. The blond hair across her forehead was still damp from the sweat of their lovemaking. Slowly, he propped himself up to look at her, flat on her back, naked. This was the fifth time they'd been able to do this, sneaking away and grabbing anything from a few minutes to just over an hour, and he still couldn't decide if it was the best thing ever to happen to him, or the makings of the worst mistake of his life.

It wasn't just fear of discovery that gnawed at him, or the inevitable pain, loss, and probable damage that would result. He'd suffered all three so often they'd acquired a natural taste. It was more the uncertainty of when they'd smack him in the head. Ellis didn't consider himself a born loser, as Mel so often insisted, but more a man un-usually prone to poor luck. It was the constant hapless-ness of his state that dogged him. He was forever feeling like a vole in the middle of a busy highway, unsure which way to turn and all but certain to end up under someone's wheels.

He continued to admire Nancy's sleeping form, recognizing also that perhaps his tendency to self-destruct wasn't always quite as random as he liked to think. He'd made choices along the way, often loaded with risk, of which this was a perfect example.

This time, however, he felt pretty good about the result, and used that to all but disable his natural wariness.

He leaned over and whispered in her ear. "Rise and shine, Nance."

She stirred slightly, bending one tanned leg.

"Gotta get going."

She rolled his way and snuggled up against him, murmuring something into his chest that he couldn't hear. He stroked her back, running his hand down over her hip. She responded instinctively, reaching down between his legs.

He was sorely tempted, not to mention encouraged by his own quick response, but the lingerings of his uneasiness held sway. He followed her hand down and moved it away, kissing her at the same time. "Gotta go," he repeated. "We don't need him hunting you down. He thinks you're out shopping, right?"

She sighed and rolled away to the edge of the bed, dropping her feet over and sitting up, her back to him. He watched her with regret as she rose and quickly replaced her clothes, her movements reflecting both her natural energy and a touch of anger.

She finally turned as he too began dressing. "Why're we so worried about him all the time?"

Ellis pulled up his jeans and paused, saddened that the inevitable had finally been broached. It wasn't that the subject had never occurred to him, or even that it seemed a problem without solution, which it did. It was more the familiarity of that dreaded, oft-encountered moment when a decision was called for and he felt himself quailing.

"Don't you think we should be?" he asked, as if ducking a small thrown object. He reached for his T-shirt.

Curiously, this actually seemed to stump her for a moment. "Other people break up all the time," she said quietly. "Mel and me don't even have kids, and it's not like we own much. He could keep the trailer."

Ellis said nothing, sitting back down to put on his socks and boots.

"You'd like that to happen, wouldn't you?" she asked, her voice almost timid. "For you and me to work out?"

He looked over his shoulder at her, one boot in hand. "Jeez, Nance. What d'ya think? Sure I would."

But Mel might as well have been standing in the room for all the strength of their conviction. Such was his hold over them.

Nancy appeared to collapse in the face of an argument that hadn't even begun. "It's so unfair," she said miserably.

He rose and circled the bed to put his arms around her, an awkward bear hugging a child. "It'll work out."

But he hadn't the slightest idea how.

Far to the south, in Hartford, Connecticut, Joe Gunther was ushered into a basement office with a picture window overlooking not the outdoors but a vast, low-ceilinged room lined with metal filing cabinets. Sitting behind a desk decorated with an incongruously colorful vase of cut flowers and a carved wooden nameplate was a tall, middle-aged woman with suspiciously uniform black hair. The nameplate spelled out "Jennifer Joyce."

"Special Agent Gunther?" she asked, extending her hand.

He shook hands but moved to the window rather than sit opposite her. "Holy smokes, this is impressive."

Joyce laughed with embarrassment. "Looks are deceiving. It's just a huge graveyard, really."

He turned toward her. "But where exhumations are as steady as burials, I bet. What amazes me is that most people think facilities like this don't exist anymore—that everything's on computers."

"Don't I wish," she said. "It would sure make my life easier." Her face brightened. "The index is computerized, at least. That's something. We used to have to walk up and down the rows, hunting for what we were after."

Joe smiled back agreeably, although in truth he had a preference for just that kind of digging. It appealed to the hunter in him and satisfied his need to see things as they really were rather than as shimmering characters on a screen, as seemingly evanescent as the electricity giving them life.

But he didn't need to fear any debate on the subject. His hostess had already returned to the task that had brought them together.

"Dr. Hillstrom's fax seems perfectly in order, and the director just e-mailed me his approval allowing you access to the case, so I guess there's no more to it than to give you a cubby and let you have at it." Joyce finally rose from her desk and crossed to the door, revealing a combination of tight skirt, black fishnet stockings, and stiletto heels that Joe hadn't seen in more decades than he cared to remember. Retro was alive, at least for one enthusiastic participant.

She led him down the hall to a metal door marked with

a number and showed him a room reminiscent of a high-end bank vault. "Make yourself comfortable," she said. "Be right back."

The room was an exaggerated closet in size and decorated solely with a table and chair. The walls were bare and the ceiling lined with fluorescent strip lighting. He felt like a human subject about to undergo an uncomfortable experiment.

His connection to the outside world reappeared some ten minutes later, bearing an inch-thick folder.

"Here you go," she said brightly. "Everything we've got about Judith Morgenthau. Any questions or problems, just push the button by the door."

With that, she was gone, softly closing the door behind her—he hoped not hermetically.

He stared at the closed file for a moment. It was old, slightly yellowed, and soiled along the edges, indicating considerable use a long time ago.

Taking a small breath, he flipped back the cover.

Such dossiers have a system, usually a chronology and a department sectioning, combined. The police have their piece of it, the ME's office theirs, then the hospital, and on down the line, depending on the case and how far it extends. This one, despite the cost it had exacted from Hillstrom, had still been pretty straightforward—a body found on the road, autopsied and identified, had been ascribed a cause of death in coordination with the police investigation that had eventually located the initial offending car.

That was merely the nutshell. The trick was going to be in finding and analyzing the nut.

He began, out of habit, with the photographs—first those of the scene, showing an initially unrecognizable lump, until details like a hand or foot eventually became discernible. Then the autopsy shots—here the body, or what was left of it, was washed and carefully laid out. The damage was horrendous. Body parts had been pulled apart and scattered over several hundred feet, and only placed in their proper position at the morgue. The prior mess at the scene now looked like a female body made up of bits and pieces. He certainly understood why it had been difficult initially to tell the difference between this poor woman and a dead dog.

He skipped the rest of the ME's findings for the moment, knowing that was where he would have to be most thorough, and opted instead for the police reports.

These, too, had a comforting feel to them, even though the paperwork was both ancient and different from what he knew in Vermont. He traced the investigation from the initial call to the summoning of an investigative team to the arrival and findings of the forensic techs. Reports and narratives followed, detailing how, once the deceased's name was made clear, her lifestyle and habits were painstakingly reconstructed through a blossoming of interviews.

Here Joe paid close attention, cross-referencing with some of the ME's reports, concentrating on statements made by those who might have known she was pregnant, watching for the classic what-did-he-know-and-when-did-he-know-it smoking gun of lore, hoping to pin Medwed to a precise spot on a timeline of knowledge. Hillstrom had said that she'd only been brought in after the actual autopsy, once the workload and media buzz had started building. Joe wasn't expecting a signed memo from her boss asking her to take the blame for covering up the woman's pregnancy, but some proof that Medwed had known of the condition before she did would have been nice. Nice but not likely, as it turned out, since all signs of his even being near the autopsy had been obliterated to protect him. Typically, Hillstrom's loyalty had been matched by her thoroughness.

Progress was slow and frustrating. Joe located a copy of Morgenthau's medical records from her doctor's office, entered the day before the accident, detailing what looked at first to be a routine visit. He took several tries at deciphering a notation in nearly illegible script at the bottom of a page labeled "to be transcribed," before figuring out that the doc had in fact ordered a pregnancy test. Intrigued and suddenly hopeful, Joe dug deeper, expecting to find the results, but concluded that they must have arrived after her death and thus were never added to the file. He cross-checked with the police narratives concerning the woman's medical history. The test didn't surface there, either, which all but eliminated the police from being inside the loop.

Because of a general backlog—along with the body's condition—the autopsy was delayed for two days, creating the possibility that the pregnancy's existence could have reached Medwed's ear before she'd been opened up. The victim and her husband, after all, had been political allies of the medical examiner. A discreet phone call might have been made.

But Joe could find no record of any contact between widower and chief.

He extracted the autopsy report and pushed the rest of the file off to a far corner of the desk. It was typed and anointed with arcane language he could only just follow. He tried his best to accompany the narrator on this specialized tour of a human body, but when he finally did come upon the mention of a fetus in the first stage of development, he felt no particular elation. For while there was no allusion to Hillstrom's connection with this case until a day later, the fact remained that her signature adorned the bottom of the autopsy report.

On paper, regardless of where he looked, it seemed that his friend Beverly had been the first to know of Judy Morgenthau's impending motherhood.

Joe sat back in his chair to rub the bridge of his nose, letting his hands drop into his lap afterward. He stared sightlessly at what he couldn't prove was a forged document.

And then he leaned forward, his eyes narrowing, not only seeing something he'd been staring at all along, but recalling, too, his own experiences visiting the Vermont ME's office. Almost always in those situations, there had been at least one other person in the room with the doctor and the body, and sometimes more. In his myopic efforts to distinguish Medwed from Hillstrom, Joe had completely overlooked the documented presence of a third person: Susan Bedell, here listed as "lab assistant."

Joe rose to his feet and pushed the button by the door. Barely two minutes later his exotic handler appeared, her eyebrows raised inquiringly. "You all set?"

"Almost. I need a favor. There's someone mentioned as a lab assistant in the medical examiner's office, named Susan Bedell. Is there any chance you could make your computer cough up anything on her? Like where she might be now?"

Jennifer Joyce looked thoughtful for a couple of seconds, and then conspiratorial. Her voice dropped as she said, "Come with me. We'll make it happen."

He followed her back to her special fishbowl and

joined her as she dragged her guest chair around so that it nestled next to hers before the computer screen.

"Okay," she said, settling down and wiggling her fingers as if preparing to play the piano. "Let's see what we can find out. What's this person's name?"

"Susan Bedell." He spelled it out.

"No birth date, I guess?"

"Sorry."

Joyce was already typing. "Not to worry. It's an unusual name and you know where she worked. What date, by the way?"

He gave it to her.

She straightened slightly in her chair, looking pleased. "Okay, got her. Now I copy down her PID, since names don't count for diddly in this system, and . . ." She paused dramatically as they both waited for a new screen image to appear. "There you go. She retired four years ago."

Joe squinted at the document before them. "Any idea where she might be now? I'd sure love to talk to her."

The fingers resumed their skittering across the keyboard. Once again Joyce allowed for a triumphant smile, even adding, "Darn, too easy. I thought I'd be able to show off a little more than this." She tapped the screen with a remarkably long crimson fingernail. "This is where they mail her checks. Suffield. Nice town."

Suffield, Connecticut, is a curious mix of a town, a spread-out collection of odds and ends that forms only fragments of a suburb, some farmland, a small shopping center, the tiniest of business districts, and a couple of rows of huge old mansions, all floating around a private school campus of pristine perfection. It's picturesque, fashionable, and has several signs attesting to its antiquity.

But for all the colonial and Victorian architecture, ancient trees, and several churches boasting graveyards filled with black-clad, austere people fond of wool and buckle shoes, the entire town has a scrubbed, fresh-out-of-the-box feel. Joe wasn't sure whether it was his own background or the general condition of his home state, but he found he preferred a little grittiness in his surroundings. From what he could see of it, this place was so clean, he felt he might bounce off it.

The street address he'd been given was on the far end of town, past the school and the churches and the Playmobil downtown mall, just beyond what looked to be the place's only gas station. He approached at a snail's pace, searching for the right number, confused by every building's looking exactly like its neighbors. In fact, if it hadn't been for those numbers, he couldn't have distinguished the address.

He pulled up at last opposite 346 and sat quietly for a moment, enjoying the warm breeze wafting through the open window. Joe, a Vermonter by birth, had a northerner's innate sense of weather, and an appreciation for those few months every year when the ambient temperature wasn't life threatening.

He got out and stretched, surveying the scene. The buildings all appeared to be narrow two-story apartments, their height supposedly compensating for what he imagined was tiny overall square footage. He walked up this one's immaculate path and rang a doorbell labeled "Bedell."

"Are you looking for me?" a voice asked him.

He stared at the still-closed door and turned to look at the empty street.

"Up here."

He stepped back off the stoop and looked up. Directly above him was an open window framing the face and torso of a thin, white-haired woman with a pleasant expression.

"I am if you're Susan Bedell," he said, smiling. "I feel like I'm in a play."

She laughed. "Right—Romeo, my Romeo, turn up your hearing aid."

He told her his name, showing his badge.

"Come on in," she said with no apparent surprise. "I'll meet you downstairs. And don't walk too fast or you'll find yourself out back."

He had been worried about the kind of person he'd be relying on for old memories. This, he thought hopefully, held some promise. He showed himself inside.

She hadn't exaggerated by much. The place was minute. It was also tidy, wonderfully decorated, and smelled of the best that a summer day has to offer.

"Sorry about that," said the woman, coming downstairs. "I was working on my computer and was too lazy to come down, in case you were a Bible thumper. I get a lot of them for some reason."

She gave him a firm handshake and introduced herself. "I'm Susan Bedell."

"Joe Gunther," he repeated. "I really appreciate your seeing me."

She slipped by him and headed into what was more a galley than a kitchen. "Believe me, I get so few guests that I'm even reconsidering the Bible folks. Coffee?"

He accepted and leaned against the doorjamb as she set about making two mugs' worth.

"You said you were from Vermont," she said, not looking up. "You hot on the trail of someone?"

He hadn't been sure how to broach the subject. He'd gotten no idea from Hillstrom of the general mood of her old office, and had certainly never heard of Bedell before today. For all he knew, this woman and Hillstrom had hated each other.

"Something that dates way back," he began carefully. "To when you worked with Medwed."

She paused in midmotion to glance at him. "Wow, you're not kidding. What are you working on?"

He hesitated, which was clearly all she needed. "Don't worry about confidentialities. I have no one to tell. Of course, that might work both ways, depending on what you want."

He nodded several times. "I realize that. I'm hoping the passage of time will make some of those issues moot."

She'd gone back to fixing the coffee, pouring hot water into the mugs. "Either that or make me the most useless interview you've had in a long time. Go ahead. Shoot."

"Do you remember someone named Beverly Hillstrom?"

To his relief, her face lit up. "Beverly? Good Lord, yes. Such a serious young woman, but one of the truly decent souls. I never saw such focus, before or since." Her expression darkened. "Is she all right?"

"Fine, fine. At least physically. I'm actually trying to help her through some political trouble."

Bedell looked relieved. "I had to ask. All those years hanging around the dead. It kind of gets under the skin—makes you morbid."

She handed him his coffee, squeezed by again, and led the way through a perfectly appointed, if child-size, living room and out into a backyard just a little larger than a Ping-Pong table. They sat around a white-painted wrought-iron table and admired a carefully nurtured array of flowers and plants.

Bedell took a sip before resuming. "I always worried a little about Beverly. She never took half measures and never let herself off the hook. Actually, to be honest, I'm not surprised she's in some political trouble. What's she doing nowadays?"

"She heads up the OCME in Vermont."

"Really? Good for her. I'm not surprised. Not surprised she's a chief, and not surprised it's in a little place like that. No offense."

"None taken." It was very good coffee. "How did she get along with Howard Medwed?"

"That was your classic master-student relationship. I sometimes felt that had it been with anyone else, it might have ended up wrong, but Medwed had no idea what power he held over her. He just duffed around, doing his thing, being a brilliant mess and letting us clean up after him."

"I think that's why I'm here, to be honest."

"One of Medwed's screwups? Which one?"

Gunther laughed at her attitude. "Flat-footed" was one word for it. He wondered if Medwed had ever fully appreciated her.

"I think it was actually a pretty big deal, at least locally. Hillstrom told me people got all worked up over it."

Bedell's eyes had grown big. "You're not talking about the Morgenthau case, are you?"

"That's it."

"Good golly. Talk about an old ghost. That *was* a big deal. Almost got Medwed fired, and it did force Beverly out the door. I guess you already know that."

"But not much more, I don't. That's what I'm looking for—the gory details."

She laughed. "You would use that word."

He shook his head apologetically. "Oh, right—sorry . . ."

"No, no," she interrupted. "If I'm used to anything, it's stuff like that. We got so good sounding respectful outside the office, while we were so completely not that way behind closed doors . . ." She waved it off. "Brings back memories, that's all. Good ones, I might add. Okay, what did you want to know?"

"It's not that difficult," he admitted, "but a lot hangs on it: I need to know when Medwed found out Morgenthau was pregnant."

"Right off the bat," Susan said immediately. "He's the one who did the autopsy. I was there when he made the discovery." She saw the question forming on his face and answered, "And no, Beverly wasn't in the room. I have an absolute memory of it, not only because of how it all ended up, but because I kept a daily journal and I put it all down."

Joe couldn't believe his luck. "You still have that?"

She smiled at him. "God knows why, but that's what we diarists do—like we were Eudora Welty or somebody. I don't even have kids to pass them on to. No," she added after a brief pause, "Medwed and I were alone. I saw him straighten suddenly as he reached Judy's lower abdomen, and he said something like 'Oh, my dear,' with real sadness, which was unusual for him. He was pretty much all business when he was working. And that's when he told me."

"She wasn't far along, from what I hear," Joe commented.

"Eight to ten weeks. You know she was fifty years old, right? They'd given up years ago."

"So I heard."

"It was a big emotional deal. Medwed was close friends with the Morgenthaus—that's why he was doing the autopsy, in fact, as a favor to Mr. Morgenthau, which probably wasn't appropriate. And then to find this out. Medwed just stood there for a while, staring down at the body, shaking his head and muttering to himself."

"He'd just lost his own wife, hadn't he?"

"Yes," Bedell answered. "And been diagnosed with cancer. Loss was pretty much all he was thinking about in those days."

"Including losing his job," Joe said softly.

Susan raised her eyebrows. "Yes, that was the crux of the whole thing later. At the time, when we were both together in the autopsy room, he swore me to secrecy—said that Judy's death was bad enough, but that news of her being pregnant would put the last nail in her husband's coffin."

"He was ill, too?" Joe asked.

Susan laughed. "No, but you have to consider Medwed's state of mind. He could be very sentimental. Anyhow, whatever his reasons, that was the end of Mrs. Morgenthau's pregnancy, at least officially."

"But it got out," Joe reminded her.

"Well, that was just stupid. I was going to type up the report from his taped narrative. It wasn't really one of my jobs. I just did it now and then, to fill in for the secretary when she was out or on vacation. After I'd finished, though—avoiding all mention of the pregnancy—I left the original tape to be destroyed. Incredibly stupid. I even offered to resign over it later, except Medwed wouldn't hear of it, nor would Beverly."

"What happened?" Joe was confused, having read the autopsy report just that day. The pregnancy was quite clearly stated.

"I had the following day off," she admitted sadly. "Like I said, I didn't often do the reports. The regular girl came in, found the original tape, typed it up all neat and tidy, and only then discovered my doctored transcription, which hadn't been filed according to her own system. Now she had a decision to make, and she went with her own report as the more complete one. She never even asked around. Surely, she must have been curious. But she just filed it. I never could prove it, but I always wondered if she was paid off by someone. Anyhow, that's when the heat got turned onto Medwed, and when Beverly stepped up to sign the report in his place. In those days the notes were just that—they didn't reflect the actual physician until they'd been typed and formalized. Not even the secretary knew at that point." She took a meditative sip of her coffee and added, "I never liked that woman."

"And Medwed died a few months later?" Joe asked.

"Yes," she said sadly. "After Beverly had landed a new job elsewhere—I don't remember where now. That's why I never told anyone. There was no point to it, except to get me fired. I never got over it, though, since I held myself responsible for the truth getting out. I felt so guilty for years."

She suddenly brightened. "Which is why I'll do whatever I can to help Beverly any way I can. Would you like that diary?"

"A copy would do, along with a sworn statement. You could mail it to me."

"No, no," she said, rising and heading back inside. "It won't take me a second. I'll do the statement whenever and with whomever, but take the journal now. You can mail it back. It's not only got the day of that autopsy, but everything else, too. It's a real smoking gun. And they can test it for when it was written and anything else they want, too, if it comes to that. Like I said, if I can help Beverly all these years later, maybe I'll get to rest easier when my time comes."

She vanished into the house and went upstairs. Joe finished his coffee and returned to the front hallway to await her, pleased with how things had turned out. With the diary in hand and Bedell's testimony available if needed, Floyd Freeman back in Vermont would suddenly discover he had no ammunition against Hillstrom.

That was probably enough to get Hillstrom back in fighting trim, not to mention have her run those additional tests on Michelle Fisher. But knowing, as he did, about Hillstrom's marital and job security concerns, Joe began thinking that something more than just neutering Freeman might be a nice touch—perhaps even a little role reversal, giving Hillstrom his previous advantage.

And Joe had a good notion of just where to find it.

Susan Bedell returned downstairs and handed him a battered fake-leather notebook, labeled with the relevant year. "Here you go. Use it to good effect and tell Beverly I was tickled pink that I could help her out. No way is the ledger balanced. I'll always feel bad about what happened. But maybe this'll count for something."

Gunther flipped through the pages of tight, careful handwriting. "Not to worry, Susan. I'll make sure this makes her day."

Bedell opened the front door to show him out. "You know the final irony?" she asked him as he stepped out onto the walkway.

"What's that?"

"Morgenthau, the grieving widower. For all the pain that Medwed thought he'd feel by losing a wife and child both, he went out and married a young thirty-something within six months and had two kids just like that." She snapped her fingers. "We could've ducked the whole mess just by being honest from the start."

Joe nodded and thanked her again, pondering the truth of her last assumption. He'd simply gotten too old to believe that honesty would set you free. He'd seen too many people destroyed as a result, at least politically.

He was a fatalist nowadays, more burdened by what people did than by how and why they did it.

Chapter 10

Mel stared sourly at the shot glass he'd just smacked down onto the bar top. "You're not much fun since you stopped drinking."

Ellis glanced up from his Diet Coke and took in the rows of bottles across from them, his face suddenly flushed with guilt. "Feel better, though," he said in a neutral tone, hoping the poor lighting would shadow his expression.

"I don't give a shit about that," Mel answered him, not moving. "You're lousy company. That's all I know. You and Nancy, both. Might as well be goddamned Holy Rollers."

Ellis pursed his lips. He didn't like Mel referring to Nancy. He felt he wore his feelings for her like a scent, available to anyone who took the time to notice. He found himself not mentioning her around Mel, and then worrying that the other man might pick up on the omission. Like the booze—he'd stopped taking it for her sake. This whole thing was driving him crazy.

They were at Piccolo's, a bar near Benmont, Bennington's old mill district and its perpetual low-income neighborhood. It was the kind of establishment that hard drinkers retired to after the polite bars had called it a night. Tellingly, the sheriff's office was just around the corner. Ellis had resisted Mel's invitation to join him, fearful of how the atmosphere might undermine his newborn abstinence. But now that he was here, he'd discovered that the old urge was less strong than in the past—something he ascribed solely to Nancy.

Not that there'd been much choice in the matter. Mel's invitation had amounted to a command—at least as Ellis had treated it.

"There," Mel said suddenly. "That's the guy."

Ellis looked up into the long mirror reflecting the dark room behind them. A young man with long, greasy hair and a soiled red baseball cap was walking among the decals of beer logos adorning the mirror's surface.

"See him?" Mel insisted.

"Yeah," Ellis acknowledged carefully.

"That's High Top—the one I was telling you about."

Ellis watched the man, dreading what might be coming next. "Dumb name."

"It's 'cause his brain's fried. Too much dope. Doesn't even need it anymore to get where he's going. Not that *that* stops him."

"What do we want with him?"

Ellis's tone clearly lacked the enthusiasm he once might have shown. Mel straightened and gave him a painful jab in the arm. "What the fuck do you care? You his mother? You actually give a shit if he lives or dies?"

Ellis hesitated. There was a time when he might not have. But the past couple of weeks had felt like a rebirth. Not that he could admit any of that to this man. "No."

"What we want with him, douche bag," Mel continued, "is information. That's the key to a good business deal. I told you that already. How many times?"

He expected an answer. Ellis rubbed his arm. "A bunch."

"It's like asking a food nut about the best place to eat," Mel said. "This guy's a drug nut. Guess what we're going to ask him?"

Ellis covered the small lurch in his stomach by taking a sip of his Coke. Another job in the works. Not exactly a surprise, but it still struck home with a dreaded familiarity. He didn't answer.

Mel didn't notice. He was winding up, his eyes tracking High Top's journey around the room as he glad-handed a collection of acquaintances. "What do you think about when you think about Bennington?"

Frankly, Ellis thought, it was Nancy. "I don't know," he answered.

"It's a port of entry," Mel told him. "Like a place where cargo ships have to enter and declare what's on board. You know? Like a customs . . . whatever they call it."

Ellis got the point. "Right."

"And guess what's entering?"

Gee, Ellis thought, the dread deepening. "Drugs?"

This time it was a slap on the back instead of a jab. "You got it. Now guess who they got to declare to?"

Ellis didn't bother. Mel was already laughing. "That's it, ol' buddy—you and me. We're going into the taxing business. Steal from the rich and give to the poor, and we're the poor. Those guys wanna get off the interstate and avoid Brattleboro and the state cops and come sneaking in the back door, they gotta pay us a little off the top."

Mel signaled to the barkeep to bring him another shot.

Reluctantly, Ellis looked at High Top with more interest, now that he knew they would inevitably meet. He was scrawny, in his early to mid-twenties, unshaven and unwashed, with the bright eyes and nervous smile of a man with damaged synapses. Not much as a single target—below even the bingo guy they'd rolled a couple of weeks ago.

But Ellis was less sure of what he'd lead to. Mel's hypothetical about what they would eventually ask this man had him worried. There were several key drug portals into Vermont, and Bennington, with major highways into both Massachusetts and New York, was one of them—all the more prized because it didn't straddle a high-visibility interstate.

And where there was that kind of traffic, there also tended to be some very ruthless men. Not the kind of people they'd dealt with in the past.

"What's High Top know?" he asked.

Mel laughed. "Not *what*, Ellis, my man—*who*. In his messed-up, brain-fried way, that pathetic little toad is the keeper of the keys—the guy who'll lead us to the land of the pharaohs."

Ellis didn't comment. His view of how to reach the promised land was beginning to lie elsewhere, and for the first time in his life, he was pretty sure someone like Mel would not be his passport—with or without High Top.

But old habits die hard, and Ellis was having difficulty formulating how he could forge a new path. If he was lucky enough to end up with Nancy, he'd also have to be ambitious enough to get a full-time job, something he'd never done. In the meantime, while dreading the inevitability of the familiar, he found himself just going along.

"You been hearing about all those car radio rip-offs?" Mel was saying.

"Yeah," Ellis answered vaguely, not sure that he had.

Mel motioned with his chin at the reflected scene in the mirror. "Well, he's the guy doin' it. I saw him. He's actually pretty good. Real fast. Made me wonder, though, what he was up to. I mean, why so many, and why all of a sudden?"

Ellis was unsure if the question was rhetorical or demanded a response. Hedging his bets, he muttered, "Yeah."

That seemed adequate. Mel nodded. "Right," he said, and went back to watching his quarry. A few minutes later, he nudged Ellis in the arm again, this time less violently, and pushed a ten-dollar bill onto the bar top. "Let's go."

Ellis looked up, startled, and saw High Top in the mirror, angling toward the front door. He let out a small groan, unheard by his companion, who'd already shoved free of his stool and was taking off like a raptor.

They reached the sidewalk on Depot Street in time to see their angular prey doing a jittery march down County Street, heading away from Benmont.

"Where's he going?" Ellis asked, regretting the question instantly.

Mel glared back at him. "The fuck do I know? Just keep your mouth shut and hang back."

But it was Mel's voice that made High Top glance for just a split second over his shoulder at them. Half fried, perhaps, but still clinging to self-preservation. Despite the two of them looking as if they'd merely left the bar at the same time, High Top nervously crossed the street to put some distance between them.

Mel cursed under his breath. He gestured to his younger colleague to come abreast of him. "Say something loud and give me a push," he ordered quietly.

Ellis understood and began a playacting skit that made them look like a couple of drunks sorting through an argument as they staggered down the sidewalk. Across the way, they saw High Top give them a second look and noticed the tension fade from his gait.

Once more, as so often in the past, Ellis felt the adrenaline beginning to stir in him, along with the self-loathing that increasingly accompanied it.

The charade lasted as far as the intersection of County and the heavily traveled Route 7 corridor, one block up. There, whether because he was still pursuing his original destination or merely testing them again, High Top suddenly bolted across the still significant traffic to the far side.

"Little shit made us," Mel swore, snapping out of his role and looking for a gap in the flow of cars before them. "Not as brain-dead as I thought. Come on."

For a man of his build, Mel could move fast when he had to, and Ellis was hard put both to keep up and not get run over. In the latter effort, however, he caused an oncoming driver to lean on his horn, and like a bell at a horse race, that signal made High Top put his head down and take off.

They were in an unusual part of Bennington, given the burgeoning development on both sides of them. Here, just north of County Street, in a demilitarized zone separating where the malls were settling in and where the original town was located, there was an undulating spread of lawns and parkland bordering the banks of the Roaring Branch Brook—an offshoot of the Walloomsac that had once powered the area's many mills. This was open land, a park dotted with a few trees and the scattered buildings of the veterans' home and the State Office Complex, but it was dark and quiet and easy to get lost in.

Which was clearly High Top's intention.

By the time they hit the other side of Route 7, Mel and Ellis were loping like lumbering hounds after their quarry's flickering shadow, all subterfuge evaporated. Each was an unlikely choice for a footrace—where the prey appeared light and wiry, he'd been handicapped by self-abuse and poor health, and where the hunters should have been slowed by their bulk alone, their ambition more than compensated.

All three dove deeper into the park's gloomy embrace, the latter two closing in.

A single slip finally ended it. High Top hesitated as he approached a small hedge by the water's edge, cut right too late to get around it, and felt his feet go out from under him.

Mel pinned him to the ground like a mastiff on a hare.

"Jesus H. Christ, you little bastard," Mel panted, spitting into the grass by the other man's ear, "what the fuck you take off like that for?"

"What d'you think?" High Top coughed, squirming to get free. "You came after me. What d'you guys want?"

Ellis was standing bent over, breathless, his hands on his knees, watching the two of them, unable to speak.

Mel shifted around so that he sat astride High Top's waist, his large hands keeping the other man's shoulders pressed to the ground. The sound of the water nearby forced him to lean forward to be heard. Around them, barely visible between the screening trees and bushes, the town's lights glimmered like cautious fireflies keeping their distance.

"We want to find out what you been up to."

"I haven't been up to nuthin'. I don't even know you guys."

"You didn't need to," Mel told him. "Now you do."

High Top's eyes moved from one to the other of them fearfully. He was clearly at a loss.

"Okay," he said cautiously.

"Why you been stealing radios?" Mel asked.

A split second of calculation crossed High Top's face, virtually unnoticeable, before he smiled and said, "For money, duh."

But Mel had seen it clearly. His hands moved in, closer to the small man's throat.

"You sure you want to stick with that?" he asked, adding, "Duh?"

"Maybe some drugs, too," High Top conceded.

Mel swiveled his shaggy head toward Ellis. "Maybe some drugs, too, he says."

Ellis didn't respond, still watching. Waiting. Unsure of what was happening, as confused as their victim about exactly why they were doing this.

Mel returned to High Top. "Who're you getting these drugs from, little man?"

Again that tiny crafty glimmer, instantly suppressed. "You know—people. Around."

Mel's thumbs caressed High Top's carotids. "Let me tell you what I heard. How 'bout that?"

The smallest of nods, followed by an almost inaudible "Sure."

"I heard there was a new pipeline in town. A coupla guys from New York—cousins. That they take in trade and money, both."

High Top looked up at him, expecting more.

So did Ellis, surprised by this new intelligence, but Mel merely asked, "So?"

High Top hesitated. "So what? I don't know."

"They're not why you're stealing radios? A freak like you? How many radios you steal so far?"

The question caught the kid off guard. "Fifty, maybe."

Mel laughed. "You're a one-man crime wave. Jesus, man. What're their names?"

High Top scowled. "Who?"

For the first time, Mel applied his thumbs where they'd been simply poised. High Top's eyes snapped open, and he struggled under Mel's considerable weight.

Mel let off and let the boy gasp for a few seconds before saying, "You get what's going on here, you little shit? This is not a conversation. This is where you answer what I ask you. You got that?"

He was met with a silent nod, and Ellis saw in the addict's face that his appreciation of the situation had sharpened.

As had Ellis's. He looked around nervously, as if hoping a staircase might appear from the night sky to give him a way out.

"Okay," Mel said. "Let's try it again. Who're the two guys?"

"What're you gonna do?" was the response.

Mel straightened, his surprise obvious. "What d'you give a fuck what I'm gonna do?"

"You don't wanna mess with them."

Mel leaned forward again, applying pressure to High Top's throat. "You stupid goofball, I don't need a guardian angel. Give me the goddamn names."

He held on longer than last time, until it looked as though his victim might pass out. Ellis was pacing back and forth, shoving his fists in and out of his pockets, gripped equally by panic and indecision.

Once more, Mel let go. High Top's recovery was slower, more measured. His hands, which before had thrashed against Mel's brawny forearms, merely fluttered to both sides, as if following commands radioed in from far away.

"I only know one," he finally said in a whisper all but swept away by the passing water. "Name's Bob."

"Bob what?"

"Don't know—funny last name . . . sounds like Nemo or something."

"Where's he live?"

"Benmont." High Top gave the number.

"What's the routine?" Mel demanded. "How do they check you out?"

"They got people they trust."

"Who are they? You must've passed muster."

Ellis didn't know how the young man managed it, but he actually sneered up at Mel. "You gotta know them, dummy," he said.

Ellis never knew what prompted the remark. It seemed like such a foolish thing, to gamble everything on a one-liner.

But without a doubt, High Top had made a choice, as was clear from his final expression. As Ellis stared in horror and Mel, in disgust, bore down one last time with both thumbs, the look in the kid's eyes, just before they dilated and went lifeless, was triumphant.

Mel grunted afterward, placed one hand flat against the body's chest, and used it to shove himself back up to a standing position.

Ellis had to remember to breathe. "Mel. You killed him."

Mel shrugged. "Yeah. Little asshole."

Ellis took a step back, the realization of what had happened in the proverbial blink of an eye overtaking him like a nightmare. "You killed him," he repeated in a whisper.

Mel was gazing down at his handiwork appreciatively, as if what decorated the grass was just another project. Ellis had seen the same look that day in the woods when they'd reduced all those glass bottles to silvery glints with the machine guns. Mel's face was the embodiment of pure pleasure following a job well done.

"Why?" Ellis asked, transfixed by the corpse.

Mel seemed genuinely baffled. "Why not? Who's gonna miss him? I got what I wanted."

"We could've followed him. It was just an address."

Mel scowled. "What the fuck is your problem? You know this kid?"

Ellis shook his head, tearing his eyes away from High Top and finally looking straight into Mel's shadowy face, studying it as if it had sprouted new features.

"That's not the point. You killed him. That's huge."

Mel took two steps toward him, making him flinch. "What d'you think we're playing at, Ellis?" he asked.

The answer was absolutely honest. "I don't know."

"You think we just been jerking around, banging people, ripping them off, waiting till we can retire to three hots and a cot and all the butt fucking we can handle in some federal lockup? That what you think?"

Ellis didn't answer.

"That's your dream, bucko. Not mine. My idea of success is not a shit-hole trailer and a bitchy old lady whose butt is starting to sag. I got a plan." He tapped the side of his head before pointing at the body nearby. "And that little cockroach doesn't amount to shit on my shoe along the way."

Ellis was momentarily distracted by some of what he'd heard. "You goin' to dump Nancy?"

Mel's eyes widened. "What the . . . ? You got a tongue out for my wife?"

Ellis held up both hands, feeling his face redden and hoping the darkness would provide enough cover. "Jesus, Mel. Where'd you get that? You're like one person to me, the two of you. What you just said surprised me, is all."

Mollified, Mel shrugged. "Fuck, I don't know. What do you want to do with him?"

They both returned their attention to the body, Ellis suddenly grateful for its presence.

"Whatever it is, we better do it now," he suggested.

Chapter 11

Joe Gunther followed the receptionist across the very room imagined in most visions of bureaucratic hell: huge, no windows, an oppressively low acoustic ceiling, and rows of harsh fluorescent lighting, inhabited by people nestled in tiny chest-high cubicles. It made Joe think of refugees crowded into a sports arena, their identities reduced to a cot in the middle of the floor. In that light, the decorations in the work spaces he passed—family pictures, flowers, posters portraying Hawaii—became life preservers.

The receptionist reached the far wall and stood aside at an open door labeled "Director," beyond which a second woman sat at a desk near yet another door.

"Mr. Gunther for Director Freeman," she intoned before giving Joe a quick smile and disappearing.

Joe didn't look back, passing instead into the anteroom and smiling at the new factotum. "He's expecting me," he told her, repeating what he'd said to the first one.

She looked vaguely irritated as she rose and moved to the inner door. "Of course."

She mimicked her predecessor's motions, twisting the knob and stepping back with a small flourish, announcing him to the person inside. For a split second, he saw this happening eight times in a row, with eight women each going through the same motions, and with him suddenly standing back out on the street.

But there were no more doors ahead. Just a man rising from his desk with the smoothness of a limousine leaving the curb, circling around to shake hands and point out which chair to occupy, as his secretary faded away.

"To what do I owe the honor?" Floyd Freeman asked, staying out in front of the large desk and taking the companion guest chair. Very polished, in fact literally—Joe noticed he had manicured fingernails. "It's not often the state's top cop drops by." Freeman laughed and concluded, "I hope I'm not in any trouble."

Gunther had considered this moment, even anticipated some of the language. But instead of responding as he'd thought he might, he merely extracted a small tape player from his pocket and laid it on his knee.

Without a word spoken, he pushed the Play button.

Beverly Hillstrom's precise voice entered the quiet room. She was speaking on a phone in the middle of an ongoing conversation.

"I realize that we've had our professional differences, Mr. Freeman. And I'm sorry to say that it appears we've had our personal ones, too, dating back to the death of your au pair, Ellen Turnley . . ."

Freeman slid forward in his chair, but was stopped in midreach for the recorder by the fierceness of Gunther's glare. "What is this?" he asked instead, his eyes narrowed, as Joe hit the Pause button.

"It's something I'd like you to hear."

"That was a private conversation," he said. "I doubt this is even legal."

"That's an interesting place to go," Joe answered him. "Before we do, though—and we will—I'm hoping you'll humor me."

Freeman hesitated, his imagination snagged on Joe's possible meaning. Finally, he slid back and made a show of crossing his tailored legs casually. "Fine," he said. "Carry on."

Joe rewound the tape a few inches. ". . . had our personal ones, too, dating back to the death of your au pair, Ellen Turnley—"

"That has nothing to do with this," Freeman's recorded voice cut her off. "What you did back then was unprofessional and clearly politically motivated, but I have totally put it behind me. My complaints against you and your department concern the way you hemorrhage money for frivolous reasons." He let out an exasperated sigh. "Beverly, for Christ's sake. I've told you all this before: You stop wasting money, and I'll stop slapping your butt. Unless you're into that kind of thing."

"What I'm not into, Mr. Freeman," she answered icily, "is being blackmailed."

"Oh, come on," he burst out, his voice bright with superiority. "The fact that you were a bad girl once probably shouldn't be held against you. God knows, I don't. But then, a lot of people are nastier than I am." He paused before adding, "And you've pissed off a ton of them, Bev."

Freeman held up his hand. "Can we stop this?" he asked Joe.

Joe interrupted the tape again. "Why?"

"Because I don't see the point," the other man went on. "You're obviously an ally of Hillstrom's, and by either challenging my integrity or trying to scare me, you're hoping to force me to betray both good management practices and a matter of principle. But like I said to her: Nothing personal. You've been a cop for a long time. Maybe too long, from what I'm seeing right now. Be that as it may, I think someone with your record should be respected for what he's done, and maybe forgiven a lapse of judgment. You leave now and I'll let bygones be bygones, with no reprisals against you or Hillstrom."

He laughed and tilted his head as if he'd just heard a good joke. "I mean, Christ, Joe. A man with your mileage must see what a slippery slope this is, right?"

Joe had actually been of two minds about going this route and had sympathized with Beverly when she bridled at his suggestion to bug the phone call. So while he'd believed her cause to be just and reasonable, he'd also needed some insight into Freeman's point of view before proceeding.

There had indeed been questions concerning a slippery slope. They'd been quickly rendered moot. On tape, Floyd Freeman had struck him, just as he was doing now in person, as a manipulative, amoral opportunist. A crook who simply hadn't yet been caught. Perhaps Freeman was correct in one thing, though: Maybe Joe had been a cop for too long. However, he'd convinced himself that a career dedicated to doing the right thing was an adequate counterbalance for running a little fast and loose with a slimy guy like this.

He appraised Freeman with a long, quiet look and commented, "I think you chose the slope long before I got here."

He started up the tape again to head off further debate. ". . . You've pissed off a ton of them, Bev," they heard Freeman say.

That was followed by a long pause as Hillstrom struggled to maintain her composure. When she spoke next, her voice was tight. "The medical examiner's office is made up of seven employees and a few dozen part-time death investigators who might as well be volunteers. The law enforcement agencies, the attorneys, the funeral homes, the hospitals, and the public we serve have, year after year, commended us for our efficiency, courtesy, professionalism, and integrity, despite the fact that we are almost continually understaffed, underfunded, and over-tasked with responsibilities."

"Spare me the sob story, Bev," Freeman interrupted. "Everybody in state government has the same bitch-and-whine, and everybody has had to learn to do more with less. You've just been too coddled and spoiled by people who won't say no to you."

"That's because I say no before they can," she came back. "My office efficiency audits are the best you have. I've even heard you quote them when you need to brag. That's why none of this has anything to do with my abilities. You simply want me gone for personal reasons. You may say it's not the Turnley case, but we both know it is. You blame me for ending your political rise to fame."

"That's nonsense," Freeman retorted, but in those two words alone, Joe could once more hear the frustration and anger, sharp and hard.

So had Hillstrom at the time of the actual conversation, and it had kept her on track, away from the managerial doublespeak that Freeman kept using as a stalking horse.

"How can you say it's nonsense?" she asked. "If my performance was as terrible as you claim, you could fire me. It's not and you can't. So you've retrieved the Morgenthau case in the hopes that political pressure will do what a job assessment cannot. All because you cheated on your wife with a teenager whose blood will be forever on your hands."

At this point, the present-day Freeman snapped. He took a lunge at the recorder still balanced on Gunther's knee and sent it skittering across the carpeted floor as Joe half rose, grabbed his wrist, and twisted it to force him back into his chair.

"I want to hear this part," Joe said, his face inches from Freeman's.

From near the wall, the thin sound of the recorder still reached them. "Listen, you stuck-up bitch," Freeman was saying, "that fucking little whore threw herself at me. She spread her legs and I took care of her, something you'd have no clue about. The fact that she was a mental case had nothing to do with me, until you made it your mission to ruin me. I cannot tell you how happy I was when that idiot governor of ours gave me this job. I made it my *mission,* lady, to fuck you like you fucked me, and I am on top of the world that it's finally working."

Gunther had crossed the room and picked up the machine in the middle of this diatribe, placing it carefully on the edge of Freeman's oversize desk and perching alongside it so that he was now staring down at the other man.

"You think I'm blackmailing you?" the voice was still ranting. "That doesn't even touch it. I'm giving you the butt fuck of a lifetime."

At last, Joe turned off the recorder.

Freeman sat motionless, his defeated body language at odds with the furious scowl on his face.

"None of that's legal," he repeated, his voice a verbal pout.

"Nobody'll care, if it gets out," Joe told him, extracting some documents from his jacket pocket. He handed one of them to Freeman. "It's a matter of principle, like you said earlier, just like this—it's a sworn statement from a retired lab tech in Connecticut attesting to the fact that it wasn't Beverly Hillstrom who cooked the books all those years ago, but her boss, and that she took the blame to protect him. I've got a whole case file backing that up."

Freeman didn't bother reading it. "Who cares?" he said unconvincingly. "She still broke the law."

Gunther nodded. "That's the second time you've invoked the law. Tricky instrument sometimes. Can come back to bite you."

He handed over another copied document, which Freeman did look at.

"That's a certified British government birth certificate for Ellen Turnley. Turns out she lied about her age to get the au pair job. According to the law you just quoted, you raped a child."

Freeman was looking ill, all fight drained out of him.

Gunther picked up the recorder and carefully retrieved all the paperwork, bundling them together as he walked to the door.

He paused with his hand on the doorknob. "You might want to call a lawyer, Floyd. I think you're going to have bigger problems to tangle with than Beverly Hillstrom."

Lester Spinney tore the latest arrival off the VLETS Teletype and read it quickly to determine where to file it. Primarily the harbinger of BOLs, or "Be on the Lookouts," for the state's wandering, as yet unaccounted for miscreants, the Teletype also served to deliver relevant news of all stripes, including, as here, a missing-person report.

"High Top," he murmured quietly. "Now, there's an alias."

"High Top?" Sam asked from across the small room.

"Can't really blame him," Spinney sympathized. "His real name's Conrad Sweet." He crossed over to a row of in-boxes, each reserved for different crimes or events, and deposited the latest arrival. Lester Spinney was the only one of the four Brattleboro-based VBI agents not to have come from the police department downstairs. His background was the state police, where he'd felt increasingly stifled by bureaucracy and oppressive oversight, and which he'd exchanged—all benefits intact and with a sigh of relief—for the freer, more autonomous style of the Bureau. He was a very tall and angular man of almost perpetual good humor, and jokes aimed in particular at his physique, mostly images of storks, festooned the area surrounding his desk, testifying to his easygoing demeanor.

"Where're you putting him?" Sam asked, her irrepressible curiosity surfacing.

"Missing persons," he answered, adding as an afterthought, "He's from Bennington."

That caught her attention. She turned toward her computer console. "Conrad Sweet, you said? Common spellings?"

There were only the two of them in the office at the moment, explaining why there'd been no rejoining wisecracks from Willy Kunkle.

Spinney changed directions and laid the report on her desk with a smile. "Go get 'em, tiger."

She laughed and typed the name into Spillman. "Ooh, bad boy," she said moments later. "Earned that nickname, too. Major druggie. Not too bright, either, according to the times he's been busted. Looks like he fed his habit the old-fashioned way—by stealing."

"Think we'll end up with him?" Lester asked from his desk.

Sam picked up the fax and read it carefully. "His probation officer reported him missing, added a footnote that High Top's never missed a meeting in the past—not once."

Lester nodded meditatively. "Guess we will, then."

Sammie Martens sat back in her chair, still gazing at the screen. "What interests me is the Bennington connection. You know what they say about how things come up in clusters . . ."

She leaned forward suddenly, as if yielding to some internal debate. "What the hell," she muttered, "I'm going to run his involvements. See if any names come up that might be interesting."

Lester looped a gangly arm across the back of his chair and looked at her. Without comment, he'd also brought up High Top's record on his screen. He raised an eyebrow. "You wanna work from the top as I work from the bottom?"

She laughed at him. "Gotcha. Go for it."

Joe was in his car, heading south on Interstate 91, when his cell phone rang. He pulled over to the shoulder before answering. This wasn't so much for safety, since he couldn't swear that actually speaking on a phone was any more dangerous than chatting with a passenger—unlike dialing the damn things, which he thought was suicidal. He was simply being practical—there were so many mountains and so few cell towers in Vermont that maintaining a clear connection while in motion was unlikely. "Can you hear me now?" was no joke around here.

Not that he minded stopping. Two of the perpetual joys of working in this part of the world were the scaled-down pace and the sheer beauty of the surroundings. Pressing the phone to his ear, he had the pleasure of seeing the Connecticut River snaking away before him in the distance, marking the political boundary between Vermont and New Hampshire and looking for all the world as it might have two hundred years ago, when farms similar to these crowded the water's edge, for both the sustenance and the flatter ground.

"Gunther," he answered.

"Joe, it's Beverly Hillstrom."

He smiled at the familiar formal tone combined with the use of his first name.

It had been several fast-moving days since his encounter with the now free-falling Floyd Freeman, and Joe and Hillstrom had spoken several times, as much exchanging information as working out a new middle ground in their relationship. There was no question of their ever repeating what had happened that one night. They both knew that without discussion. But at the same time, referring to each other as "Dr. Hillstrom" and "Agent Gunther," as they had for decades, now seemed childish. Always the diplomat, however, he'd left it to her to set the new ground rules. He'd been flattered and touched by her choice to stick with first names.

Nevertheless, he knew he shouldn't get carried away, and thus kept to business. "Hi," he said, "you got something for me?"

"I think so," she told him. "Since my hands have been untied, I ordered the extra tests on Michelle Fisher. In fact," she added with a touch of vindictiveness, "I ordered a five hundred test panel on her, plus a few others for safety's sake. Good thing, too, because what came up wouldn't have appeared short of that."

"And what is it?" Joe asked, allowing her some theatrical buildup.

"Volatiles in the bloodstream—through the roof," she answered him simply. "I've faxed the lab results to your office, but from my experience, I'd look at that gas stove again."

Joe didn't respond, his brain fogged in a tangle of new calculations.

"You there?" she finally asked.

"She died of a propane overdose?" he finally asked.

"That would be consistent," she answered carefully.

"Wow," he said softly. "I guess that's what they mean by hearing the other shoe drop."

"It couldn't have been accidental?" she asked. "It's been known to happen."

Although sitting alone in his car, Joe shook his head at the phone. "The stove was off, the furnace, too, and all the windows were open. Plus, she would've smelled it. She wasn't sleeping."

"Oh, that's interesting," she mused. "I hadn't thought of that."

"It's like a suicide that isn't," he said.

"Which officially makes it a homicide," she agreed.

"At long last," he murmured, reflecting on the path he'd taken to reach it. "I'm not sure I've ever worked so hard just to get to the starting block."

She laughed gently in his ear. "Personally, I'm glad you did."

After he'd left Freeman, all but sure of the man's

fate—certainly in terms of his hold over Hillstrom—Joe had visited her at her office to break the news. There, with the door closed, she'd given him what they both knew would be a final kiss—something to savor in the future.

"So am I," he told her, and resumed driving toward Brattleboro.

Chapter 12

They weren't in bed, weren't naked, hadn't even kissed since Nancy's arrival. Which was a first as far as Ellis could remember. So far, their affair had been so torrid that sex had been the prelude to every meeting, as if nothing could proceed without it—like gulping air before plunging underwater.

Not this time, though, which was just as well. He doubted he could have performed, given his state of mind. And he wasn't alone, ever since he'd told her what he'd witnessed.

"Jesus, Ellis," she said, sitting on his sofa beside him with her legs tucked up beneath her. "What did you do with the body?"

"Buried it."

Her eyes grew even wider. "Where? With what?"

"Right there, by the river. We got sticks and stuff—a piece of board I found in the mud—and dug a grave."

"Are you crazy?" she asked. "That's not going to work. A dog'll find it, or the water'll wash it up in a flood. Something'll happen. You buried a man in the middle of a *city*, for Chrissake."

Ellis became a little resentful. "What the hell would you've done?"

She didn't bother answering that. "Why'd he do it?" she asked instead.

He shrugged. "One moment he was talking to the guy; the next, he'd strangled him. It was like an impulse. He was trying to find out who the kid was selling his stolen radios to."

"And the kid refused?"

"No," Ellis said emphatically, shifting around to face her. "That's the thing. He told Mel what he wanted to know—names, an address. It was only at the end, when Mel asked him how to approach the buyers, that he said something snarky, and that was it." He snapped his fingers. "Just like that. I mean, I thought the conversation wasn't even finished, but it was like Mel had just had enough. It was weird."

"You didn't think Mel could kill somebody?" Nancy demanded incredulously.

But Ellis was already shaking his head. "No, no. I meant that Mel was making headway. He'd found out about the kid, staked him out, planned how he was going to squeeze him, and then, just as he was getting what he wanted, he kills him. Why?"

Nancy was looking glum. "We are so screwed. That crazy bastard is going to put us all in jail forever."

Ellis didn't have an answer to that. It came too close to his own premonitions. "Yeah—probably," he finally muttered.

Nancy suddenly looked up at him, her face hard with anger. "Why? It's not fair. He's the one who does all this shit. When was the last time you cooked up one of these stupid deals?"

Ellis looked dumbfounded.

"Exactly," Nancy continued raging. "We just do what we're told so he doesn't rip our heads off. We let ourselves get pushed around like nothing. But that's not how they're gonna look at it when we get caught. You know that, right? We'll be lumped with him just like soldiers are when the boss gets into trouble for telling them to do stuff they're not supposed to. That's exactly the way it is with us." She readjusted herself on the couch, getting up onto her knees, moved by her own growing enthusiasm. "You hear about that all the time. Some lieutenant tells his people to blow something up, or kill a bunch of villagers, and next thing you know, they're all in shit up to their necks. Why? Because they had to follow orders. They don't do it, they get court-martialed. They do it, and the judge throws the book at them anyhow." She placed both her hands on Ellis's shoulders for emphasis. "That's what's gonna happen to us. Mel's like that lieutenant."

Ellis was processing what she'd said. He didn't disagree with any of it, but he wasn't sure he saw her point. She was merely voicing with more passion the same feelings he had every time Mel launched one of his plans. But it still didn't mean anything. Mel always went ahead anyway, and so did Ellis.

He put his hands on her waist, hoping to show support, and nodded. "Yeah," he said.

Her expression brightened. "So we need to do something. To fight back. We can't let him do that anymore." She suddenly kissed him, hard and fast. "Especially now that we've found each other. We need to figure out how to turn the tables. There's gotta be a way we can make sure he gets what's coming to him without being caught in the same wringer."

"Like call the cops?" Ellis asked.

Nancy laughed. Her face was flushed with the excitement of having located at least the outline of a solution. She kissed him again, this time longer, more passionately. He began to respond, his hands searching out her blue-jeaned bottom.

She broke away again, her lips moist. "No, silly. The cops'll just lump us all together. What do they care? Bunch of trailer trash. We gotta make it easy for them. Give 'em one single target, so big and juicy they don't even think of us."

"Like an anonymous call telling them he did the kid," Ellis mused, moving his hands up under her tank top and around to the front. Nancy arched her back in response but kept talking.

"No. You're too close to that one. You've seen those shows. They'll find people who saw you there, or they'll get hair samples or something. If anything, we should go back to where you buried him and make sure there's nothing left that'll point to you."

He worked his fingers in under her brassiere and swept it out of the way. She let out a moan and with one clean jerk pulled off her tank top, pulling his face between her breasts.

"Jesus, Ellis, I know we can do this. We can get rid of him forever and have all the time in the world."

She was yanking at his shirt as he fumbled with the snap of her jeans.

"Think of it. No more Mel. Just you and me. Christ, I can almost taste it."

Ellis succeeded and yanked her fly open, simultaneously laying her on her back.

"Yeah. Me, too," he said, figuring they could work out the details later.

"I wondered when this would come back to kick us in the ass," Willy said sourly. "Soon as I heard he was poking his nose into someone else's case. What's he want us to do?"

Sammie gave her companion an exasperated look. "You know you love this shit. Why do you raise a stink every time?"

They were heading down the Municipal Building staircase together, she having turned him around in the hallway with a crook of the finger as he was coming in for the day, along with the words "Road trip to Bennington—boss's orders."

"We're supposed to interview some folks," she continued. "Supposedly, they alibi a guy named Morgan. I forget his first name."

"Newell," Willy said under his breath.

"*Ha.*" She burst out laughing, punching his good arm. "I knew it. God, you are easy. I knew you'd read the file. You're dying to get into this; admit it."

He shook his head. "You are so full of it."

She paid no attention. "It's perfect for VBI. I bet the boss saw that from the start—smelled a rat, just by instinct."

"He got lucky."

"Oh, right. That's why he's already put so much time into it." They reached the lobby on the ground floor and headed out toward the parking lot to the rear of the building.

"Give me the keys," he said.

She laughed again. "Like I'm going to trust my life to some gimp? You have *got* to be kidding."

"Better me than anyone else you know," he growled, but he let her keep the keys. "So what finally did her in?"

"Fisher?" Sam asked, turning the key and checking the mirror. "They're thinking the gas from the stove."

That caught him by surprise. "No shit?"

She barely waited for him to settle in before moving out of the parking lot at a rapid clip. "That's where Joe and Lester are headed, to meet up with the crime scene people in Wilmington—see if they can figure it out."

"Good luck," he said, but didn't pursue it, already considering the case in its new light.

"You get enough sleep last night?" Sam asked, seemingly out of the blue.

Willy looked over at her. "Sure. Why?"

"You thrashed around a lot. More'n usual."

He slapped his forehead dramatically. "Jesus H. Christ. How many cops get to hear that—from their partners, no less? 'Gosh, honey, you tossed all night.' There are times this really creeps me out."

She laughed. "Right. You really look like it when I'm giving you what you want."

He groaned and rolled down the side window.

"You getting hot?" she asked leadingly.

"Enough," he told her emphatically. "We're on the job. None of that here, okay? You know how I feel about that."

"Okay, sweet pea. Anything you want."

His frown deepened, and he shifted abruptly in his seat. She cast him a quick glance, recognizing the signs. "What about Morgan?" she continued seamlessly, nimbly sidestepping a land mine. "Since we now know you read the file."

He didn't answer at first, pretending to stare out the window at the passing scenery. She had a knack for pulling his chain like that and then letting go just in time, leaving him nothing tangible to complain about.

"I read what the boss wrote. But who cares? You were right there with him when he grilled the man," he said sulkily.

"Yeah, I was," she admitted. "I'm asking how it looks on paper. From a distance."

He understood what she was asking, and worked to consider it more carefully, his emotions disentangling from their earlier conversation. That was another thing she'd figured out how to do.

"I think he's playing us," he eventually said. "There're too many angles that don't add up."

"The convenient trip to Frankfort, complete with buddies and credit card receipts?" she suggested.

"For instance. But the big one, too—that she died just when he wanted her out of the house." He pursed his lips thoughtfully. "And from what I could read between the lines, it sounded like he was super cranked about her doing the son in the sack."

"God, yeah," Sam agreed. "Kept calling her a whore. Joe even asked him if *he'd* made a play, or vice-versa."

Willy laughed. "Bet that went over well."

"He blew up."

"That's what I mean," Willy continued. "I think he was jealous, which maybe led to something he can't cop to now."

"Meaning her death had nothing to do with the house?" Sam suggested.

Her companion wobbled his hand back and forth equivocally. "It's possible. With the son out of the way, the old man might've seen himself as the perfect replacement. Must've driven him nuts that the love nest was his by mortgage only."

"If that's true," Sam reflected, "then he had to have visited her—he wouldn't've leaned on her long-distance. Could be someone saw him. Joe was thinking along those lines, too."

Willy, to his credit, then argued against his own theory. "Wouldn't she have mentioned it to the girlfriend, Rubinstein? They were thick, right?"

"Supposedly," Sam agreed.

"Except that it didn't come up in Joe's report of his conversation with Rubinstein. Either he didn't ask or she didn't say, or both."

"She did say she'd never set eyes on the man," Sam said.

Willy merely grunted, unhappy about the ambiguity. Pointedly, his discontent wasn't directed at any lapse by Joe. He had too many years on the job not to know that these kinds of holes were endemic to an investigation. Still, it was a gap of knowledge, and he would have liked it filled.

"Maybe someone should reinterview her," he suggested.

"I think that's one of the reasons they're out there. The mother's being contacted, too. Lester's driving down to Fall River to talk to her."

They fell silent for a few moments, each lost in thought. He, however, was pondering what they'd just been discussing, which was why it surprised him yet again when she returned to an earlier topic.

"The nightmares just as bad?" she asked, her voice neutral and her eyes studiously on the road. This was not an area she was comfortable in.

Now he understood her comment about his sleeping habits. Instinctively, he bristled. A war vet, a recovering alcoholic, and a cripple with a lifelong history of poor interactions with his fellow human beings, Willy Kunkle was nothing if not quick to man the barricades.

And yet, he'd allowed this woman inside, if grudgingly— a gesture she repaid with forbearance and patience. He changed the rules according to his moods, opening up or shutting her out almost at whim, often finding her attachment to him more baffling than flattering. But still she hung on.

He knew it wasn't because of any great encouragement from him. He wouldn't have said it out loud, but it was in part her balancing this tolerance with her own self-respect that impressed him most—something she often did simply by speaking her mind. Years before, he'd been unhappily married. His wife had eventually left him—not that he blamed her for that—but while they'd been together, she hadn't known enough to forcefully stand her ground, and in the absence of such limits, he'd ended up diminishing her and forfeiting their marriage.

It wasn't something he wanted to repeat.

Reluctantly, therefore, almost struggling with the effort, he tried answering openly. "Not as bad," he admitted. "Is that what woke you up last night?"

"Yeah," she answered truthfully, "but it wasn't over the top. You didn't slug me or anything." Now she risked a glance at him, privately pleased by his response, which wasn't always so benign. "The only reason I mentioned it is because they've gotten rarer."

He continued looking straight ahead and made no comment, but he nodded ever so slightly.

She reached out and squeezed his thigh, quickly returning her hand to the wheel. He made no overt movement, but she noticed the hint of a smile and was happy to count it as progress. This might turn out to be the labor of a lifetime, but however subtle the signs, she was content to think she wasn't working alone.

Mel Martin left his pickup and looked around cautiously, watching for anything out of the ordinary. He was on the edge of town, parked off the road behind an abandoned tumbledown barn, the likes of which decorated the Vermont roadsides like billboards did farther south, in the urban flatlands.

Except that up here they weren't advertising anything besides the slow disintegration of a culture.

Satisfied, Mel approached the back wall of the barn and removed a few carefully piled-up boards barring the door, noting by the tiny indicators he'd left behind that they hadn't been disturbed since his last visit.

He stepped inside, glancing up at the small flurry of birds taking flight as they did every time he entered, their tiny outlines flickering against the sky as they streaked out through the shattered roof high overhead.

In the resumed quiet, he crossed the debris-strewn floor to another pile of boards, which he methodically shifted to reveal a small trapdoor. This he hefted to one side before removing a flashlight from his back pocket and shining it into the hole at his feet. He smiled at what he saw—an undisturbed and innocuous sprinkling of twigs and dry leaves that only he knew disguised the rusty jaws of an open bear trap.

No one had been here.

Gingerly, he lowered himself into the hole, with difficulty avoiding the trap and, bent over double, worked his way for about ten feet toward the cellar's earthen wall.

There he unhooked an ancient Coleman lamp from an

overhead beam, took his time lighting it and then, by its hissing glare, addressed his final obstacle, a beaten-up piece of plywood that looked as if it had all but become one with the dirt.

Behind it, in a small hand-dug cavern, lay the box that he and Ellis had removed from the armory.

He pulled it out, sat back on his haunches, and flipped back the lid to reveal the two M-16s.

"Hey there, my babies," he murmured, running his fingertips across one of them as he might have stroked the head of a child. He'd been here several times after he'd hidden them away, unbeknownst to Ellis or Nancy. He visited them as a collector might, handling them, admiring them in the harsh gleam of the light, and working the actions with practiced ease. But whereas a collector often conjures up the culture that yielded his prize, Mel saw only the future—when he'd use them to secure something better.

Along these very lines, he didn't replace the weapons in their box for the next time. Instead, he fitted them awkwardly under his arm and began retracing his steps, careless of the open box and its gaping hiding place.

Time was getting near, and he wanted these close at hand.

Chapter 13

Lester Spinney had been to Fall River only once before, to take his family to see the U.S. Navy vessels moored there as a floating museum. Wandering happily for hours around the harbor, touring a battleship, a submarine, and assorted other artifacts, including an unexpectedly large PT boat—Lester's favorite—he'd been perpetually aware of the gritty, rough-and-tumble industrial city looming just over their shoulders, poised as if threatening to spill across the nearby docks and bridges and take them all down into the opaque dark-colored water.

The feeling must have been catching—much as he and the family had enjoyed the outing, none of them had suggested afterward extending it into the town itself.

Now, wrapped in heavy traffic, Lester was far from the bulkily elegant vessels caressed by the ocean's breeze, immersed instead in a tangle of crowded, stifling back streets, a map clutched in one sweaty hand as he negotiated looming obstacles with the other.

Spinney's idea of a city was his hometown of Springfield, Vermont, where a traffic jam meant having to wait twice to get through the one red light in the middle of town. After the two and a half hours it had taken him to drive here in a car with a broken air conditioner, this was not his idea of an improvement.

Finally, some twenty minutes after finding the address, he also located a parking spot and walked back to a three-story wooden building of typical nineteenth-century triple-decker design, complete with strung-up laundry hanging limply like a banner from the second-floor balcony.

He climbed a set of stairs to the building's recessed entrance and paused there, overlooking the neighborhood while removing the stifling jacket he'd just put on out of habit.

"Hey, Mr. Policeman," a young voice instantly called out. "Ya gonna arrest somebody?"

Lester shifted his gaze to two boys loitering on the stoop next door, one of them holding a ball. Their comment caused a couple of passersby to cast a look at him. Only then was he aware of having exposed his shield, gun, and handcuff case with the removal of his jacket. The second-nature aspect of the equipment often made it all but unnoticeable to him. Now, however, he became acutely aware of being in full sight of every window and parked car up and down the block.

"Not this time," he said uncomfortably.

"Who ya lookin' for?"

He spied the name "Redding" above one of the five doorbells near the front door.

"I got it," he told them, and quickly pushed the button.

To his surprise, the front door lock immediately began buzzing, while the speaker above the bell remained silent. Gratefully, Spinney pushed the door open and stepped into the building.

It wasn't as hot as he'd expected, the hallway's window-less gloom being forever spared the sun's direct onslaught. But it was dark, and he stood there blinking for a few seconds, his sense of vulnerability now expanded in scope.

"What d'ya want?" a woman's voice asked, directly but not unkindly.

He squinted up the hallway to a shadow outlined against a door opening. "I have an appointment with Adele Redding."

The voice was clearly surprised by his gangly appearance. "You the cop?"

"Yes." He motioned toward the shield on his belt.

"Wow," the voice said, its amusement clear. "That, I never would've guessed. Come on back."

Lester walked slowly, not sure what he might stumble into on the way, and approached a small, squarely built gray-haired woman who emerged from her surroundings like a photograph surfacing in a tray of developer.

Face-to-face, he stuck his hand out. "Lester Spinney. Vermont Bureau of Investigation."

Her handshake was surprisingly firm. "Adele Redding. Come inside."

He followed her through a cluttered, dark entryway and along a narrow hall before turning a corner into a bright, sun-filled living room whose windows were crowded with stacked shelves of healthy plants. Lester wasn't to know this, not having been to the Wilmington house of Adele's daughter, but the propensity for successfully growing things evidently ran in the family.

The contrast between this virtual greenhouse and the gloomy corridor brought him up short. It also gave him a much clearer view of Redding's face, which, despite its smile, was etched with grief.

"I'm really sorry for your loss," he blurted out.

She seemed to understand that his words came from deeper than their blandness suggested.

"Thank you," she told him, gesturing to an armchair. "Would you like something to drink? Or to use the bathroom?"

He shook his head, sitting down and draping his jacket across his knees. Despite the warmth, there was a pleasant breeze wafting in from the windows. Through the clutter of plants, he could make out a small backyard and an alleyway beyond a wooden wall. The room was filled with old furnishings, carefully framed pictures, and assorted treasured objects ranging from vases to family photos to a dark, heavy grandfather clock. None of it was expensive, but the place was clean and tidy and proudly maintained, which seemed to reflect the woman, who took a rocking chair next to a basket full of knitting to face him.

"You're here about Michelle," she began. "Like I said on the phone, I'm happy to tell you what I can, but can I ask something first?"

"Of course," he said, having expected this.

"What did she die of?"

He didn't avoid the predictable question, and now, having met her, he also didn't worry about sugarcoating his answer.

"Mrs. Redding, I'm afraid she died from too much propane in her system."

Her brows furrowed. "Like from a stove?"

"That's right, or a gas leak of some sort. We're still looking into that."

Her hands sought each other out on her lap and curled up together for comfort. "Oh, my goodness. I thought . . ."

"Yes?"

"Well . . ." She hesitated. "That she might have just died. You know?"

"Of natural causes," he suggested.

"Yes."

"So this comes as a surprise?" he asked gently.

She frowned and considered that. "You're asking if she was suicidal."

"We know she was sad about Archie," he said, using Morgan's first name on purpose, increasing the moment's intimacy.

Adele looked down at her hands, as if checking to see what they were up to. "She was sad," she told them, "but I never thought she was going to do that." She looked up, her expression drawn, as if guilty. "We spoke every morning."

Lester felt sorry for her. "I didn't say she did, Mrs. Redding. We're still investigating."

"But how else?"

He held up his hand. "I'm also not saying she didn't. I'm sorry. I don't mean to torture you with this. We simply don't know right now. That's one of the reasons I'm here."

She pursed her lips and nodded. "All right."

"We understand Michelle was in financial straits," he said as an opener.

"She was, yes. I was trying to help with that, as much as I could, and I know her friend Linda was, too. They were talking about moving in together, into Linda's place."

"Because of the troubles with the landlord?"

Her expression darkened. "Yes—horrible man."

Lester chose to hold off on that for the time being. "Was Michelle at all upbeat about living with Linda?"

"They liked each other a lot. They had some experiences in common."

"The alcoholism?"

Adele ducked her head down again, and Lester worried that he might have overstepped here. "We've interviewed several people already," he said vaguely, hoping that would spread the guilt around a bit. He knew from Gunther's notes that Adele had also struggled with the bottle.

"Yes," she finally murmured. "I was worried at first that's what might have killed her."

"We have no evidence of that," he said.

"Good. I'm glad. She'd been doing so well. She never joined AA, like Linda told her she should, but she seemed to have come up with her own way of dealing with it."

"That's saying a lot," Lester commented. "What with Archie dying, the money running out, and the troubles with Archie's father, the pressures to slip must've been huge."

That seemed to bolster her a little. "Maybe Linda and I made the difference." Her eyes suddenly welled up. "I felt so bad about that part of her problems. I used to drink when she was little and needed me most. I failed her and I passed that on to her, too. A terrible thing for a mother to do."

"You were there for her later," Lester soothed her. "And she obviously really appreciated it. Linda said your daily phone calls were a big help."

He wasn't actually sure of that but figured it couldn't hurt.

It didn't. Adele smiled wanly. "That's nice to know."

"Tell me a little about Newell Morgan," Lester finally said. "Why did things go so wrong there?"

She made a face. "Michelle said it was envy—that he hated his own life and wished it was more like Archie's."

"Was Archie's life that wonderful?" Spinney asked innocently. "I don't know much about him."

She shook her head. "It wasn't on that level. He was a school custodian. He didn't have big dreams. He was just happy being alive. What Michelle meant was that they had each other. All the father had was anger. He hated everybody."

"But he still let them live in that house. Why was that?"

"Michelle said it was just so he could have a free workman to fix it up until he could sell it out from under them. He charged them rent on the one hand and expected Archie to improve it on the other, free of charge except for materials. And Archie did good work."

"Sounds like Michelle wasn't too thrilled with the deal."

"She loved the house and she loved Archie. She told him what that man was up to, but I think Archie needed to think his father loved him, too. She said Archie lived one day at a time, and I guess if you do that, other people's motives don't matter as much."

"Except that they did after Archie died," Lester suggested.

He paused, thinking back over what he'd read about this case so far.

"Was that all it was?" he asked. "The house? I mean, was that the only reason Newell went after Michelle so hard once she was alone?"

Adele gave him a thoughtful look. "You're wondering if he propositioned her."

"Yes."

She touched her chin, as if considering a single item from among many. "I'm not sure. It was the one thing I wondered about that she never told me."

"You never asked?"

"No, no," she said with some emphasis. "That's not the way these talks went. You have to understand, it took a long time for us to get where we were."

"A lot of history?"

She let out a short, humorless laugh. "A lot of bad history. Like I said, I was not a good mother. I did my best to be one." She paused, as if eavesdropping on some inner piece of dialogue, before adding mournfully, "Too little, too late."

Lester didn't know enough to argue the point. There was, however, one last question that Joe had requested he ask.

"Mrs. Redding, this is going to sound a little weird maybe, but did your daughter have any trouble smelling things?"

Adele looked at him with her eyebrows raised, startled out of her melancholia. "Yes. She couldn't smell much at all. She got really sick, years ago, landed in the hospital and everything. They said it was the flu, but I'm not sure they knew. Anyway, whatever it was ruined that part of her breathing system. I forget all the words now, but it was a known condition."

She paused, thinking back, and then asked in turn, "Why?"

This time, Spinney lied, not wishing to drag her back once more to the source of her sorrow. He feigned taking a glance at the notepad he'd been consulting. "You know? They didn't tell me. It was just a detail I was supposed to ask about."

But it was more than that, and as he took his leave shortly thereafter to return home, it was the one piece of information that kept coming back around in his head.

Joe stood at the door of the converted schoolhouse once more, revisiting the scene that now seemed so familiar and yet ancient. No trace of the cat droppings remained, apart from a single faint floor stain. The plants were the worse for wear, ghosts of their former selves. And the air, because of the closed windows, was stale and vaguely musty. No one had been inside the place since the state police sealed it shut that first day.

With him this time, also reminiscent of ghosts, were white-clad crime scene technicians, outfitted from booties to hats, who methodically traveled through the building gathering whatever scraps they deemed relevant.

It was a formal requirement, given the case's upgraded stature, but Gunther didn't expect much to come from it. Any fingerprints would probably belong to people who had legitimate access. There'd been no gunfire, so no holes or errant bullets were there to discover. There was no reason to think any bloodstains would surface, and he and Doug Matthews had already gone through the papers.

DNA was always a possibility, however remote, but he remained doubtful of any context it might fit. Supposedly, Michelle had been living alone for half a year. Nevertheless, wearing a crime scene suit himself, he returned to the attached bedroom, where any such evidence was most likely to be found.

There, to his surprise, he discovered David Hawke standing on a stepladder, taking a bird's-eye photograph of the oversize bed. The room had utterly lost its intimacy, not just with the absence of its occupant but with the addition of so many intruders.

Hawke was the forensic lab director and therefore not a man to be found often outside the office. Joe waited until he'd taken his shot before commenting, "You know, many a private eye would love a vantage point like that."

Hawke looked at him and laughed. "Hi, Joe. Wow. Why didn't I ever think of that? You have a devious mind."

He carefully climbed back down the ladder, watching his awkwardly dressed feet on the steps.

"You find anything of interest?" Joe asked. The bed's covers had been pulled back to reveal the bottom fitted sheet, which, to his eye at least, looked pristine, if a little wrinkled.

Hawke shrugged. "Nothing at odds with a single woman living alone, and nothing to challenge the findings I read in your report."

He packed his camera into a black plastic suitcase and snapped it shut, resuming: "I always hate it when we get called in so long after discovery."

"We didn't know it wasn't a natural."

"I know, I know," he said. "I wasn't complaining. I also read how this all played out—plus," he added with a smile, "a few little birds are already adding some interesting political tidbits. I wonder who Hillstrom's new boss is going to be? Rumors are, Freeman resigned so he wouldn't have to fess up to some huge skeleton in his closet. Big mystery."

Joe laughed. "Forget it. I'm not touching that. Was the stove the source of the propane?"

Hawke shook his head, still amused. "Very good. Nice, elegant change of subject. Okay, yes, the stove fits as a possible source. How's that?"

"There's another one?"

Hawke led the way into the big room and over to the linear kitchen, speaking as he went. "Not that we've found, but that doesn't mean a portable one couldn't have been removed. You have to start thinking like a scientist, Joe."

He stopped before the stove and pointed at its row of control valves. "These are all off, the gas tank out back is three-quarters full, consistent with the delivery schedule, and the pilot lights are on and burning."

"Meaning that if the stove was used to kill her," Joe interpreted, "not only did the killer turn the controls back off, but he relit the pilots, too."

"And opened the windows," Hawke added. "Probably ran the ceiling fans, too, to speed things up."

Joe turned to look at the long bank of windows across the room. "That does make you wonder, doesn't it? Why bother? Why not just blow out the pilots, turn on the gas, and walk away?"

"So the house doesn't explode," Hawke said simply.

"Right," Joe agreed. "Which would make sense if you had a vested interest in it."

"Or were just a neat and careful person, which this one was."

Joe looked at him inquiringly.

Hawke smiled. "I think we figured out how it was done," he explained. "Follow me."

They went out the back door at the end of the kitchen, stepped off the small, cluttered porch there, and circled back along the outside wall, eventually reaching two small, curtained windows located near where the stove was situated inside.

There Hawke stopped, pointing at a large cylinder of

propane gas, whose feeder line vanished through the building's wall. "Our theory right now is that the killer cut the gas here initially, which knocked out all the pilot lights. He used a wrench or some mechanical device to turn the valve. We found the tool marks. He probably did this while the victim was in the bathroom, getting ready for bed, which—what with the noise of running water and all—would have isolated her acoustically from any sounds he was making, or from any sounds the cat might have made in reaction."

"But just turning the gas back on and letting it seep in through the pilots wouldn't have been enough, would it?"

"True," Hawke agreed. He crouched down and pointed out four small, deep impressions in the dirt. "A stepladder," he explained. "We matched these holes to the ladder we found on the back porch." He glanced up at the window beside the tank. "The gas gets turned off, the pilots go out, the gas gets turned back on, the killer climbs the borrowed ladder, leans in through the window, which is unlocked, reaches across the top of the stove, turns on all the valves, and then sits back and waits. The victim continues doing her thing in the bathroom, steps out into the bedroom, does whatever she does, eventually feels woozy, sits on the edge of the bed, and is overcome."

"Plus," Joe added, "I just heard back that she had no sense of smell."

Hawke's eyes widened. "Anosmia? Really? Interesting twist. Well, that would definitely explain it. I was wondering about that."

He straightened and returned to the back porch, pointing out the small stepladder that Gunther hadn't noticed earlier. "In any case, our bad guy replaces that, enters the building, which, I gather, was usually unlocked, opens the windows, runs the fans, shuts the valves, relights the pilots—"

"*Hey, Dave,*" a voice shouted at them from near the woods at the property's edge. "*I got it.*"

They both turned to see one of the technicians pointing down at a small pile of dirt at his feet.

"Thanks, John," Hawke answered. "Be right there." He then turned to Joe and finished his sentence: ". . . and buries the dead cat that crapped all over the place before it died."

Joe's eyes widened slightly, as if suddenly recalling a long-forgotten tune. "Man, that cat's been driving me nuts. Georgia."

"First thing I asked myself when we got here," Hawke agreed. "That's why I had John go looking. Georgia, huh?"

"After Georgia O'Keeffe."

They began walking toward the tiny burial site, which the technician was documenting with a camera of his own.

"Oddly sentimental thing to do," Joe wondered aloud, "especially fresh from killing a human being."

"Yeah. People are funny that way."

Joe suddenly stopped and looked back at the house. From where they were, they could see down the length of the exterior wall to the gas tank and the small window.

"What kind of shape would you have to be in to do that little stunt?"

"Reach in through the window?" Hawke asked. "You don't have to be a gymnast. But somewhat agile. It is awkward, and the trick was to be quiet, even with the bathroom walls and the running water acting as a muffler. I think that's why he didn't just walk in—that and Georgia, who might've made a fuss."

"So a fat man on disability is unlikely."

"I'd say so," Hawke said.

"On the other hand," Joe went on, "a familiarity with the layout and Michelle's routine was key, all the way down to the kitchen window's location and when she was most likely to use the bathroom."

David Hawke nodded thoughtfully. "From what I've put together so far, this is way too calculated to have been done on the fly. Somebody planned this and took their time doing it."

Chapter 14

Willy dropped heavily into the car's passenger seat as Sam fitted the key into the ignition.

"Damn," he said peevishly. "If you can tell what a guy's like from his friends, like they say, then old Newell must be a grade A, prime-beef, award-winning asshole."

Not actually starting the car, Sam rolled her window down to let in some fresh air. She consulted her notes.

"Four down, two to go."

"Screw it," he said. "I'm sick of these jerks. All red-white-and-blue on one side, and all fuck-you-cop on the other. We know Newell is clean, Sam. He made sure of it. Let's give it a rest."

"Be nice to know they're all on the same page. Maybe one of them's willing to rat the others out."

Willy slapped the dashboard in frustration. "What's to rat? The son of a bitch was in Frankfort, like he says. We called the places they ate at and stayed in, we compared four of their stories with each other, and we even looked at those stupid pictures the last one showed us, so conveniently stamped with the time and date. I mean, okay, fine, so maybe they're all in it together, but if they are, they were also in goddamn Frankfort when they said they were. There's not a frigging thing we can do about that. We're working the wrong angle. We're doin' what they want us to do."

It was the opening gambit for a ready-made argument between an impulse-driven reactionary and a by-the-numbers solid soldier, except that in this case, although usually playing the latter role, Sammie Martens didn't have it in her to disagree.

She tossed her notes onto the seat between them and said, "You're right. Fuck it."

Willy stared at her. "Huh?"

"It's a waste of time. You're right," she repeated.

He absorbed that for a few seconds, pleased but surprised, his brain in sudden need of an alternative plan.

"Maybe we should hit him again—directly," Sam suggested, thinking along similar lines.

Willy shook his head. "We don't have anything to hit him *with*." He paused again, looking out at the street. "But I wouldn't be surprised if he'd pissed off some of his neighbors over the years."

Sam laughed and turned the key.

"They really let you be a police officer?" she asked, pointing at Willy's limp arm. "That doesn't sound very safe."

Willy either was too stunned to react or was reaching deep for something properly weighted. Sam decided she didn't want to know which.

"He passed the physical, ma'am. He can definitely do the job, just like he's been doing for the past two decades."

"Really?" the woman asked, her face open and smiling.

"Well, good for you. Why don't you both come in? And you, little girl, you're such a slip of a thing, I'm not sure I see how you can do it, either."

"I used to be in the military, ma'am. Combat trained."

"Isn't that nice? Would you like some tea?"

"I'll take a Coke," Willy said, his expression dark.

The old woman paused in the hallway and peered up at him. "You speak? That's very good. How do you know I have any Coke?"

Once again he was stumped.

"We're all set," Sam said, starting to rethink their entire strategy. This was the fourth of Newell Morgan's neighbors they'd met, and so far, they'd gotten nowhere. This time it looked as if they were headed for an assault on an old lady by a cranky cop.

"Nonsense," their hostess said, resuming her course. "He wants a Coke; that's what I'll get him. I like a man with direction."

Willy nudged a secretly grateful Sam and waggled his eyebrows as they fell in behind and ended up in the kitchen. Sam ignored him.

"Sit, sit," the woman ordered, and guided them toward a wooden table set into a windowed nook. As they slid onto the bench seat, Willy pointed out the window. They were overlooking Gage Street and Newell Morgan's house.

"I'm so sorry," their hostess said, placing a Coke before Willy, "but I've already forgotten your names."

"I'm Sam. The one with direction is Willy."

The old lady laughed. "Well, I'm Mary Ann Gagen, and I'm very pleased to meet you both. You sure you don't want something now that he's all set?"

"I'm fine, thanks," Sam told her.

Mary Ann Gagen sat at the head of the small table and shook her head. "No wonder you're so tiny." She smiled suddenly and leaned forward. "Now, tell me, are you two romantically involved, too?"

Sam's face went red as Willy muttered, "Jeez."

Gagen burst out laughing. "I thought so." She reached out and patted Sam's hand as it rested on the table. "He must be a tough one to handle. Bossy, right?"

"This is not happening," Willy said, and began getting up.

But Sam arrested him in mid-motion with "He has his moments, but I'm getting used to him."

He stared at her incredulously. Their relationship, while not an absolute secret, was known only by a very few. They'd certainly never shared it with a stranger before.

Gagen looked up at him questioningly. "Did you want something else, dear?"

He pressed his lips together angrily and then managed to say, "This is private stuff."

She repeated her gesture with Sam, reaching up and laying her hand on his arm. "You're quite right. But you're cross with me and not her, I hope."

Slowly he sat back down. "Yeah."

"Well, that's all right, then. Drink your Coke." She then turned to Sam. "What was it you wanted, by the way? I'm sure it wasn't just to get all worked up by a nosy old woman."

In a sudden change of tack, Willy took her up on her one-liner, cutting Sam off as she opened her mouth to speak. "A nosy old woman is just what we were looking for."

Gagen's eyes came alive. "Really? Who do you want to know about? I practically live at this table."

Willy tilted his head toward the street. "How 'bout Newell Morgan?"

Gagen sat back and laughed. "Oh, ugh. What an awful man. Why on earth would you be interested in him?"

"Can we say that's confidential and not hurt your feelings?" Sam quickly asked.

"Of course, sweetie. I've always thought he must be up to something, but I very much doubt I want to know what. He's such a terrible fellow."

"How so?" Willy asked, finally taking a sip of his drink.

"He yells at his wife, for one. I cannot tolerate that in a man. I hope you never do that."

"He's more the silent type," Sam said with a smile, not being entirely truthful.

"Well, I wish Newell were more silent, but I wish even more that Lillian would just leave him. She never will, though. She's a God-fearing woman, and that man is her cross."

"How 'bout other people?" Willy asked. "Does he have friends drop by?"

"Oh, Lord, yes, usually when she's not around. Large, lumpish men like him. Never women, thank goodness. I have no idea what they do in there, but it's usually noisy, and the trash he puts out afterward is mostly empty bottles. He's on disability, so called—probably his brain— which means he has way too much free time. He spends most of it watching that enormous TV set. You can see the glow of it at night—and hear it, too. So rude."

"Do you know who the friends are?" Sam asked her. "Maybe seen them around town? Or where they work?"

Gagen shook her head. "No, but they come here often enough."

Willy took a shot in the dark. "Did they come by as a group a couple of weeks ago and all pile into a car together, like they were going on a trip?"

"Yes, they did," she said excitedly. "Were they off to rob a bank or something?"

Willy looked sour. "Hardly. They spent four days getting drunk."

Her expression matched his own. "Oh, poor Lillian."

Sam was thinking back to their last update from Gunther, who'd called them this morning with the crime lab's findings in Wilmington.

"Mrs. Gagen . . ."

"You can call me Mary Ann. I'd like that."

"Okay. Mary Ann, have you ever seen him with someone else? Maybe recently? Someone who caught your eye in particular?"

"There was the truck man. At least, that's what I called him."

"He drove a truck?" Willy asked.

"No. He bought one. Newell had it for sale."

"Oh." Willy nodded, his disappointment obvious.

Once more Gagen reached out, her eyes bright again. "No, you don't understand. He was a mean-looking man, and he came by a couple of times. I remember thinking at the time that I should pay attention. You know how some people just strike you that way? Like they're up to no good? This man was like that, and he dressed like a biker, complete with tattoos. He even arrived on a motorcycle."

"About how long before the big trip was this?"

"Maybe three weeks, and there was something else. I didn't really think about it until now. But after the truck was sold, I saw Newell get in his car a few times—

several days apart—and drive off for an hour or two each time."

"He doesn't drive much?" Sam asked.

"That wasn't it," Gagen continued. "It was the way he did it, just on those occasions. It was sneaky. He looked around really carefully. I had to make sure I was hidden by my flower boxes. I just knew he was up to something."

Willy pulled a photograph from his pocket of a laughing Michelle Fisher and Archie Morgan, posed together at some beach. He passed it over to Gagen.

"Ever see either one of them?"

She tapped the picture slowly with her fingertip, her face grave. "That's Archie, poor boy. Died half a year ago—maybe a little more. I don't know the woman . . . Don't they look happy, though? I hope this is a recent picture. I'd like to think of Archie being happy toward the end."

"Wild guess," Willy said. "He and the old man didn't get along."

Gagen returned the photograph slowly. "What they had made Lillian's relationship look normal. I always wished Archie had been underage. Then I could have called on you folks to have his father arrested for abuse. The way that man treated that boy . . . Shameful."

"Did it ever get physical?"

"Not that I saw. It was just the way he talked to him, like he was less than dirt. But I haven't seen Archie in years. This is all ancient history."

Sam and Willy exchanged glances.

Half an hour later, they were back in their car.

"God bless busybodies," Willy said. "What do you say we drop by the local PD and follow up on some of this?"

The Bennington police occupy the old post office building, just a block south of the town's infamous major intersection. An enormous, hulking marble edifice, it looks like a leftover from a Hollywood sword-and-sand epic—a wannabe Greek Parthenon. For all that, however, it probably helps to endow this one department with more immediate awe and stature than any of its sister agencies across the state, including the federal field offices. And the impression doesn't stop on the front stoop. The lobby is a vast, vaulting echo chamber, fronted on one wall by a row of bullet-resistant windows from which dispatchers and office personnel can peer out at any visitors.

Sam and Willy showed their badges and were soon ushered into the inner sanctum by a tall, affable plainclothes officer named Johnny Massucco.

"What can we do you for?" he asked after introductions had been exchanged.

"Got a computer, Johnny?" Willy asked, looking up and down the hallway they'd just entered.

Instinctively, Sam moved to soften Willy's standard effect on people. "Sorry about him," she said, drawing Massucco's startled attention. "He gets a little overly focused. We're in town doing homework—got a homicide outside Wilmington that's touching on a few Bennington folks."

Massucco nodded distractedly, still studying Kunkle. "I heard about you," he finally said.

Willy turned at that. "Me? Nothing good, I bet."

Johnny laughed. "Well, yes and no. Everybody hates you and everybody wants to be like you."

Willy shrugged. "Everybody's stupid. Got that computer?"

Massucco shook his head and began taking them down the corridor, saying, "I think I'm starting to get it."

He led them into a small office with a couple of desks equipped with monitors. "Take mine. You use Spillman?"

"Yeah." Willy sat before the computer and quickly entered his password, his one hand moving in a blur across the keyboard.

"Who're you after?" Massucco asked Sam.

"Guy named Newell Morgan. Lives on Gage. That ring a bell?"

But the young man shook his head. "Nope, but it's not a bad neighborhood—kind of the Joe Blow street. The average citizen."

"The average jackass," Willy said, studying the screen. "According to this, he either rats on his neighbors for noise and parking complaints or gets them to squeal on him for yelling at his wife."

"Pretty much what we already knew," Sam commented, watching Willy shift over to the vehicle table.

"You like working for VBI?" Johnny asked.

"Best job in the state," Sam said without hesitation. "It's major cases only, you work border to border, and you don't have to belong to the state police."

"I was thinking they might be my only option if I ever want to leave here."

"Do you?" she asked.

"Not really, but if the state cops are the only way to go, I better start early—it's hard to move through the ranks with them."

"Screw 'em," Willy said without turning around. "Stay where you are, bust your hump, and join us when you hit top of the class."

Sam stared at the back of his head. Never before had

she heard him say anything positive about any job he'd held or anyone he'd worked with.

"Got it," he said, sitting back, cutting off anything she might have been tempted to say. "Newell sold that truck to Melvin Curtis Martin, who lives in one of the local trailer parks, at least according to this."

"That he does," Johnny agreed. "Him I do know. Go to the names table and I'll fill you in."

Willy did as suggested while Massucco continued, "Martin's a New York import. Albany area. Came over a few years ago. He's done federal and local time both, has a biker background, and is into drugs and stealing and beating the crap out of people."

"Says he's married," Willy read, surprised.

"Wife's name is Nancy," Johnny confirmed. "She's calmed down lately, at least according to her arrest record, but she used to be a biker babe recruiting poster. No kids. With their lifestyle, they probably fried whatever was in the gene pool long ago."

"He ever kill anyone?" Sam asked.

Johnny pointed his chin at the screen. "You won't find it in there, but there're some serious thoughts along those lines. Over in New York, they're pretty sure he did a couple of people at least, but nothing was proved. Among other things, witnesses dried up. Wonder why?"

Willy had been rapidly scanning narrative after narrative on the computer, familiarizing himself with the cops'-eye view of this new interest. From what he was learning, Mel Martin was his kind of bad guy.

He finally swiveled around in his chair and looked up at his partner.

"I like him," he said.

Chapter 15

Doris Doyle looked up smiling, her pleasure fighting clear of the pain and dullness that cancer and medications had made of her life.

"Ellis. Nancy. What a surprise. I didn't know you were coming." She touched her temple. "Oh, Lord, I bet I forgot. I'm so sor—"

"Mom, Mom," Ellis quieted her, kissing her hollow cheek. "It was just something we decided. Spur of the moment. You didn't forget anything."

Nancy followed suit, placing a small package in her lap. "Got you a little something. Probably against the rules."

Doris tore at the wrapping and revealed a box of chocolates. She immediately opened it and offered them some. "I love these. You are so nice. I'll keep them hidden."

They each dutifully selected a sample before Doris closed the box and tucked it away. They noticed that despite her enthusiasm, she didn't take one herself. She gave them a conspiratorial and unconvincing wink, adding, "For later."

"How've you been, Mom?" Ellis asked, as he always did, increasingly embarrassed by what he saw as the obligation of exchanged lies.

"Not too bad," she said as if reading the script. "Sleeping better now that all that radiation nonsense is over. That was a real piece of science fiction."

At least the room was friendlier. They'd moved her back upstairs among the living. Nothing was covered in plastic, the windows were normal-size, and one, in fact, was even half open to let in the warm summer air. It wasn't a single. That would have been too much to expect, but for the moment at least, the second bed was unoccupied.

Nancy sat down opposite Ellis's mother, casting a glance in his direction. He walked over casually to the door, from where he announced, "I'll let you two talk for a bit. I gotta sort out some paperwork."

"Is everything all right?" Doris asked, alarmed. "Is it money?"

Both of them laughed. "No, Ma," Ellis reassured her. "I promise. You know how bureaucratic these places are. It's like I just told you—junk."

He stepped out into the hallway, content that with that last comment, at least, he'd actually told the truth.

Nervous before he'd even arrived here, he now found himself feeling the way he did with Mel, hypersensitive to the slightest sounds and motions. He wandered down to the exit sign, struggling to look like any other hallway stroller, and took the stairs to the floor where his mother had been moved for her radiation treatment.

As before, it was quiet and virtually empty. The nurses' station at the far end showed little activity—someone sitting at a desk, talking on the phone, but that was it aside from a few muffled conversations coming through a door or two. He checked his watch. He had three minutes and thirty seconds.

He left the stairwell and stealthily walked the length of the hall, keeping his eyes on the station ahead. There was only one nurse on—Ann Coleman, the one who had helped him earlier—and her back was turned to him. He made it to the bathroom just shy of her area and quickly ducked inside without being seen.

A very long three minutes later, during which he conjured up every possible setback, he heard Nancy's voice just outside his door.

"Hi. Nice to see you again. I'm here to see Mrs. Doyle."

He heard Ann Coleman's more muted response: "Oh, hi. We moved her upstairs. They only stay here while they're being treated. She's in a regular room now."

Nancy's voice was hesitant. She didn't have much time. The plan had been for her to tell Doris that she was stepping out for a soda from the machine. "Do you know the number?"

There was a pause, followed by "Three-oh-four."

"Great. Thanks. Sorry to have bothered you. How do I get there?"

"Elevators are at the end of the hallway."

"Where?"

"Down there."

A second pause. "I'm sorry. I forgot my glasses. Where?"

Ellis couldn't actually hear it, but he imagined a sigh. He heard footsteps approaching and Coleman's voice saying, "Straight on down."

"Could you show me?"

It was childishly transparent, and now that he was actually overhearing what they'd rehearsed, he half expected the bathroom door to fly open and Nurse Coleman to ask him, "And you thought this would work?"

But instead, he heard her kindly comment, "I've had days like that. Come with me, and don't feel bad."

He waited five seconds and opened the door without a sound. The two women were retreating down the hall, no one else was in sight, and all the doors he could see were closed. He cut to the left, toward the nurses' station, went straight to the desk drawer he remembered from the last time, and pulled it open, his hand trembling.

The key was where he had hoped it would still be.

He quickly slipped it into his pocket and returned to the bathroom, the sounds of their conversation still echoing down the hall. Moments later, he heard Nancy's parting thanks as she returned to Doris's side, and the soft footsteps of Ann Coleman getting back to her post. As soon as she passed, he reversed his earlier move, leaving the bathroom silently and cutting right, making a beeline back to the stairwell.

There he leaned against the wall and wiped his face with his sleeve, wondering if he'd remembered to breathe during the whole ordeal. One obstacle down, two more to go. He headed toward the subbasement.

Downstairs, he felt slightly more comfortable. This wasn't a medical part of the hospital but the heart of its services area—food preparation and delivery, laundry, the custodial system, and what he was after: waste management.

He retraced the steps he'd taken with Coleman days earlier, blending in with the steady flow of other people who reminded him of himself, with rough hands, work clothes, or homebuilt haircuts, until he reached the same unmarked door they'd commented on at the time.

Looking as self-confident as possible, he fitted the stolen key to the lock and let himself in.

The last time he was here, they'd been alone, so he was startled to find one of the previously closed doors wide open at the end of the short corridor and to hear both music and conversation coming from it.

He stood stock-still for a moment, wondering what to do, expecting someone to appear at any second.

But no one did.

As Coleman had done before, he used the key again to unlock the storage room door and confronted the familiar, randomly stacked pile of thrown-together garbage bags, their apparent chaos mitigated by each one's having a carefully labeled tag attached at the throat.

Suddenly, he was stumped. Did it make any difference which one he took? He knew that the contents of this room fit a sliding radioactive time frame, but what if his choice was only hot for a few hours, versus one that would percolate for several months?

Standing there, stalled, he suddenly heard a thump behind him, and two voices bursting into the tiny hallway. Instinctively, he glanced over his shoulder as two white-coated lab techs appeared behind him, chatting, one of them fiddling with a key ring that he'd fished out of his pocket. Fighting panic, Ellis took a big step farther into the closet and laid both his hands onto the nearest bag before him, putting on a great show of shoving it about, as if he were attempting to tame the unruly pile.

It worked. After the one with the keys locked his own door, both men passed by Ellis without a glance, still deep in their conversation, and exited into the central corridor outside. Breathing hard, his forehead damp with sweat, Ellis grabbed the nearest bag, shut the closet door, left the stolen key in the lock where it could be found later, and followed the two men outside. Only there did he remember about the telltale tag that cinched the bag shut.

Feeling as if every passerby were staring at him, Ellis nervously positioned his hand to cover the bag's throat and walked rapidly toward a turnoff he'd passed on the way, leading to a cul-de-sac with three closed doors. There, his back to the central corridor, he fumbled to tear off the tag, ripping part of the plastic in the process.

Now breathing through his mouth like a sprinter, fully expecting alarms, shouts, and the appearance of armed men, Ellis followed the signs to the central waste management area in a near daze. He entered a two-story-high room as big as a warehouse, complete with a yawning loading dock door looking out onto the hospital's rear delivery lot. All around, in orderly piles, were garbage bags, cardboard boxes, recyclables, returnables, bundles of office paper, and all the other paraphernalia of a major municipal trash-handling plant.

But he had eyes only for that open door.

As he was halfway across the room's vast concrete floor, however, the alarm he'd been dreading finally went off—a blood-chilling, hair-raising Klaxon that cut right through his skull. Ellis stopped dead in his tracks and waited for the command to drop the bag and fall to his knees.

Instead, all he heard was an explosive oath from a fat man stationed near a ceiling-mounted, cylindrical trash chute in the far corner.

"*Stan!*" the man shouted to a colleague, pointing at the chute's latest deposit. "We got a glow-in-the-dark special."

Ellis watched the two men converge around a bag like the one in his hand, scoop it up, and drop it into a lidded wheeled cart. It had appeared from the chute, presumably from one of the upper floors, and had triggered an alarmed sensor right by the large man's station, which was also near where Ellis had been planning to exit from the building.

"Shit," he muttered, realizing that his plan was now in tatters. How the hell was he supposed to get out of the building without tripping a similar sensor?

He retreated from the cavernous room and stood in the hallway, thinking. What, exactly, had happened? he wondered. Something inappropriate had apparently been introduced into the normal trash stream and had been intercepted according to protocol. Judging from the reaction he'd witnessed, this was not a rare event and had been handled in a routine fashion. No doubt, people on the floors above were expected to screw up now and then and mix lightly radiated waste in with regular trash.

So what did that mean for him?

He rubbed his forehead, trying to think this through, striving to ignore the certainty that the longer he stood here, the greater were his chances of being caught.

Finally, shaking his head in frustration, he retraced his steps back to the central corridor and returned to the stairwell. Better to be brazen and get this over with than simply get busted for standing around. He remembered Mel once telling him that the best way to overcome this kind of roadblock was simply to walk through it as if you owned the place. He didn't worry about the irony that the very reason he was doing this was to dispose of the source of such wisdom.

Ellis reached the main floor, took a deep breath, stuffed the bag high up under his arm as if it were so much bundled laundry, and strode purposefully toward the front entrance.

He made it, feeling like a man treading through waist-high water, the target of a hundred invisible tracking monitors, all linked to a central room filled with TV sets and eager federal agents.

By the time he reached his parked car in the lot, into which he tossed his hard-won trophy with relief, he was drenched in perspiration. Now all he had to do was return to his mother's room, pretend nothing had happened, and hope that her usual ability to see right through him had succumbed to her medications.

Shaking his head at the paradoxes that seemed to constitute his life at the moment, he trudged back toward the hospital.

Outside Burlington, Vermont, several days later, William French sat staring at his computer screen, digesting what he'd just read. He considered forwarding the information in e-mail form to the appropriate party—in this case someone from JTTF, the Joint Terrorism Task Force—but then reconsidered. He hadn't been assigned to the Fusion Center for long, still thought it a real feather in his cap, and didn't want to run the risk of messing it up with an avoidable stupid mistake.

Better to appear overeager than to drop the ball, and God knows, they'd been told enough times of the latter's cost. There were posters aplenty of the smoking Pentagon and the ruins of the World Trade Center decorating the walls to make the point without any lectures.

The Fusion Center was an information-gathering

point, one of several on the books or already in existence across the United States, designed to integrate and exchange any and all snippets of intelligence of any interest to law enforcement. Clearly, the stimulus and primary focus of the centers was information that might even vaguely pertain to possible terrorist activities, but no cop saw any point in stopping there, an attitude that naturally had most of the nation's civil liberties groups up in arms.

William French didn't care about that. A young man, upwardly mobile, already equipped with a file full of supportive letters from superiors, he was a believer in having a clean desk and in documenting where everything went as it left his hands. To say that he was as unloved by his colleagues as he was back-patted by his bosses puts it about right. To the former, he was not a cop's cop but a pencil pusher with a gun, and a man who could get them into trouble—not just a few of them saw their jobs here with paradoxical ambivalence, as both cushy and a little embarrassing. The William Frenches of the world, tingling with efficient dedication, made them nervous.

French walked down the hall from his cubicle, printout in hand, and rapped on the door of an older man sitting glumly at one of two desks in the room. He was alone, which he preferred, since, unlike his junior associate, he felt trapped in this building and cherished all the private time he could get. His name was Milton Coven, and he had been with the FBI for more years than he wished to recall, most of them unhappy ones.

"Agent Coven?" French asked.

Coven stared up at him. "How long we known each other, Bill?"

"Six months."

"I rest my case. What do you want?"

French blinked once, deleted from his brain what he clearly didn't understand, and marched into the room, proffering the printout.

"This just came in from the NRC. I thought you should see it."

Coven reached out tiredly and took it. The NRC in this alphabet-happy world was an old-timer—the Nuclear Regulatory Commission—the watchdog for nuclear reactors, waste disposal, matters of security, and just about anything else having to do with awful stuff that made your balls drop off.

He read the missive slowly, deciphering its many parts—who and where it was from, its level of importance, the topic it discussed, the date at its top, and the nature of the threat it addressed. French stood patiently in place throughout, his irritation growing.

Coven finally laid the sheet down. "Bill," he asked, "this got you cranked up for what reason?"

French hesitated. "I'm not sure I understand."

"You got this off the screen, printed it out, hand delivered it to me, and now you're standing there as if you expect me to order up a fleet of black helicopters. I just wanted to hear what you know that I don't."

French thought for a moment. "Well, it's an event. It might be significant."

Coven sat back in his chair and placed the sole of one shoe carefully against the edge of his desk. "It's a report of a single garbage bag of incredibly low-level medical waste gone missing in Bennington, Vermont."

French nodded. "That's right—potential makings of a dirty bomb."

"For about three days," Coven agreed, "assuming someone was crazy enough to wrap a stick of dynamite with some old Band-Aids, underwear, a couple of pillow-cases, and maybe a diaper or two."

"I thought maybe JTTF might want to know," French said, losing conviction.

The Joint Terrorism Task Force did admittedly handle a lot of wild-goose chases. They were made up of any number of participants, from fellow FBI agents to members of ATF, ICE, the state police, and anyone else deemed relevant.

In the silence that fell between them, Coven looked at French and eventually sighed, giving up. "Good thought, William. I'll pass it along."

As French left, Coven dropped the printout into his out-box, knowing full well that his young messenger was already mentally formulating the memo that would both cover his butt and put Coven's in the hot seat. Not that the older man was worried. He knew all too well how items like this got lost in the system, follow-up memo or not.

Chapter 16

The VBI office in Brattleboro rarely contained all its occupants at once. Not only their assignments but their personalities dictated that they spend most of their time in the field.

It felt cramped and crowded to Joe, therefore, merely having everybody at their desks on the day he'd assembled them for a staff meeting.

"Okay," he began, speaking over the exchanges and friendly insults that further filled the small room. "It took a long time to get here, but it's pretty clear that Michelle Fisher is now officially a homicide."

"Let's hear it for the wheels of justice," Kunkle said quietly.

"At least we caught it," Spinney commented, forever striving for the upbeat.

"On the face of it," Gunther continued, ignoring them, "it seems pretty straightforward. Man wants house back so he can sell it. He can't do that because of a cranky tenant. He kills tenant."

Kunkle merely laughed.

Joe nodded, smiling. "Right. Or maybe not. For one

thing, given the mechanics employed, Newell Morgan, our suspect, is too fat."

"Plus, he has an alibi," Sam added.

"A suspiciously airtight one," Willy threw in.

"Right again," Joe agreed. "How many times have we met an otherwise total slob with such perfect recall, not to mention documentation, for the one recent event that'll save his bacon? Not often."

"Although not impossible," Spinney said. "That trip was a big male-bonding moment. And according to what Willy and Sam got from the interviews, planned in advance."

Willy rolled his eyes, but Joe conceded the point. "Granted. Although it seems the murder was planned as well. Still, we have to watch out for tunnel vision. Since we're already thinking Morgan couldn't have done this on his own, that means he either had help or is totally innocent."

"God, I hope not," Sam murmured, half to herself. "I'd love for him to go down for something."

Joe used that as a cue. "Well, if we are going to focus on him initially, we should dig into two areas: the actual killing of Michelle Fisher, and what led up to it."

"His wanting the house back?" Spinney asked.

"No," Sammie corrected him, understanding what Joe was suggesting. "Why he wanted the house *all of a sudden,* after years of Archie and Michelle living in it. There's the smell of revenge about it."

"The fat bastard wanted a piece of his son's honey," Willy spelled out in predictable fashion.

"And we know that for sure?" Lester asked reasonably. "It could also be exactly what he's claiming: His son died; the girlfriend became a nonpaying squatter with an attitude, leaving him no other option than to evict her.

Could be he did need the money. Do we know anything about his finances?"

Sam laughed outright and Willy readied for a response when Joe cut him off. "Right now that's as valid a position as any. We have to prove our case here, folks. We need to go into Michelle's neighborhood and start interviewing people. Flash Newell's photograph around, and his truck's, and see if he was a regular visitor. I spoke with Michelle's friend Linda and got nowhere there, but that doesn't necessarily mean anything. Michelle might not have told her, for some reason, or Linda may have been coy with me."

"I didn't get anything out of the mother on that subject," Lester added. "I asked her flat out if her daughter fessed up to Newell going after her sexually, and she said it never came up. She wondered but didn't ask. And Michelle never said."

"I wouldn't've told my mother," Sam said sympathetically.

"I wouldn't have told your mother if a truck was headed at her," Willy cracked.

"Fuck you," she said without much emphasis, and threw a pad at him, which he swatted away.

Lester was still speaking, as used to their antics as Joe was. "She did say one funny thing—that she thought Newell probably hated his own life and wished it was more like Archie's."

There was a sudden stillness in the room. For all their casual interactions, every person here was a trained investigator, and phrases like what Lester had just quoted carried a telling weight.

"More like Archie's, how?" Willy asked just as Joe inquired, "How did she know that about Newell?"

Spinney answered his boss first. "From what I could tell, everything she knew came from her daughter. Michelle told her Newell was fueled by envy. According to Adele, that meant that while Michelle and Archie had each other, all Newell had was anger."

Lester turned to Willy. "Which means 'I don't know.' What Archie *had,* quote-unquote, might've just been old-fashioned peace and quiet. It might've also been his sexual relationship with Michelle."

"That's my bet," Willy answered. "Screw peace and quiet."

"Don't we know it," Sam murmured, smiling.

"Which brings us back to finding out if he was a regular visitor after Archie died," Joe commented, adding, "and when we do that canvass, let's avoid Linda Rubinstein. I'd like her put on the shelf for the time being. Let's concentrate on less involved people first."

He glanced down at his notes before resuming on a slightly different tack. "Sam and Willy, you dug the most into Newell. The crime lab established he couldn't have done in Michelle, at least not alone—not according to my description of him. How can you make him the bad guy?"

"Mel Martin," Willy said simply. "He's on top of my list."

Joe frowned. "Sam mentioned him in her report. He bought a car from Newell?"

"Truck. He'd be perfect for this."

Joe shrugged. "Educate us."

Willy crossed his feet, which were already resting on his desk, his chair leaning against the wall behind him. "Ever since the Bennington PD tipped him to us, kind of by accident, I've been checking him out. Took all the state CAD records apart, ran him through NCIC, finally called a buddy with the New York State Police, who then put me together with a guy on the Albany PD. Turns out there's as much against Martin off the record as there is on. He's suspected of a ton of bad stuff, including murder."

He waved vaguely at the jumble of paperwork strewn across his desk. "I've got printouts if you're interested, but my guess is, he and Newell got together on the truck deal, and then like birds of a feather, one thing led to another and Newell popped him the question."

Joe paused a moment, waiting for more. Hearing nothing, he asked, "And you've got them meeting together, building this friendship? Maybe even some kind of financial exchange?"

"Not yet," Willy admitted affably. "But I will."

Joe nodded. In another context, with another cop, he might have at least questioned the foundation of what was sounding like a wild guess. But with Willy, he knew better. Willy was holding back. Possibly nothing of enormous obvious merit—certainly something that wouldn't stand Joe's scrutiny. But his ego was such that he wouldn't have said what he had without some basis. Willy didn't like being caught making mistakes, and he was flagrantly sticking his neck out here.

Joe glanced at Sam for some form of confirming body language, but she was sitting stolidly at her desk, fiddling with a bent paper clip, her eyes down. Apparently, Willy was on his own.

"Okay," he said, "then let's divide and conquer. Lester, I'd like you to take a crack at Michelle Fisher's neighborhood. Doug Matthews at VSP has some information from their preliminary canvass. That can be your starting point. We're now not only looking for sightings of Newell

Morgan, but Mel Martin, too. Willy will supply you with mug shots, vehicle descriptions, and the rest.

"Sam," he continued, causing her to drop her paper clip and look up, "you and Willy go after Martin. Given his record and who you're likely to meet, I'd like you to team up on this. Do not split up unless it's totally safe to do so, right?"

"Yes, boss," she said, while Willy merely looked at him.

"One other thing," Joe added. "Do your best to tiptoe around this guy at first, okay? I don't want him to know we're checking him out until we know what he's up to, if anything. Try to figure his action from the inside, maybe."

"Undercover?" Sam asked, surprised.

"Not exactly," he corrected her. "But you've both had experience in that line. I'm saying superlow profile for now.

"For my part," he continued, already unhappy with the pleased look on Willy's face, "I want to look at Newell beyond the field trip to Frankfort. I'll meet with his wife, talk to his former coworkers, try to find out about his fi—"

Judy, their administrative assistant, opened the door from her small cubicle just off the hallway and peered around the corner. "Joe, I've been holding calls like you asked, but I thought you'd want this one. Milton Coven, from the Fusion Center?"

Joe nodded. Of the various ways the Fusion Center chose to communicate, direct phone calls were few and far between. In addition, Coven was a friend he hadn't heard from in years. "Thanks, Judy."

He picked up the phone. "Milt. The Fusion Center? They give you a double-O number to go with that?"

"Very funny," Coven's familiar voice said. "It's more like they finally found me a chair to sit on instead of a cardboard box—I'm liaison here, probably until retirement next year. Your lady there said you were in a staff meeting, so I'll cut this short. I promise I'll call later so we can catch up."

"Okay, shoot."

"I heard through the grapevine that some of your people were working in Bennington, on what I don't know, but I got a few recent hits over there you might find interesting, just in case."

Joe raised his eyebrows, impressed and a little startled at what he was hearing. He wondered just what and how Coven knew of their activities. They all shared the same law enforcement tent, but this had a quasi-creepy feeling to it.

"Milt," he told his friend, with just a touch of perverseness, "your timing couldn't be better. We were just discussing Bennington. Since you've been keeping an eye on us anyhow, I'm going to put you on speakerphone so you can tell all of us what you've got."

"What? Joe . . ."

The last word filled the small room.

"Go ahead," Joe said. "I'll spare you introductions. Suffice it to say the squad's all ears."

There was a telling silence as Coven scrambled to think. "Okay, okay. Hey, everybody. I'm Milton Coven, FBI, assigned to the Vermont Fusion Center. As you probably know, we serve as a kind of clearinghouse for intel, hoping to avoid the black holes that preceded nine-eleven. Anyhow, a couple of days ago, one of our gatherers handed me some information about a bag of low-level hospital waste that went missing from the Bennington area—technically radioactive but with a short enough half-life to be harmless. I almost . . . Well, never mind. I thought I'd do a quick follow-up, just to be thorough, and found another Bennington blip. Like I was telling Joe, I knew some of you were in the area poking around, so I thought this might be helpful. Sort of kill two birds with one stone."

Joe watched Willy slowly remove his feet from his desktop and sit up, scowling. Trained by years of exposure to such body language, Joe signaled to him to keep his mouth shut.

Coven's voice went on, oblivious. "Keep in mind that all we do here is pass stuff along. We don't know its value necessarily, and we don't know how or if it connects to anything."

"What've you got?" Willy cut in, irrepressible.

"What? Oh, right. It *may* be the mugging of a night guard at the armory. The guy actually doesn't know if he fell or was pushed—he didn't see—but he went down a flight of stairs. He survived, obviously—a concussion only—and nothing was stolen or otherwise disturbed. But since it happened at the armory, we and the locals took notice. The PD probably has some back-burner investigation going into the guard's story, just to be sure."

"That's it?" Willy pressed him.

"Along those lines, yeah. I mean, Bennington's like any other town—something happening all the time. But we look at things that might go bigger, like the missing bag. I mentioned the armory because it was offbeat and I thought you should know."

Joe knew that Willy was cranked up because of the Big Brother implications, although he suspected that the outrage was more because Willy wasn't the one working the microscope. But the possibilities of what Coven was telling them got Joe's brain working along other lines.

"You filter everything, don't you, Milt, to get to the good stuff?"

Coven's voice was guarded. "What're you after?"

Joe laughed. "I don't know. That's the point. Anything else that's hanging around without a solution."

Coven paused. They could hear him rustling through paperwork. "Well," he eventually reported, "there's the disappearance of a young dope seller and user named Conrad Sweet, street-named High Top."

"What've you got on him?" Sam spoke out, caught by surprise, glancing at Lester Spinney, who was staring at the speakerphone. Their own research into High Top earlier had ended nowhere.

"That's about it," said Coven's disembodied voice.

"Anything else?" Joe asked.

"Nope . . . No, hold it. There's a mugging of a local firefighter, a little north of Bennington. Almost missed that, being out of town. He was robbed of their weekly bingo money, to the tune of a little over a thousand bucks. He has no idea who hit him.

"Like I said," he repeated, sounding back on track, "I don't know how or if there are any linkages, but it struck me as interesting that there were two unusual, so far unsolved events, in the same area and at the same time you guys were in the neighborhood. I know it's unlikely, but that's the kind of thinking that got us jammed up before nine-eleven. You stirring anything up?"

"You heard about that Wilmington homicide?" Joe asked.

"Michelle Fisher?" Coven responded immediately.

Joe knew this time that the response had little to do

with high-grade intelligence gathering. There were so few homicides in Vermont that the average well-read newspaper subscriber might have come up with the same quick answer.

"Her case is looking like it may have ties to Bennington," Joe explained, his eyes on Willy's increasingly clouded face—not a man given to sharing information.

Seemingly by honed instinct, Coven knew enough to quit while he was ahead. "Well, like I said, I figured you might be interested, and I wanted to say hi anyhow. I'll e-mail you what I got and call you later at home."

"Thanks, Milt," Joe told him. "I appreciate it. One question, though: What're you thinking was behind the theft of the garbage bag?"

Coven hesitated, weighing his response. "Well . . . I suppose the natural reaction is a dirty bomb, but that seems pretty unlikely. I mean, this stuff was medical trash—old IV tubing, dressings, junk like that—all slightly tainted. Even if you sprinkled it from a helicopter, it wouldn't do any harm. On the other hand, if you cancel out the dirty bomb idea, you don't have much left—somebody stole somebody else's trash. That's why I didn't hit the red button and alert my fellow feds."

"It could've been misplaced," Lester suggested.

"My point exactly," Coven agreed. "The hospital says not. But like I said, we just pass this info along, no matter how small it looks."

Joe saw Willy warming up again and so wrapped it up quickly. "Thanks, Milt. It might be worth a lot. Thanks for thinking of us. Give my best to Sue."

"Oh, yeah. Thanks. Love to Gail, too."

Joe hit the Off button, causing Gail's name to float in the air.

"Guess his intel isn't all *that* great," Willy smirked.

Sam glared at him. Her words could barely be heard, she spoke so quietly. "You are such an asshole."

Joe cleared his throat. "I'll fatten my own assignment with the garbage bag and the missing dope dealer, just for what-the-hell."

"Lester and I can give you a little background on that," Sam admitted. "We spent some time checking him out when the BOL first came out."

Joe nodded, giving his team one last appraising look. "Okay—looks like we're heading for parts west."

Chapter 17

"Where is it?" Nancy asked quietly, as if being discreet in a roomful of eavesdroppers.

They were both in Ellis's apartment again, alone. In bed.

"In my trunk," he said.

She propped herself up quickly on one elbow, her eyes wide, all discretion gone. "*What?* It's been days. I thought . . ."

He covered her mouth gently with his fingertips. "I did, too. But I started thinkin' about somethin' else."

She slowly removed his hand. "What?" she asked, her confusion clear. "You were going to hide it in his toolbox."

He nodded. "And then call the cops."

"The feds," she corrected.

"I know, Nance. I know. Let me finish."

She pressed her lips together, fighting the urge to protest.

Ellis took a small breath before continuing. "The plan was to have Homeland Security take him away like they did with that guy we heard about on TV—lock him up forever and not even give him a trial, like a terrorist."

"But you gotta plant the stuff, Ellis, like we discussed—put the cheese in the trap."

His face darkened slightly at her persistence. "Yeah, Nance, I gotta bait the trap. And whose prints are on that bag? And whose DNA? I sweated on that thing."

"We wiped it off."

He shook his head. "You seen what they can do on TV. Plus, where did that bag come from?"

She stared at him, wondering what the trick part of the question was.

"From the hospital where my mom is," he finished. "How hard do you think it'll be for them to figure that out? I drop a dime to the feds, telling them Mel is a wack job aiming to blow up the Bennington Monument or something, and first thing they'll do is take that bag apart. They'll figure out where it's from, and nail us instead of him. Far as I know, Mel's never even *been* in that hospital."

Nancy untangled her legs from his and sat up in the bed, leaning against the wall, her expression hard.

He tried winning her back. "Sweetie, we can still do it, or something like it. We just need to be more careful."

"Give me a cigarette."

He rolled over toward the night table and retrieved a half-empty pack. He extracted a cigarette, lit it up, and handed it to her.

"It's still a good plan," he reiterated.

She took a deep pull, held the smoke for a few seconds, and then let out a long contrail between her lips. She was staring straight ahead.

"I guess," she finally said.

"We need to figure out how to make them look only at him and not us."

She was silent a while longer, her eyes still on the far wall, working on that cigarette.

"I just want it done, Ellis," she said.

"I know. Me, too."

Joe glanced down at the buzzing cell phone in its dashboard charger. He didn't recognize the number on the small display, but it was a Montpelier exchange, which gave him a pretty good idea who was calling him.

Conflicted, he glanced ahead, saw a pull-off at a souvenir stand parking lot, and stopped his car. He was on his way toward Bennington, on Route 9, and had just passed the road's apex over Vermont's tree-covered, hilly backbone—complete with a view stretching out for hundreds of square miles. His ambivalence about the upcoming conversation was compounded by a small regret that he'd just missed the best place to have it.

"Hello."

"Hi, Joe. It's me."

Gail Zigman had a low voice, and from the first time he'd heard it, it had always hit him the same way, with a stirring he imagined animals responded to in the wild.

Almost despite himself, he smiled. "Hey, Gail. This is a treat."

"Where are you?" she asked.

He laughed. "I was just thinking about that. I'm a few hundred yards past the top of that long downslope into Bennington, between Searsburg and Woodford, staring at some tourists buying stuffed animals and pricey syrup. How 'bout you?"

Her voice flattened somewhat. "Oh, in the Executive Building somewhere. I had a little time between meetings. I'd rather be where you are."

That was perhaps a little richer in meaning than either of them wanted. "Oh, I doubt that," he said lamely. "Bennington hasn't changed much."

She played along. "Big case there?"

"Maybe. We have something percolating we need to figure out, but right now we're just fumbling around."

In fact, this was his favorite part of an investigation, when not just he but the whole team had the pull of a strong scent encouraging them. They were largely ignorant, that was true, but motivation was taking care of itself.

"You still having fun up there?" he asked, moving the conversation along, its emptiness palpable. They were being guarded to an extent that they'd never been before. Their past involvement had epitomized intimacy, and had included their jobs, where each of them had found the other to be a natural sounding board. It was the aspect of their relationship that Joe missed the most—and which was now making him feel awkward. In fact, the depth of his ignorance about what she was doing these days was startling.

"Oh," she said with no great enthusiasm, "I wouldn't call it fun. Worthwhile, though. Definitely that." She paused before adding, "There are times, though . . ."

"Right," he said, not knowing where to go next. Looking out at the parking lot, oddly mirroring this conversation in his head, he envisioned two picnickers in a minefield.

"I miss you, Joe," she said after a long silence. "I miss us."

"I know," he admitted, thinking back to his night with Beverly. He didn't regret it, not even now. But he missed what would have accompanied it had the woman been Gail. It reminded him how much he was in limbo.

"Well," she added sadly, interrupting his thoughts, "I guess I only have myself to blame."

He knew that deserved some response, a one-liner designed to make the jagged edges less painful. But for the life of him, he couldn't come up with it, not to his own satisfaction.

"I don't see blame going anywhere," he said, not liking how that sounded.

But it seemed to work. "You were always very sweet that way," she said.

He wasn't sure he had been, or even exactly what that meant.

Mercifully, he heard some feeble electronic sound in the background of her phone, a bell of some sort, that prompted her to say, her voice defeated, "I have to go. Thanks for talking. You sound good."

"You, too," he lied. "Knock 'em dead."

He replaced the phone, checked his rearview mirror, and returned to the road.

Time to get back to something he knew how to do.

"I never liked that look," Willy said, glaring at her from the passenger seat.

Sam stared at him. "Is that what's been bugging you all the way over here? My hair?"

"That, the tight jeans. You look like a hooker."

She laughed at him. "No hooker you ever knew. What I look like is fashionable. These are sixty-dollar jeans. And the blond hair works like a charm to open guys up. You just don't like how other men appreciate me," she added in a teasing, lilting voice.

He shifted his gaze to the scene outside. They were parked on a side street in Bennington, not far from Piccolo's, the bar that their local PD contact, Johnny Massucco, had told them was a likely watering hole for men like Mel Martin.

"They don't appreciate you," he said sullenly. "They just want to jump your bones."

"And you don't?" she asked.

"Not the same."

She watched his profile, knowing what was bothering him. Her change in appearance wasn't new. She'd used it before, once when she'd masqueraded as a ski instructor, and again when she'd pretended to be a drug dealer in Holyoke, Massachusetts. On both occasions, he'd become surly and aloof. Over time, she had come to understand both his insecurity and his deep conservatism, and how they combined sometimes to wind him up tight. It was a pain—he was difficult enough to live with when he was feeling fine—but given her own quirky needs in a mate, she'd actually come to see his moodiness as sweet . . . some of the time.

"Well," she told him, "you sure won't have the same problem in that getup."

He swung back to face her. "What? I look normal."

She poked him. "Normal for a bum."

With a flash of anger, he reached for the door handle and yanked it open. "Let's get going."

She caught hold of his arm. "Whoa, hang on. I don't want to lose sight of you."

"Fat chance of that. You'll be in the middle of an admiring crowd."

She didn't let go. "Willy."

He caught her change of tone and was quieter in his response. "What?"

"I've stuck by you this long, haven't I?"

Willy wasn't overequipped with moments of grace, but he did have them, as both Sam and Joe knew. They came fast and vanished faster for the most part, but when timed right, they could linger.

As an example, in a gesture scented with faint but reliable virtue, he quickly ducked his head, kissed her fingers, and said, "Come on, babe, we ain't got all night."

They headed off in slightly different directions after leaving the car separately, blending into a section of town at once bruised and polished. Bennington was full of such contrasting overlays, with haves and have-nots virtually sharing the same fences. This area featured low-income housing down one street, a fancy restaurant and a state-of-the-art fire station up two others, and one of the town's busiest commercial strips one block over.

Piccolo's appealed to customers of all stripes, being a place where the younger, slightly rough-edged gentility might go for a nightcap after the evening had officially concluded—to where the hard-core drinkers had been hanging out all night. It wasn't a classic biker bar—those tended to be short-lived in towns like this—but it was definitely working class.

It was also a place where Sam and Willy each could reach a combat-ready comfort level. As with those few soldiers who discovered that the adrenaline of battle afforded a certain simplified clarity, so these two had found that slipping disguised into the twilight between the good guys and the bad freed them to act more spontaneously, without fear that their bosses were one citizen's complaint away.

Cops, especially those in uniform, were more conscious of maintaining the badge's reputation than they were of the gun most civilians stared at. It was the claim of misconduct, whether real or imagined, that dogged them most, not the misuse of a weapon they rarely fired. For these two, therefore, there was a paradoxical sense of liberation in their identities being hidden.

So Sam and Willy, several minutes apart and via two different entrances, came into Piccolo's looking cheerful and glum respectively, supposedly in search of either company or respite, but in fact as keen as dogs on the hunt, ready for anything and on the scent for Mel Martin.

Mel Martin, not surprisingly in a town this size, was a couple of streets from Piccolo's at that very moment, sitting in the cab of the truck he'd bought from Newell Morgan. He was watching the front of the oddly named Green Mountain Vista Lodge Motel—a fleabag with no vista of anything except the traffic on Route 9.

The Vista, as it was colloquially known, was C-shaped in the traditional manner, surrounding its own parking lot on three sides. All the rooms led onto two stacked walkways, the upper one belted in by a balcony, a row of cars hemming in the lower one like sucklings lined up against one gigantic, sleeping pig.

Mel's point of interest was the door to number 32, on the second floor, slightly closer to the right-hand staircase. It was indistinguishable from its neighbors— brown, battered, and accompanied by a tiny, occluded window to one side—but Mel stared at it as if seeking enlightenment.

Which, in one sense, he was. He'd witnessed a blade-thin young man, street-named Banger, enter the room twenty minutes earlier, intending to conduct a minor piece of business in the illegal drug trade, and he was awaiting his reappearance.

Mel knew what was happening behind that door. He'd even caught a glimpse of the young couple who had opened up to Banger's knock. They'd be sitting around feigning coolness, feeling each other out on issues of quantity and price, and either doing a deal and parting company or joining together in a group indulgence where Banger consumed most of his profit on the spot. Whether sex entered into it often depended on a crucial few creating the right mood. Mel remembered times when he'd woken up atop a naked woman with no memory of what might have gone on between them.

The source of his fascination, however, had nothing to do with such reminiscences, or even any yearnings to relive them. Mel was more interested in where he'd picked up Banger's tail—the same address High Top had given him just before dying.

Which made of this innocuous encounter inside a faceless motel a beacon toward Mel's major score. Of that, he'd convinced himself.

Banger worked for the mysterious two cousins who had captivated Mel's imagination the way the lottery drives others to gamble away their life savings. And just as he had snuffed out High Top to get a simple address, so he was now willing to do whatever was necessary to extract the next level of knowledge from this source. His first knowledge of the elusive cousins had created something akin to a quest in him, based less on their reality than on the dream they represented.

In truth, Mel had no idea if Banger's suppliers made any more money than he did conducting his much ballyhooed raids. The mere rumors that they did were good enough. And, perhaps incongruously, his sacrifice of High Top for so little was not a reflection of any concerns about insolvency. He was far more careless than that—if a single influence could be blamed for his growing thirst for violence, it might just as easily have been boredom.

He had killed before. High Top had been the third. The first had been an inebriated bum in an Albany alleyway one night when he'd been in his early teens. That had been mostly experimental—and a disappointment. He'd come upon the passed-out old man by accident, on his way from having broken into a hardware store only to find the till empty. On a whim, he'd closed off the bum's mouth and nose, hoping for some paroxysm of death he could then add to his mental scrapbook. All he'd received for his efforts was a cessation of breathing. Presumably, the guy had been so drunk, he was already at death's door.

The second time had been a slight improvement, if dissatisfying in other ways. Too much booze, an argument, a handy baseball bat. He didn't remember much beyond feeling the bat's reverberation as it contacted the other man's skull. He'd stumbled away from that one, making no effort to avoid capture. But while there had been cops and an investigation, they'd touched him only peripherally, the victim having led a complicated life too full of potential lethal enemies. The whole affair had slipped away like the stupor that had given it birth.

High Top had been the best one yet, even though merely the result of a spontaneous urge. Still, Mel had been sober, and his victim had responded well, the obnoxious little shit.

Mel shifted in his seat, growing impatient. Apparently, Banger was hitting it off with his customers—either that or they'd knocked him off and made their escape through the bathroom window.

The thought made him uncomfortable. Had he brought Ellis into this, he would have had someone watching the back—a maneuver he'd certainly used in the past to good effect.

But he didn't have Ellis. He hadn't wanted him. Ellis was getting weird on him, changing in a way that made him uneasy. He'd once been the perfect student—cooperative, appreciative, submissive, and willing. He'd never challenged Mel's primacy, never come up with ideas of his own, never done anything other than be the textbook sidekick. He was strong, obedient, held his liquor, and was good in a fight.

But not since they'd all moved to Bennington.

The Three Musketeers. That's what Mel had once called them, but whatever that had meant then, it was no longer true.

Which made him think of his wife, another pain in the ass. The list of disappointments with that one was growing daily, and he knew in his heart that before much longer, the habit of having her around notwithstanding, he'd have to dump her.

Or maybe do something more creative . . . He smiled in the darkness of the cab, considering the possibilities.

There was movement by the door of number 32—a reflection from the distant streetlights as it swung open. Against the dim glow of the room inside, a shadow appeared briefly before vanishing just as fast. For a moment, watching Banger's dim outline slipping along the balcony, Mel regretted that his plan hadn't been simply to kick into the place and work all of them over, like in a movie, maybe even threatening them with one of the M-16s.

But even he had enough tactical sense not to do that.

Too many unknowns. Plus, he wouldn't have gotten away with it, not for long. Burying a little toad like High Top was easy enough—nobody to miss him, even with Ellis wringing his hands. But a roomful of people?

Best to stick with the plan—just as with High Top, go after the nobodies, the people who, in the eyes of those who knew them, were just as prone to go wandering as to go missing.

Mel slipped quietly out of the truck, his eyes on the shadow working its way down the stairs, his heart beating to the call of his own primordial lethal urge.

Chapter 18

Joe rose from his plastic seat as a tired, heavyset woman entered the employee break room and blinked at him without curiosity. She was wearing a brightly colored vest adorned with a large sticker announcing, "Hi, I'm Lilly, I'm Here to Help."

Rarely had Joe seen a person more in need of what she was professing to offer.

He approached her with his hand held out. "Mrs. Morgan?"

She didn't smile, and her hand was soft, moist, and cold in his. "I go by Kimbell."

He hesitated. Not only did this differ from what he'd been told, but it made him wonder what might be going on in the Morgan household to have prompted it.

"I'm sorry," he said. "I was misinformed. No offense, I hope?"

"I just changed it back," she said, standing before him like an upended duffel bag.

He stepped back and swept his hand over a scattering of chairs adorning the otherwise empty room. "Would you like to have a seat?"

The faintest sign of a smile appeared. "I may never be able to stand up again."

Still, she sat, surprisingly daintily, on the nearest chair.

"Can I buy you a soda from the machine?" he offered.

"I'm fine."

Joe sat opposite her, a synthetic table between them. The room was a display of bland colors and polymers. Joe assumed that every aspect of it, from the acoustic tiling to the fake wood paneling to the rows of robotlike vending machines, was the result of either a metal press or a plastic molding machine.

He introduced himself, slipping a business card across the table to her. "Do you prefer to be called Lilly?" he asked.

She took the card but didn't even glance at it, holding it instead like something she'd found on the floor and didn't know how to throw away. "No. They call me that here."

"Ms. Kimbell, then?"

The faint smile returned. "That sounds nice."

"Great. I guess you know why I'm here."

The smile faded. "Michelle, I suppose."

He sat back and crossed his legs, hoping to introduce an element of friendliness into an otherwise sterile environment. "Yeah, that's right. I heard she and Archie were very much in love."

The approach caught her off guard. She stared at him for a moment, nonplussed, before answering, to his own surprise, "I guess that's right. I wouldn't have thought of that."

He raised his eyebrows. "Really? Why not? Wasn't it true?"

"I think it was." She seemed to be considering it for the first time.

Joe didn't say anything, letting the silence work for him, as he often did.

"We didn't talk about them much that way."

"You and Newell?"

"Yeah."

"He didn't like her much?"

This time she actually produced a noise like a laugh. It was her only response.

"Was that always the case?" Joe asked. "I mean, I know it was after Archie died and Michelle wasn't paying any rent, but how 'bout before?"

Lillian Kimbell tightened her lips before saying slowly, "There was always some tension."

Joe thought back to his one visit to the Morgan house on Gage Street, and to the disparity between the grubby TV set–chair combo and the rest of the room, jammed with delicate figurines and kitschy bric-a-brac, all dust free and neatly arranged. Tension, indeed.

"How about you, Ms. Kimbell? How did you feel about Michelle?"

Her expressionless eyes settled on his for a long, measured moment while she appeared to weigh her options. Joe considered the possible reasons behind her taking back her maiden name and hoped that one of them might play in his favor now.

"I liked her," she finally said, adding, "right up to the end.".

He tried tipping her a little further. "Your husband wouldn't like hearing that."

"Screw him."

It was said softly, almost tentatively, but Joe burst out laughing anyhow, creating the happiest expression he'd seen on her yet.

"That must've been tough on you," he said then, "being so at odds with Newell."

"I'm always at odds with him," she said, this time bitterly. "First with Archie, then with Michelle. Now with everything."

"Is that why the name change?"

She nodded without comment.

He paused before suggesting vaguely, "The thing with Michelle really did something, didn't it?"

"Yes." The word was said so quietly, it almost vanished in the hum of the overhead lighting.

"Marked an end?"

"I guess it did."

"Are you going to leave him?"

She hesitated before admitting, "That's not what women like me are supposed to do."

"But you're thinking of it." He said it as a statement.

"I guess so, yes."

Now that he had her on the threshold, he tried opening the door wider. "Why?"

The potential was there for her to close down and ask him to leave. She'd never met him before, he'd been asking strange questions, and the entire point of the interview remained as unclear as ever. And yet, not only had she kept pace with him, not challenging the reasons behind his visit, but she seemed to be warming to the age-old comfort of confiding to total strangers what you'd hesitate to tell your closest friend.

It clearly wasn't easy for her. Joe watched as his business card was unconsciously reduced to a small lump between her kneading fingers. She studied the tabletop, forming her thoughts, before she finally said, "Something happened—changed."

"Between you and Newell, or him and Michelle?" Joe asked pointedly.

"Both. All of it. He got so angry."

"At her?"

"Yes. It was more than the money. We're not that bad with the money. There's enough."

Joe leaned forward, suddenly tense, fearful that now would be the very moment when a coworker would come barging in and destroy the mood. "Ms. Kimbell, I hate to pry here. This is all so terribly personal. But it means a great deal to me to really understand exactly what happened. Did you ever think your husband's fury at Michelle might have been for another reason? I don't want to be insensitive here, but I also don't want to tiptoe around—do you think he might've made a pass at her?"

To his relief, she took it in full stride. "I wondered that. If he did, I don't think it worked."

"Is that why you said you liked her up to the end?"

She nodded. "Like you said, she always loved Archie. So did I. I'll always feel in my bones that it was Newell who killed Archie."

Joe was comfortable with the assumption that she wasn't being literal—that the father's harshness had merely driven the son to drink and an early grave. It was a startling one-liner, though, given what he suspected Newell had done to Michelle.

"Did Newell go out to see her after Archie's death?" he asked, keeping on track.

He knew he shouldn't have been so unreasonably hopeful, but he was still disappointed when she looked up at the white acoustic ceiling and gave a hapless shrug. "I'm here most of the time. I barely noticed when he went on a trip with his buddies a while ago."

"How 'bout right after she died?" Joe persisted. "How did he react?"

She scowled. "That's what really did it for me—made me decide. He was so happy, it almost made me sick. It was the first time I saw him as a cruel man. Before, I always thought he was just kind of useless."

Joe reviewed what he'd learned—supportive of their theory, but frustratingly shy of hard evidence. He considered asking her outright if she thought Newell had killed Michelle, but he knew that it would merely upset her and result in nothing useful. Besides, she had enough in her bag of dark thoughts.

Instead, he extracted a mug shot of Mel Martin and slid it across the table. "Have you ever seen this man in the company of your husband?"

She looked quite startled at the harshness of the image before her. "Lord. I've met some of Newell's friends. None of them look like this. Newell's been with this man?"

"He sold him his truck."

She made a face. "Oh, that old thing. I was happy to see that go. Always left oil on the driveway. Noisy and smelly, too."

"So he never even described the man he'd sold it to? Or discussed him in any way?" Joe asked hopefully, knowing he was grasping at straws.

She settled the issue by smiling gently at him. "Newell and I don't discuss."

Lester Spinney wasn't having much luck. He'd checked the few dirt roads that might reasonably house anyone who'd notice traffic going to and from Michelle's, and hadn't hit a single person yet who'd even known of her or Archie, much less seen Newell's ex—and Mel's current—truck. People lived isolated from each other out here by design, it turned out. Everyone he met was perfectly happy not to know the first thing about their neighbors.

It was therefore with no great optimism that he finally pulled up to his last planned stop—a complicated jigsaw puzzle of Swiss chalet, Norman keep, and modern glass—and swung out of the car to make his pitch.

But he never got to it. Before he'd traveled halfway up the front walk, a bright-faced, spindly couple capped in matching snow-white hairdos threw open the broad wooden door and stood beaming at him like something out of a B-level fairy tale.

"Don't tell us," the male half ordered, his hand in the air like a circus barker's. "The car looks strictly standard issue."

"And the clothes," his companion chimed in, adding, "I hope you won't be offended, but they're practical and inexpensive, aimed toward respectability."

"Yes," agreed her mate. "Like an aspiring junior clerk out of Dickens."

She laughed as Spinney stood there, smiling politely and waiting for the routine to wrap up, although as a cop, he had to appreciate the way they thought.

"So what do you say, George? The poor man's on pins and needles."

George looked thoughtful for a moment. "Hard to say with any certainty . . . State employee, for sure."

She clapped her hands once and kept them clasped against her narrow chest. "Yes, just what I was thinking. But from what branch?"

Lester, far from pins or needles, nevertheless hoped all

this would play to his advantage. "Police," he confessed. "Vermont Bureau of Investigation."

The couple burst into laughter, George saying, "Oh, I never would have gone there. Thank you so much. You don't look like a policeman at all, young man. I was just about to embarrass myself—I won't tell you how."

Lester waved that away with his hand, displaying his badge with the other, for the record. "Not a problem. I have that effect on everybody. My name is Spinney, by the way."

"Mr. and Mrs. George B. Heller the Third," said the woman, extending her hand before abruptly withdrawing it with the words "Oh, my. Does one shake hands with the police? I don't know the rules."

"You do with this one," Lester said, playing out the formalities with both of them.

George Heller asked, "To what do we owe the pleasure, Officer? Have we done something wrong?"

"No, no. Not at all. I just wanted to ask you a couple of questions about the neighborhood."

Mrs. Heller laughed. "You mean the neighbors, not the neighborhood."

Lester conceded with a smile. "You got me."

"Is it poor Michelle Fisher?" George asked. "We knew the police were looking into that. We even heard they'd been by when we were out of town for a couple of days. We were sorry to have missed out."

Spinney felt an instant warmth for both of them, like a thirsty man might who'd finally reached water. "It is. Strictly routine—something we do with all unattended deaths. Do you mind talking about it?"

Mrs. Heller broke into a broad smile. "Goodness, no. George and I live to gossip. We love to watch the comings and goings around here—gives us something to do in our old age. But before we go on, wouldn't you rather come in and have some tea or something?"

Lester accepted, and they all trooped into the eccentric house, eventually settling in a nicely appointed living room–kitchen combination with a huge picture window overlooking the road.

"This is where George and I do most of our busybody business," his hostess explained as she went to work preparing the tea.

Her husband and Lester chose deep armchairs facing the view. In fact, Lester did feel a little as if he'd just bought a skybox seat at a ballpark. The house sat up high over the road, and the vegetation had been trimmed to afford the best advantage over quite a piece of real estate. The peaks of several houses could be seen nestled among the treetops.

"This is beautiful," Lester murmured.

"We like it," George stated. "We could have set it up to take in just the woods and fields, but we like people. We're from the city originally, and we've always enjoyed watching our fellow human beings."

His wife chimed in, "We used to walk in the park every weekend, trying to come up with little life stories for everyone who caught our eye."

"And sometimes," he added, "when we could get away with it, we'd even ask them about themselves, to see how much we got right. We ended up being pretty good." He paused before admitting, "Of course, around here it's a little harder. We only get to see cars go by—sometimes strollers walking their dogs or something. And people are a little more reserved here, too."

"Oh, yes," she agreed. "They think we're very strange."

Lester was taking this all in while he surveyed the

room, inventorying the usual assortment of family pictures and decorative artifacts. At some point, quite clearly, someone in this family had done a lot more than simply look out the window. The whole house spoke of serious income.

"So," he began, feeling that the niceties had been given enough free play, "what can you tell me about Michelle Fisher? Did you know her well?"

"Didn't know her at all," George said flatly.

"We never got to meet her or her boyfriend," his wife agreed, still hard at work at the butcher block island separating the kitchen from the room's observation platform. "We just watched their comings and goings—got a feeling for their life. They seemed very happy together. We always noticed that."

"That's true," George concurred. "And you could tell that Archie especially had been around a bit, which made us all the happier that he'd found her. It's hard to believe they're both gone . . ."

"How do you know so much about them?" Spinney asked.

"Oh," she admitted, finally bringing over a tray laden with tea things, "you ask around; you eavesdrop a little. Once the postman even dropped off some of their mail here by mistake. That's how we found out his name— Archie Morgan."

Lester was fascinated by how guileless they both were about their snooping. "Did you notice if they had a lot of visitors?" he asked.

"There was Linda," Mrs. Heller said immediately. "She was a regular. Very nice woman. She's from the city, too. We met her a couple of times, out walking. She was a good friend of theirs."

"Anyone else?" Lester persisted.

The couple exchanged searching looks. George finally shrugged and handed Lester his tea. "I guess not. Like I said, people tend to keep to themselves—part of the point of living here. We're not so different, when you get down to it. We love being nosy, but we hardly get out of the house, we're such hermits."

"That's true," his wife said happily. "This is our cave."

Lester reached into his inner pocket and pulled out two photographs, one of Mel Martin, the other of Newell Morgan. He laid them flat on the low table between them. "Do either of these men ring a bell?"

"That one does," they both said, with George tapping Newell's picture. "Nasty-looking fellow, at least from what we could see in passing. He was Archie's father, Newell, according to Linda. We heard his personality matched his appearance."

"What was he driving?"

"An old, beaten-up pickup truck."

"You never saw him in anything else?"

Again they exchanged baffled looks. "Nope," George said, speaking for them both.

"And when was the last time you saw him around here?" Lester asked, keeping the timetable of the truck's sale from Newell to Mel in mind.

"What would you say, George?" she asked. "Two months ago, maybe three?"

He nodded. "That's what I would say—closer to three."

After the eviction notice and before the truck sale, Spinney thought. "Did you see him often?"

"Well," George answered slowly, "over the years, we saw him now and then. You know he actually owned the house, right? That Archie and Michelle rented from him."

"Yes."

"We always figured he was just being a landlord, dropping by to make sure everything was okay. He never stayed long."

"And after Archie died," Lester asked, "how often did he come by then?"

George shrugged. "Half a dozen times, maybe."

"Really?" Lester reacted, surprised. "Over a six-month period?"

Mrs. Heller nodded. "About that, yes."

"Were the visits evenly spaced?"

Her brow furrowed. "That's interesting," she said. "They weren't. Isn't that right, George?"

"Yup," he agreed. "There were about four visits that we saw over something like a week and a half, just before they stopped altogether."

Lester suddenly thought of something else. "When you saw him driving by, was he always alone?"

They both hesitated. George finally said, "Can't say for sure. From this angle, we could see through the driver's window, but not to the other side of the cab. And sometimes, when he drove back, it was too dark to see anyone inside at all."

The old man suddenly leaned forward in his chair, as if hoping to dispel any disappointment. "So, Detective, by your expression, I can tell you're pleased overall. Have we given you something valuable?"

Spinney hesitated before answering. The question made him uncomfortable, and not just because he didn't want to answer it. It also suggested the possibility that these two informants had been feeding him what they thought he wanted to hear. In fact—not that they would know this—they'd been the only ones to say that Newell had ever visited the area, at least to the degree they claimed. Cops, like responsible reporters, didn't like hanging their narratives on the say-so of just one source.

"You've been very helpful," he therefore said blandly.

Mrs. Heller pressed a little harder. "Do you always dig this deep for all deaths? You've made us think something bad might have happened to poor Michelle."

Spinney had to struggle to remember that they'd never actually met poor Michelle.

"That's exactly why we do it," he explained. "To make sure nothing did happen." He tried shifting the focus by picking up Mel Martin's mug shot. "You're sure you never saw this man around here?"

George Heller replied cautiously, as if reading Lester's silent reservations about their enthusiasm. "We never did, but that doesn't mean he never came by. We don't actually spend all our time staring out the window. It's just a hobby."

"I understand," Lester told them, "and I really do appreciate your being so helpful."

Mel Martin was grateful, too, as he sat watching, yet again, in his truck. Banger had been good to him, not just with information but in the way he'd died. After being grabbed outside the Vista Motel, he'd been quiet at first, which had made for a peaceful departure out of town, and then he'd broken down in textbook fashion as soon as he realized what Mel had in store.

For Mel, it had amounted to a watershed. In his progression of killings, this had been the first he'd planned with care, and just as he'd anticipated it, so had he relished its execution. He'd always fantasized this level of violence—had even vaguely pushed at its boundaries during sex with Nancy—but for one reason or another, he'd never taken possession of it.

Until now.

He smiled at the memory of Banger, pleading and spent, totally confused by the violation of such an encounter's implicit contract—you torture me, I give you all I have. Hey, his expression had told Mel, I gave it up. Why're you still going?

Because information gathering had only been Mel's surface ambition. Intelligence about the cousins—Paul and Bob Niemiec, he now knew—could have been collected any number of ways, including by just asking around. They were in retail, after all, and needed to get the word out. But Mel had wanted more. That extra piece—that emotional satisfaction—had been at the heart of his desire.

Not that the promise of big money hurt. Banger had confirmed what Mel had suspected even before he targeted High Top—that the newly arrived Niemiecs were aiming to be major players, exchanging the big city with its attendant overhead and risk factors for the easy pickings of a rural state. But where such operators in the past had used Vermont purely as a retail market, these boys were hoping to create a production base as well. Better still, they'd chosen to step up in style, taking advantage of the local airport to improve importation beyond precedent. Toward the end, Banger had told Mel of a plane delivery of drugs—and of such quantity as to set a man up for decades.

This was what Mel had been longing to hear, which

explained why he was watching the Niemiec headquarters now, taking note of all the players, their habits, and their methods of operation.

When it came time to strike, he wanted to do it with military precision. If this was to be their last shot, the Three Musketeers were going to make it their very best.

Chapter 19

"Special Agent Gunther. Good to meet you."

Wally Neelor was the head of hospital security—a large, open-faced man with a camp counselor's friendliness. He greeted Joe with a two-handed shake. No doubt to quell the concerns of nervous patients, his uniform was low-key and looked only faintly official, lacking all but a couple of muted patches that identified his function here. He carried just a radio on his belt.

He preceded Joe down the broad hallway as he spoke, leading the way to his office. "You said on the phone you were checking out the disappearance of that low-level bag. Is there something I don't know about?"

"Not particularly," Joe told him, sensitive of being in a public place. It wasn't crowded, and they certainly weren't attracting attention, but people were nevertheless milling about.

"I just wondered," Neelor continued. "We did push all the required buttons here, but I didn't really think it was that big a deal. Most of our bells and whistles with that stuff are just to keep the local paranoids happy, you know?"

"I do," Joe told him, grateful to have finally reached the office. They filed past a dispatcher in the front office and ended up in a small, windowless room decorated with charts, maps, and a few pieces of memorabilia showing that Neelor had, in fact, a good deal of police experience in his background.

He waved Joe into a chair and offered him some coffee, which Joe turned down.

"So what's the concern?" Neelor asked, settling into his seat and giving Joe a calculating look.

"I'm fishing," Joe conceded. "Pure and simple. The Fusion Center told us the bag was one of several funny events in this area over the last few weeks, and we're just trying to see if there's a connection between any of them."

Neelor's eyebrows rose. "Other radiological vanishing acts?" he asked.

"No," Joe admitted, almost embarrassed by the slimness of his motivation. "That's part of the problem. We haven't figured out a common thread. It's a bunch of random stuff."

Neelor laughed. "I get it—supersecret stuff. Need-to-know only. No sweat. What do you want from me?"

Joe allowed him his conspiratorial fantasy—it was easier than trying to explain their actual situation. "Run me through how you traced the disappearance."

Neelor made a face. "Simple, really. Each bag has a tag. When the tag's attached, its number is logged in. When the bag is disposed of once and for all, the tag gets matched to the log, and everybody's happy. It's kind of like handling luggage at an airport."

"Does the tagging include the contents?" Joe asked. "I mean, can you match the contents to who it belonged to?"

"The actual patient?" Neelor came back. "No. It's more the *level* of waste than who produced it. Chances are, the same patient's stuff is in the same bag, but it could be mixed in with someone else's who was treated in the same way at the same time. Why would that matter?"

Joe honestly didn't know. "No idea," he answered. "I'm just asking. Was there anything else about all this that stood out?"

"Besides why it would happen in the first place? Nope. In fact, that's what had us going—we couldn't see the sense in it. You want to build a dirty bomb, for example, this isn't a bad place to come to. We have some real hot stuff here. But it's wrapped in lead, weighs a ton, and is harder than hell to move, even without security, which— not to brag—is pretty good."

"I'm sure it is," Joe said appeasingly, not that Neelor seemed to care. "Was there anything else—maybe not connected to the bag—that occurred around the same time?"

Neelor frowned. "Probably is connected, not that any- thing can be made of it, but one of the nurses got into a jam over her key. It was found dangling from the door lock where she left it. We're assuming that's how the bag grew feet—somebody took advantage of finding the key sticking out of the lock. She had no idea she'd left the damn thing behind—kind of thing that can happen to anyone."

"This is the same door where the bag was locked?" Joe asked, intrigued.

"Yeah, there is only one, at least for the low-level stuff. The fry-your-nuts waste is kept elsewhere."

"Is that nurse around today?" he asked.

Neelor reared back in his chair and checked one of the

charts on his wall. "She should be," he said, and gave Joe directions on how to find her.

Ten minutes later, Joe was introducing himself to Ann Coleman, who instantly struck him as the no-nonsense type of professional he most liked to deal with.

He told her why he was there.

She groaned and shook her head. "I caught hell for that," she admitted. "Sad part is, I have no idea how it happened. I don't do things like that. I'm a supervisor, for crying out loud. It's my job to make sure other people don't screw up in just those ways."

"So you have no memory of leaving the key behind?" Joe asked.

"I have no memory of using it at all," she said. "Disposing of trash is not one of the things I do anymore, unless there's a shortage of people, and there hasn't been in ages."

They were chatting at the nurses' station on one of the hospital's lower levels. It was quiet and largely empty. Joe swept his hand around vaguely. "Where do you keep it?"

She patted her pocket. "Here, now. I used to keep it in that drawer." She pointed to a section of the semicircular counter.

Joe crossed over and pulled at the drawer. It slid open without a sound, revealing a typical rabble of paper clips, rubber bands, pens, and pencils.

"Unlocked?" he asked.

She sighed. "I know, I know. But give me a break. What're the chances, right?"

Joe held up both hands. "No argument from me. But if you didn't use it, and you've ruled out all your colleagues . . . I'm assuming you have, right?"

"Absolutely," she said emphatically.

"Then," he continued, "it had to be somebody else—somebody out of the blue. Do people loiter around here at all, so they can see what you're doing and mark your habits?"

As he spoke, he saw her face transform with enlightenment. "Oh, shoot," she said. "The goddamn pendant."

He merely raised his eyebrows.

"We had a thyroid patient—a terminal. She had a pendant that got thrown away by mistake. Her son asked me what we could do about retrieving it, and I bent the rules and took him downstairs to the low-level waste room. Found it right off. I gave it back to him, and that was the end of it. I'd completely forgotten about it."

"Did he handle the key?" Joe asked, a little confused.

"No, but he saw where I kept it." She waved her arm around. "You see how deserted this place is. He could've come in later and swiped it anytime. That's why I didn't connect the two events. They happened days and days apart."

Joe smiled. "Do you remember the son's name?"

She held up a finger. "Hang on."

She moved to a computer console and quickly typed in a few commands. "I remember he was listed as next of kin. The mom's name was Doris Doyle—or still is, I should say. She's upstairs, hanging on by a thread. But the son had a different last name." She straightened suddenly. "Here we are—Ellis Robbinson."

It meant nothing to Joe.

"Too bad," Ann Coleman added.

"What is?"

"I liked him," she said sadly. "He was really nice to his mother."

*　　*　　*

Ellis stood morosely beside Nancy in the dark shadows by one of the smaller metal outbuildings of Bennington's municipal airport. Just ahead of them, Mel was pointing out the layout and talking in a hushed but excited voice. Both Ellis and Nancy had been here before, metaphorically speaking, more times than they could count—they'd even come to dub it "Mel's pep rally," where he briefed them on the next great adventure.

But whereas they'd once been as adrenalized as he, not to mention as careless of any consequences, now they felt only dread. Like hapless kids led by a dominant bully, they were reduced to finding solace solely in holding hands whenever Mel turned his back.

"Pay attention," he was telling them, "I don't want you fucking this one up."

With a last squeeze of Nancy's fingers, Ellis moved up alongside his erstwhile friend. So far, neither he nor Nancy had the slightest idea what he had cooked up, although Ellis was gloomily confident that it tied into the death of High Top the other night.

Mel pointed into the darkness north of them. "The runway's out there. Anything that lands has to take one of the taxiways over to this side, where they park the planes. See there?"

They shifted their attention to the large rectangular apron boxed in by the parallel taxiways, the landing strip, and the buildings. As if to prove Mel's point, several planes, including an old, hulking DC-3, were sitting there like oversize toys abandoned by a giant child after bedtime. Other planes were scattered elsewhere as well. The night was clear and warm, sparkling with stars. On the far side of the strip, the floodlit Bennington Monument shone eerily in the distance, a misplaced museum piece from an Egyptian exhibition, surrounded by the soft glow of the town's lights behind and slightly below it. The utter peacefulness of the scene, as much as his yearning to be elsewhere, distracted Ellis from focusing on what Mel was telling him.

"It won't matter what road they use to get off the runway, since they're not all that far apart. My guess is, it'll be the eastern one, 'cause it's closer to the parking lot. Anyhow, the key isn't the place; it's the time—we have to hit 'em just as they're unloading. That's when they'll be the most distracted."

"Won't it be when they're most on the lookout?" Ellis asked, his attention suddenly drawn.

"You watch too much TV," Mel countered. "This isn't *Miami Vice,* for Chrissake. *We're* going to be the ones with the machine guns, not those losers. They probably won't even be armed."

Ellis frowned in the darkness. Everybody had guns in Vermont. It was the only state in the Union with virtually no gun laws of its own. And a bunch of drug dealers weren't going to be packing?

"We're talking about drugs, right?"

Mel sighed. "No, stupid. We're talking about illegal squirrels. No shit."

Ellis ignored him in favor of more pressing concerns. "Why don't we wait till they're in the car, halfway down Airport Road?" he countered. "That way, they'll be contained. The road is dark and isolated. We could ram them, maybe, and be on them before they knew what hit them."

Ellis could just make out Mel's scowl in the ambient light. "You are so full of it. Ram them? With what? And how do we get away after we've trashed our car?" He reached out and smacked the back of Ellis's head with his open hand. "Moron. Leave the planning to me, all right?"

Ellis nodded, the familiar shrinking sensation he always felt around Mel setting in. He decided, as always, merely to listen instead of question. For all that Mel could sometimes seem foolhardy to the point of craziness, he hadn't gotten them killed yet.

"See how those two buildings come together, sort of?" Mel was saying now, pointing again. "They'll stop the plane there, where there's some cover. That'll allow the pilot to finish the loop and end up back on the strip, so he can take off."

"How do you know that?" Nancy asked, having moved up beside them.

Mel laughed. "I have my sources, babe, and believe me, I trust 'em. Not to worry."

He turned back to their surveillance. "They'll be expecting an attack from either corner, maybe even from across the open, so that's where they'll be looking. What they won't be watching is that hangar—right there. See it?"

They followed the line of his extended finger, nodding silently. Ellis resisted mentioning the unlikeliness of people expecting an attack also being unarmed.

Mel resumed, "That's where we'll be—inside, waiting. There are two doors about twenty yards apart. You and me'll come out at the same time. We'll box 'em in."

"How many are there?" Nancy asked.

"Four, not counting the pilot," her husband answered. "Pussies, every one of 'em." He turned back to Ellis, as if reading his mind. "Which is why, genius, you don't need to worry about firepower, 'cause even if they're packin', they won't have the balls to use it. And the same's true if the plane parks somewhere different. Everything stays the same—we box 'em in; we drive 'em to the ground. Total power."

Ellis saw an opportunity perhaps to learn a bit more about what they were getting into. "These the cousins that guy told us about down near the river?" he asked, keeping his wording vague.

"Yeah," Mel conceded. "The Niemiec boys. They think they got easy pickin's here among the local yokels. Won't they be surprised?"

He suddenly faced them both, the distant light making his widened eyes gleam pale with enthusiasm. "No screwing around, either, boys and girls. This'll be the big one for us. We get this done, and there'll be no more trailer parks or ripping off bingo games or any of that bullshit. We're talking serious money here."

Nancy and Ellis exchanged glances.

"What d'you mean, hon?" Nancy asked.

Mel laughed. "I thought that might twist your panties. I mean those crazy bastards have a deal goin' where they're taking in pounds of coke and heroin both. *Pounds.* You sell what they're talkin' about and it means a million bucks, probably more."

"So we have to sell it," Ellis said softly.

Mel made a face. "Oh, for Chrissake. You are such a fucking drag. What the hell happened to you, El? You used to eat this shit up. Now, it's all 'Golly-gee, it sounds a little hairy.' Yeah, we'll have to sell it, and we'll be able to do that anywhere we want—keep on the move, cut down the chances of getting caught. That ought to satisfy you, right?"

He punched Ellis in the arm. "Think of it. It's a fortune— more than we've ever seen. We'll be able to go anywhere, do anything. When I caught wind of this deal, I thought we'd maybe grab a few thou. But this is a home run."

Along with the wash of Mel's mounting excitement, Ellis felt the trembling light touch of his lover's fingers against the small of his back, and understood what she was thinking: What was good news for three people would be even better for two in need of a fresh start.

"Sorry, Mel," he said with a laugh. "You just caught me by surprise."

Mel smiled broadly. "Now you got it, Buckwheat—surprise is the name of the game. Let me show you the rest of the setup."

The next morning, as was his habit, Ellis phoned his mother at the hospital to find out how she was doing. He was alone—after their midnight field trip with Mel, they'd gone their separate ways, and from Mel's punchy mood, Ellis could only imagine how things would play out for Nancy.

Nevertheless, he was feeling good. As they'd crept from spot to spot at the airport, and the plan had been rehearsed, he couldn't repress the hope that he and Nancy might turn the tables after the Niemiecs had been dealt with and get away with enough dope to finance them forever. There was some irony worked into it, too—it was Mel's trap, after all, with the dope as the cheese, except that he and the Niemiecs both would end up as the losers . . . somehow. And with Canada so close, Ellis had no trouble imagining it as the stepping-off place to an island beach far away, where he envisioned them taking in the sun and catching up on the good life.

His mother, as if infected by his mood, sounded

sharper and more upbeat than recently, when the lethality of her disease had been visibly marking its progress.

"Ellis, I don't know what I did to deserve you," she said in her weak voice, "but I want you to know how happy you make me feel."

"No problem, Ma. How're you doin' today?"

"Pretty chipper. Is Nancy okay?"

"She's good. You sleep all right last night?"

"Oh, yes. After all the excitement, I was pretty tuckered out."

Ellis made himself more comfortable on the couch. He could never tell how long these conversations might last, they were so dependent on her energy. But she seemed to be riding high.

"Yeah? You guys win big at bingo or something?"

"No, no," she said. "The police were here. It was all very mysterious."

Ellis froze. "What?"

"The police. Well, one of them. A real nice man. He kept telling me to call him Joe."

"What did he want?" Ellis asked, trying to keep his voice calm, his optimism of moments earlier vaporized.

"It was pretty silly—even he admitted that. Remember the pendant I lost?"

"Yeah."

"It turns out that nurse who helped you get it back got in a heap of trouble. You might want to write her and thank her again."

"What happened, Ma?"

"Nothing much, really. Joe was saying it was just routine but that every little bit of garbage, no matter how small, is tracked. He seemed pretty embarrassed by it, but he had to do his job."

Ellis was standing up, his hand tight on the receiver. "I don't understand. What did he want?"

"Are you okay?"

He rolled his eyes, angry at himself for revealing his anxiety. "I'm fine. Just a little tired. Why would the police be interested in your garbage, Ma? It doesn't make sense."

"It's the Homeland Security thing, Ellis. You know that. Everybody's so cautious nowadays. According to Joe, the pendant being returned must have been picked up by the system somehow, so they sent somebody to check it out. It was just a conversation. You could tell his heart wasn't in it. I mean, we talked more about you than the pendant."

Ellis dropped his hand with the phone to his side and stared at the ceiling for a long moment, still hearing his mother's voice going cheerily on. He felt as if the floor had given way beneath him.

Slowly, he brought the phone back up to his ear. "Ma," he interrupted her, "did you get this guy's last name, or what department he was from?"

His mother paused. "I'm not sure. I know he was from Vermont. There was something about a bureau when he introduced himself—at least I think so."

"The Vermont Bureau of Investigation?"

"Yes. That was it. I'd never heard of them before."

"I have," her son admitted sadly, and did his best to wrap up the conversation as quickly as possible.

Afterward he sat on his couch, where he'd first made love to Nancy, and stared out the window. A row of old and battered parked cars littered the lot in the middle of the day as if in testimony of their owners' success rate at finding employment.

Damn, he thought. What was coming down the tracks at him? He knew goddamned well no cop was interested in a dime-store pendant being extracted from the trash. Especially a cop from the state's major-crimes squad. They had to have tumbled to the bag he'd stolen to frame Mel, which was still stuffed in his car trunk. But how the hell had they gotten from the bag to his mother's pendant?

He rubbed his temples with the heels of both hands. He hated sorting out things like this. He felt trapped back in eighth grade math class.

He tried to think clearly. Maybe he was being paranoid. His mother had said the guy was bored and apologetic, that he'd said his investigation was purely routine. Wasn't it possible that the VBI was given this kind of job just because of the national mood—purely routinely? Everyone *was* so cautious nowadays, like she said.

Maybe that's all there was to it.

But he didn't really believe that. Not really.

Joe stared at Willy. "You are kidding me."

Willy smirked with satisfaction. They were in a borrowed conference room at the Bennington PD, along with Sam, Lester, and the ever-affable Johnny Massucco, now assigned to them as official liaison.

"Nope," Willy said. "Ellis Robbinson and Mel Martin are joined at the hip."

"I can vouch for that," Massucco said. "They pop up in each other's files all the time. At one point they even lived together, the wife and the two guys, before Robbinson found his own place."

Sam laughed. "Well, apparently that part's gotten complicated, unless it always was."

Joe raised his eyebrows at her. "Oh?"

"We poked around Ellis's apartment complex, under the radar. Willy fits in really well over there . . ."

"You should know," Willy threw in.

". . . and we found a neighbor," Sam kept going, "who saw Nancy Martin more than once go inside for a few hours at a time. The neighbor had no doubt what they were doing."

"Does Mel ever come over?" Joe asked.

"Not with her, and not in a long time."

"Do you have a timeline for this affair?"

"We think it's new," Willy answered. "Without tipping off who we were, we talked with some of his coworkers after hours. He's been real happy just recently, and he doesn't deny it's because he's getting his rocks off."

"He mention her by name?" Joe asked.

"Didn't have to—one of his pals saw them in a pickup truck in town. He said their relationship was crystal clear."

Joe turned to Massucco. "You know anything about this?"

"News to me" was the response. "When they all shared the trailer, it never came up."

Joe nodded. "The reason I'm interested is that I traced the source of that missing radioactive garbage bag. Looks like Ellis Robbinson stole it while he was visiting his sick mother at the hospital, accompanied by someone fitting Nancy Martin's description."

He placed both hands on the tabletop for emphasis and added, "All of which means we've got even more going on we know nothing about—namely, what's the story behind the bag? The Fusion guys talked dirty bomb because that's their thing. But what if it's tied to this romance between Mel's wife and his best friend? What're Nancy and Ellis up to, and is Mel in on it in any way?"

Lester raised his hand. "We keep dismissing the dirty bomb idea. Couldn't that be an option?"

Joe shook his head. "I double-checked with the hospital. The half-life of the stuff in the bag was over almost from the start. It's just trash now."

He looked at Sam again. "What else?"

"Not much. We saw the pickup Mel bought from Newell outside his trailer, so he's still driving it. We didn't tail him anywhere, 'cause we didn't want to spook him, so we're a little vague about his movements. He is on the move, though. The pickup comes and goes all the time—'course, some of that's Nancy getting a little afternoon delight, and Mel also has his Harley."

"Does Mel work anywhere?"

Willy shook his head. "Nope—happy ward of the welfare state. He's definitely got something going, though, just from the way he's cruisin' around, looking over his shoulder all the time. You can almost see the fuse hanging from his butt."

Joe nodded, pushed himself away from the table, and began pacing the breadth of the room. "I had a small talk with Conrad Sweet's parole officer."

"Who?" Willy asked.

"High Top," Sam answered.

"He still hasn't heard from the kid," Joe continued. "One second he was there, the next he wasn't. Johnny, your department was asked to help look into that, right?"

"Right," Massucco confirmed, sitting slightly straighter in his chair. "High Top's a local boy. Been a customer of ours since he was eight or so. Parents were a mess; older brother from a different father is doing time up north for sexual assault of a minor, but he was High Top's primary influence before we nailed him. High Top himself's never gone for the violent stuff. He mostly steals, hustles small-scale dope deals, and earns his nickname. The only times I've ever seen him, he's looking like a space cadet."

"Any ideas where he disappeared to?"

"Not a one. We interviewed all his contacts and got nowhere."

"His PO thinks something bad happened," Joe told them. "He said High Top could be a smartass but was otherwise harmless, and he was regular as rain when it came to checking in, since he didn't want to go back to jail. Did any of you come across anything in your digging that might connect him to the Martin-Robbinson trio?"

"Only Piccolo's," Massucco said.

They all looked at him.

"That's—or was—one of his hangouts. It is for Mel Martin, too." He tilted his head equivocally to one side. "Of course," he added, "the same thing could be said for half the lowlifes in this town, so that's hardly a neon arrow."

"Martin's into drugs," Willy said flatly.

"True," Massucco agreed. "But it's not his primary line. He's mostly a thief and a bully—more into beating people up."

Joe was by this time leaning against the wall, his hands in his pockets, too restless to sit at the table with the others.

"All right," he said. "What about the whole reason we're here, which is Michelle Fisher? Has anyone found anything connecting her to Mel, Mel to Newell Morgan beyond the sale of the truck, or for that matter, anyone to anyone?"

Lester asked almost mournfully, "You all read my report?"

"Yeah," Willy conceded, "but that was it, right? The two old snoops that live on her road, seeing Newell's truck go by?"

"That's all I could find."

"And they weren't even sure who was at the wheel each time."

Sam tried supporting Lester. "Newell didn't sell the truck until after their last sighting of it."

"They said one thing," Lester spoke slowly, "that didn't make it into my report, mostly because they didn't actually see it."

Predictably, Willy let out a laugh. "That stopped you?"

"I asked them," Lester continued, ignoring him, "if they could see how many were in the passing truck from their angle, and they said no."

"Meaning Newell and Mel could've ridden together at some point, like on a training run," Sam suggested.

Joe rubbed his forehead. "Okay. Let's back up a little and see what we've got." He began counting off items on his fingers as he resumed pacing. "We've got Michelle dead of propane poisoning and clear signs of how that was both done and covered up. We've got circumstantial evidence pointing at Newell Morgan having an interest in her, being resentful of her, and finally benefiting from her death. We've got Newell establishing a firm alibi for the time of that death, but also selling his truck to a man with a known history of violence who could have functioned as the agent of Newell's intentions."

"Meaning we ought to lean on Mel to see if he's got an alibi," Willy cut in. "Along with a fattened bank account."

"And if Newell has a thinner one," Sam added.

"We don't have enough probable cause to get warrants for that," Joe cautioned.

"Plus, Michelle's house is for sale," Lester said.

They all stared at him.

"So what?" Willy asked.

"That may be the money—or part of it—that'll end up in Mel's pocket if this was a contract killing," he said.

Joe smiled at the notion. "Les is right," he agreed. "Newell's on disability. His wife works at a bottom-level job. They've got their own house and she says they're okay, but my bet is, that's about it. If Newell did want Michelle killed but didn't have the cash to pay for it, selling that house becomes crucial."

"Wow," Sam murmured. "So the house she lived in was the symbol of her happiness, and the grubstake to finance her death."

"Could be," Lester said.

"So how do we find out, if we can't get warrants?" she asked.

Joe was staring at the floor, thinking. "We approach them from another angle," he mused.

They waited for him to explain.

He looked up at them after a few moments. "If these two guys are in cahoots, they built a plan. They scouted the scene, maybe. They set up a cover story for Newell, and probably for Mel, too. They built all their defenses facing the direction they expected us to come from."

Willy smiled and tilted his chair onto its back legs. "Right," he said. "But we have a back door."

Joe nodded. "Exactly. We do have enough to get a warrant for Ellis for stealing that trash bag."

"And maybe enough to pick the girlfriend up as an accessory," Willy added.

Joe crossed over to the door and opened it. "Let's round 'em up and have a chat."

Chapter 20

She loved riding on the back of a bike. The noise, the vibration of the engine, the sense she always got of almost flying at ground level were all memories of her past that she didn't regret in the least and loved to revisit, especially now that she was once more with a man she believed she could trust.

At least for the moment. Not that Ellis wasn't dependable. Of that she had little doubt. But she wasn't kidding herself about the life they were facing—or, more precisely, the length of it. Even if they were successful in eliminating Mel, stealing the dope, and staying clear of the law, they were still looking at a future on the lam.

But today they were merely on a day trip. Mel was all consumed with his plans; they'd been all consumed with each other and, lately, their own big plans. Ellis had finally suggested a miniature breakout—a chance to enjoy the fresh air, the sun on their backs, just to taste what freedom might be like.

It was a great idea. Nancy's emotional claustrophobia had been worsened by the mounting gloom on both their parts. It was nice simply to ride away from it all, even briefly, and soak up the scenery and warmth of a summery Vermont day.

Perhaps presciently, they'd chosen Pownal, and the site of the abandoned racetrack there, for their trip. A huge oval laid out near where the road overlooked it, the track started life in the sixties as a horse racing venue, switching gears in midcourse to feature greyhounds. But it had closed about ten years ago, and, despite the occasional plan to use it somehow, from gambling to housing development, it remained empty, ghostly, and weatherbeaten—a testament to high hopes, big dreams, and ventures run aground.

It was a setting strangely in keeping with their mood, and they celebrated the choice by taking the Harley onto the vague grassy footprint of the track, through a break in the chain-link fence, and spinning around and around the oval, throwing up dust and scattering dirt into the banks.

Later, they sat on a hill gazing down at their handiwork, eating sandwiches and drinking beer, yielding to the temporary illusion that they had nothing to worry about.

Nancy was still enjoying that feeling on the way back north toward Bennington, wondering not just if but when the fantasy of such simplicity might become fact. This made her completely unaware of the car that swung in behind them as they passed the cemetery below town.

Ellis leaned slightly to the left, abandoning Route 7 as it began filling with traffic, and took them up Monument Avenue—narrower, tree lined, and dappled with sun filtering through the leaves. He, too, was inattentive of the following car.

Holding on to Ellis's waist, Nancy resumed daydreaming. If things did work out and Mel could be eased into the woodwork, what would they do then? Where would they move to? It wasn't the first time she'd engaged in such fantasies. If pressed, she'd have admitted to having done nothing else from the day she left home as a teenager.

The bike began to slow. Nancy looked up and saw a couple of cars in the far distance, next to each other and blocking the road.

"Cops," Ellis said.

She leaned in so her mouth was near his left ear. "They don't have lights."

"I can smell it," he said, slowing even more. He straightened slightly. "And there's one behind us. Shit."

He checked what he'd seen in the rearview mirror by swinging his head around. "We gotta get out of here."

"Ellis, maybe not. We haven't done anything."

"You haven't. I'm an accessory to murder, and they probably think I'm a terrorist, too."

He swung the bike around in a tight circle, putting their backs to the roadblock and facing the single approaching car.

"Hang on."

He gunned the throttle, and she felt the bike heave forward beneath her, its rear wheel squealing. Ahead of them, the car fishtailed slightly and positioned itself so that it could move forward or backward, depending on how the Harley tried to cut around it.

Nancy could feel Ellis's body tense.

"Okay, here we go," he shouted back at her, and launched up a driveway to their right, marked "Southern Vermont College." Behind them, sirens began to wail.

Southern Vermont College occupied the once remote five-hundred-acre Everett estate, carved into the side of

Mount Anthony. Neither Ellis nor Nancy knew anything about the place—or more important, whether there was another way off the campus.

They were aimed at a huge, pale hangar-size building up the hill and slightly to their right, opposite what looked like an apartment complex. Ahead and higher still, the steep drive continued toward something huge with multiple pointed red roofs. Ellis hung left at the complex, not wanting to go any farther up and hoping to double back somehow onto Monument Avenue. The sirens were closing in. Nancy glanced quickly over her shoulder and saw that the previously nondescript cars were now sparkling with hidden blue strobe lights.

Traversing the hillside on what turned out to be a parking lot, Ellis poured on the speed, heading around a slight curve in front of the apartments, to discover at the far end that a police car was closing in from a feeder road below and to the left. Not only that, but a large pond had appeared on the right, just past the apartments, and the parking lot petered out to a narrow drive.

Ellis took off across country at a slight angle, roughly parallel to the pond—terrain to which the Harley was poorly suited.

Nancy screamed as they hit the first series of dips and humps.

"You okay?" Ellis yelled back at her.

"Yeah," she answered before reclenching her teeth. She felt as if she were walking on a tightrope—so precariously perched, she didn't dare to look down, didn't dare even to think.

Somehow or other, in defiance of gravity and common sense, Ellis reached the upper end of the same feeder road the police car was still traveling. He hit the smooth surface with an explosion of power, causing Nancy to almost lose her grip on him, and aimed, engine screaming, for the school's showcase centerpiece, Edward Everett's eccentric, Norman castle–like mansion, built in 1914. Beyond that, however, all Nancy could see were the trees clotting the rest of Mount Anthony. It looked as though they were heading into the top end of a box.

The road ended at the narrow end of the mansion's enormous rectangular parking lot, which was located to the building's south side so as not to interfere with its view down the mountain, to the east.

Ellis, in a last desperate attempt to find a way back into the valley and Bennington beyond, shot off toward the mansion, hoping there might be a road beyond it. Nancy watched the fairy tale structure, red-roofed, ornate, absurdly otherworldly, grow in size before them as Ellis aimed for the narrow alleyway to its rear.

It wasn't to be. There was no road. It was a dead end. Again Ellis slammed on the brakes, kicked the bike into a skid, and swung the large machine around to face the direction he'd just traveled from.

For the few seconds they had left, they watched four cars abreast, all with blue lights firing like flashbulbs, bearing down on them.

"*Down the hill,*" she shouted, pointing at the steep grassy slope back down toward the main driveway, in effect suggesting closing the circle they'd begun by entering the estate.

But Ellis shook his head, patting the Harley's gas tank. "I know what she can do. It won't work with two of us on board."

Without hesitation, Nancy stepped back off the machine's rear seat, leaving Ellis alone on the bike.

"Go."

He whipped his head around. The cars were so close, they were skidding to a halt.

"You can't."

"Go," she repeated. "I'll be fine. I haven't done anything."

It took him a split second. "I love you," he told her, and gunned the throttle one last time.

The Harley roared across the parking lot, its lightened tail end slithering to and fro, before Ellis jumped it over the lower embankment, hit the downward slope like a circus performer, and, barely under control, proceeded toward the distant road far below.

Nancy stood in the parking lot, feeling utterly alone, even the growl of the bike vanishing by the instant. Her legs were trembling with exhaustion and spent adrenaline.

Seeing Ellis reach the road safely and speed off toward Monument Avenue and freedom, she turned to face their pursuers.

The violence she'd expected to follow—shouted commands, drawn guns, handcuffs, being thrown to the ground—none of it came about.

Instead, with the dust swirling around them in the sun, the four cars remained quiet, their lights flashing silently, and a single man in a jacket and tie got out and approached her at a slow, almost leisurely pace.

She watched him carefully, anxious about what he might do. But his hands were open and loose by his sides, his gait relaxed, and as he drew nearer, she saw that his face, older and friendly, was calm, almost reassuring.

He nodded his greeting as he stopped near her. "Nancy?" he asked.

She nodded back, not sure she could trust her voice.

He smiled slightly, which touched his kind eyes. "My name's Gunther. We should probably talk."

It wasn't a friendly room—small, bare, with a steel table bolted to the floor and two metal chairs. There were strategically placed bars on the wall, at waist level, that Nancy figured were used for handcuffs. The lighting was fluorescent and harsh, the floor gray concrete. There was a camera mounted high in one corner.

Nevertheless, the man who'd introduced himself at the college didn't seem any less peaceful or friendly. He'd brought her a glass of water, asked her if she wanted to use the bathroom. He'd even cupped her elbow supportively as he steered her to her chair, and asked if the temperature was all right.

"Am I under arrest?" she finally asked.

"No, ma'am," he said immediately. "You can leave anytime you'd like."

She hesitated, surprised by that, wondering what the catch might be. "Like right now?"

He smiled slightly. "Like right now."

She frowned, troubled by her own ambivalence. In the old days, when this scenario had been discussed over beers, it had always been punctuated by admonitions to keep silent, be stern, tell them all to fuck themselves.

But now that she was in it, she felt differently.

"I was hoping you might hear me out first," he then said. "Your choice, though."

Nancy eyed him cautiously. "About what?"

"Ellis, for one thing," he answered conversationally. "And Mel, of course."

"What about them?" She was struck by his familiarity

with their names, as if he'd known them for a very long time.

He gave her a slightly crooked smile—a gesture of sympathetic support. "Well, you're in kind of a bind there, I would say, caught between the two of them."

Her crestfallen look confirmed what had been somewhat of an assumption, if not a guess.

"I mean," he added, "I doubt Mel will be too happy about what's happened. He doesn't strike me as a man to gracefully fade away."

She swallowed hard, which was eloquent enough for Joe.

He leaned forward, placing his forearms on the table. "I saw what happened when we picked you up, Nancy. You took a big risk, getting off the bike so Ellis could get away. You didn't know what we were after. And yet you did it. That was a sign of love. He knew it. I know it. I think you and Ellis have the real deal with each other, and believe me, that counts for something, especially in this world."

She was visibly confused by now, confounded by what he was saying. "Why do you care about that?" she asked.

He let a small pause elapse before admitting, "Because Ellis is really jammed up, just when everybody wishes he wasn't."

"Everybody?"

Joe raised his eyebrows. "The people who count most—Doris, you. Me, for that matter, since I'm the one who could help."

"How?"

"You ever hear of officer discretion?"

"No."

"It's like when you get pulled over for speeding. You

don't always get a ticket, right? In fact, you've probably played that game a little—being nice to the cop, calling him 'sir,' trying to make a good impression?"

She flushed slightly.

"It's okay," he said. "I do the same thing when I get stopped. 'Cause it works sometimes. You get off with a warning. That's officer discretion. Law enforcement is built in large part on the trust that each officer will know to do the right thing, and that sometimes the right thing is to give good people another chance."

"You could do that for Ellis?"

"Within reason, I can do that for anyone," Joe said, sidestepping the question. "It gets trickier if some serious crime has been committed, but even then, after the state's attorney gets involved, we work as a team to the same end."

Nancy still wasn't completely buying it. "What about all that accessory stuff? If you know about a murder, it's the same as if you did it."

Joe held up a finger, like a helpful teacher. "I know what you're saying. Actually, you're a little off—it wouldn't be the same for simply knowing, not necessarily, but the idea is close. And it gets back to my point exactly: The same discretion I was talking about cuts both ways. If people try to mess with us, we sometimes mess with them right back—sad to say when they might've gotten off lighter by just cooperating."

"Doesn't sound very fair."

"It is if you look at it the other way around," he said, his expression cheerful. "Try this: You play ball with us; we play ball with you. Best of all in this case: Ellis gets the benefit."

Nancy pursed her lips, considering her options. It was

confusing, but she could sense that somewhere in all this, there might actually be some truth. She just couldn't be sure of it amid her conflicting prejudices.

"I don't think I have anything to say."

It didn't seem to faze him in the slightest. He leaned back in his chair comfortably and made an expansive gesture with his arm. "Oh, sure you do. Maybe it's a little hard to see right now, feeling hog-tied the way you are."

She felt an odd tingle along the back of her neck, hearing him address out loud the very thoughts she'd just been having.

"Take, for instance," he continued, "the thing about the stolen bag from the hospital."

She stared at him with her mouth half open. "How did you know about that?"

"Where is that, by the way?" he asked suddenly. "Is it still . . . ?" He snapped his fingers as if trying to extract a memory.

"In his car," she said softly.

"Right. Never did anything with it, did he?"

"No," she admitted. "I thought he planted it like we planned. I couldn't figure out why nothing happened. He told me later it was still in the trunk."

"Well," Joe said offhandedly, not only pleased with the conversation so far but amazed by his luck in getting the location of that bag so easily. Such a creaky old trick. "It doesn't really matter—that stuff had the half-life of a fruit fly."

"I guess," she said vaguely. He guessed that radioactivity wasn't her strong suit.

"Still," he carried on, "so much for plan A, eh?"

"Yeah," she agreed. "It didn't have much going for it anyhow."

He almost looked like he disagreed. "Which part do you mean?"

She gave an exasperated sigh. "It wasn't like Mel and that terrorist guy were exactly the same. You know? The one who got locked up all those years without a trial?"

"Right," Joe said confidently, stretching his brain to fill in the blanks. "Maybe turning Mel into a terrorist bomber was a little thin."

Nancy just stared at the floor.

"But you had to do something, right?" Joe prompted her, worried he might have miscalculated. "It's not like you could leave things the way they are."

She looked straight at him. "He's gotten worse, almost all of a sudden. And we were getting desperate."

Joe swung for the bleachers, hoping against reason to put Michelle Fisher to rest at last. "If you're talking about the murder," he told her, "you're right—it doesn't get much worse than that."

The effect was startling. Her face crumpled up with concern. He couldn't believe his luck, after all this effort. "You can't pin that on Ellis," she cried. "That's where the discretion thing comes in, right? He didn't even know the kid. That's got to count. And he just saw it happen. He didn't even touch him till he had to bury him."

Joe was stunned. This had nothing to do with Michelle. In the surprise of the moment, his brain locked and he couldn't think at all what she might be referring to.

Instead, he punted. "Guess they got lucky there. Usually burial sites get uncovered pretty fast—dogs, hunters in the woods, you name it."

She looked at him, her eyes wide. "You didn't find it?"

"It's the only missing piece," he said quickly.

"It's in the park, by the river," she said without great interest. "Behind the State Office Complex."

"Thanks," he said, hoping to match her detached tone. "The other thing was, we couldn't figure out why."

She became suddenly animated. "That's what I'm saying. And that's what Ellis said. There *was* no reason. The kid was talking, telling Mel what he wanted to know. He just killed him. Ellis said it was like he was curious, like it was a whim or something."

Joe abandoned Michelle for the moment, hoping to keep this new train on the tracks for as long as he could. At least he knew who they were talking about.

"What did High Top have that Mel needed?" he asked her.

She shook her head vaguely. "I don't know exactly, but it tied into the Niemiecs, and Mel wanting to rip them off."

She was suddenly very quiet, and he guessed she was thinking she might have said too much.

The problem was, he was stumped himself. He had no idea who the Niemiecs were. "Well, you're perfectly right," he tried, "Mel is getting crazier, and he is on a roll. The thing with High Top and the Niemiecs'll end up being just the tip of the iceberg. Know what I mean?"

She nodded thoughtfully, to his relief. "Yeah, I do. Never do it honestly if you can steal it from someone else."

Joe recognized that she was talking to herself as much as to him now. "There you go," he played along. "But it's like anything else in life. You can't keep doing the same thing again and again, especially if you're a guy like Mel. Life gets too boring. You keep wanting to stir things up. Problem is, eventually it all falls apart."

She was staring off into space.

He took a stab at bridging their two divergent trains of thought. "It can end up like a death wish nobody else wants to share."

That brought her around. She looked at him again. "That's it. That's been it for a long time. I was thinking maybe a baby and some security, getting a good job and buying a home. With him, it's always been *Butch Cassidy and the Sundance Kid.* I just didn't see it, I mean, not really."

She knocked the side of her head gently with her fist. "Stupid. I've always been stupid that way. I don't see people straight."

"You fall in love with them," Joe suggested. "That can fog your thinking."

She suddenly looked irritated. "And I'm doing it again," she said darkly.

But he didn't want her to go there. Not now. "I don't think so," he said, hoping to steer her back. "Not from what I saw." He leaned forward again for emphasis. "Just because you failed at something a few times doesn't mean it's a bad idea, Nancy. Ellis is no Mel, right?"

"No."

"He's as horrified as you about what's happened, isn't he?"

"Yeah," she admitted, half reluctantly.

"Then don't give up on him so fast. If you both get free of Mel, there's no telling what you might be able to do together."

Her expression became almost pleading. "That's what I was hoping."

He smiled broadly, grateful to be on surer footing. "Then stick with that. One thing at a time, okay?"

She nodded slowly.

"But we can't let Mel blow it up. 'Cause he can if we don't stop him. If he pulls this latest thing off against the Niemiecs, there'll be no saving anybody—everyone'll go down the tubes. You can see that, right?"

She rubbed her face with both hands and spoke through them in barely a whisper. "Yeah."

Joe dropped his voice a father-confessor notch lower and placed his last bet. "Then let's talk about what he has planned."

Chapter 21

At least the weather was cooperating. Warm, no wind, a sky full of stars but no moon, making visibility a perfect balance between seeing and not being seen. That perfection played to the strengths of all three conflicting parties due to arrive.

Joe stood slowly to stretch his legs and readjust his bulky ballistic vest, wishing he had more to do. Unfortunately, it was no longer his show, and although he had a radio whisper mike strapped to his throat, and an ear bud to listen through, he knew there would be hell to pay if he uttered a single word uninvited.

Cautiously, he edged up to the window and glanced out. As before, the place was empty. A few planes were tethered in the large parking area between the taxiways, and beyond them the paved runway shone slightly pale in the starlight. But no one moved among the shadows of buildings, planes, and assorted equipment. The Bennington airport was unmanned during nonbusiness hours, and it was certainly deserted now.

Or was being made to look that way.

In fact, elements of the VBI, the Vermont State Police,

the Bennington County Sheriff's Department, the Bennington police, and the latter's SWAT team, complete with a sniper, were secreted in nooks and crannies all across the airport grounds, from inside its buildings and on its roofs to along its feeder roads far outside the property perimeter.

And they had all been in place for hours, having infiltrated quietly, discreetly, in small numbers, just to be the first to arrive. The second group due, from what Joe had been told, would be Mel and his team of two, one of whom—Nancy—would be carrying a tiny GPS emitter so they could track at least her on a computer-mounted map. As for how they'd position themselves and what they were planning, Joe and his colleagues had only Nancy's version. And they all knew how prone to spontaneity Mel could be.

Finally, there was the Niemiecs' gang, coming in from somewhere inside Bennington to pick up what was sounding like the largest haul of hard drugs ever to be interdicted in Vermont—assuming things worked as planned. And nobody knew what the Niemiecs truly had up their collective sleeve, either, Mel's self-confidence notwithstanding. Even the choice of this particular night was in some doubt, since it dated back to Mel's last interview with one of the gang members.

It was very possible nothing would happen at all.

But Joe didn't think so. He'd spent hours with Nancy Martin on the day of the interview. At one point, he'd even gone on a walk with her, switching the recording from the video at the PD to a handheld unit in his pocket. They'd strolled outside for a time, sat under a tree, taken pauses to hear the birds sing. He'd done everything he could to coax every last memory, reminiscence, and reflection out of her, while maintaining an almost father-daughter tone to the conversation. In a move that had later caused Willy almost to lose his composure, Joe had even bought her an ice-cream cone.

But it had worked. He had learned not just about the raid on tonight's planned delivery but about the removal of the M-16s from the armory, the practice session with them in the woods outside town, the theft of the bingo money, the killing of High Top, the growing love between Ellis and Nancy, and their screwy plan to throw Mel to the Homeland wolves. He also listened to the all-too-familiar tales of young lives sacrificed for the immediate pleasures of the here and now, to poor choices and bad decisions leading into emotional box canyons offering no options and no escape. And hoping he wasn't just cynically adding to the latter, he encouraged Nancy time and again to think of a better future, to believe that she might have found at last her Mr. Right, and that he, Joe Gunther, might well be the man to make it all come about.

That last part still wasn't sitting too comfortably on his conscience.

Other things were sitting awkwardly as well, not the least of which was what they were all doing here tonight. Nancy's information had created an instant flurry of débate among the leaders of most of the agencies represented in the county. Her evidence pointing to things as varied and damning as murder, assault, robbery, and grand theft promised a healthy combination of case clearances and good press.

But none of it touched her prize offering. Being told of the Niemiecs had been like finding a solid gold nugget in an otherwise bulging Cracker Jack box, and when it came to tantalizing law enforcement, the promise of a big drug bust was hard to resist.

Thus, despite Joe's urging that a bird in the hand could just as easily be complemented by a separate operation against the Niemiecs, the decision had been made not to grab Mel separately but to sweep them all up at one time.

To pay them their due, the advocates of this approach did have a few points buttressing their position, not the least of which was that Mel had gone to ground, leaving a message to Nancy at the trailer that for security reasons he'd decided they should reassemble only at the airport on the night in question. According to the note, which she'd read to Joe over the phone after reaching home, Mel had heard there were extra cops in the area, asking questions about him.

Ellis had also proved problematic. Nancy, using the police department phone, had located him after calling a half-dozen numbers, and had stopped him from telling Mel what had happened at the college. However, he'd also refused to speak to anyone but her. He'd understood that she was making a deal with the cops and that he was the primary beneficiary, but he'd said no to coming in. An uneasy compromise had been cobbled together where he would see how things stood only after Mel was in handcuffs.

His position thus weakened, Joe had been forced to concede. But as he stood in the dark, watching the peaceful scene outside, he couldn't shake the feeling that they'd taken on something involving far too many variables.

Finally, for Joe personally, there was one last disappointment that had nothing to do with this, at least not apparently. He couldn't escape a lingering sadness that Michelle Fisher had never surfaced in any of Nancy's tellings. While she had acknowledged Mel's purchase of his truck from some "fat guy" on Gage Street, she had cast no light on any trips to Wilmington or any boasts about a lucrative hit job.

Michelle Fisher, as seemed her fate, had once more slipped into the background.

Joe crossed over to the shadowy figure of Johnny Massucco, who was, as it turned out, the team leader of the Bennington SWAT.

"Any problem with my going up to the roof?" he asked in a whisper.

Massucco, calm but focused, shrugged and pressed his throat mike. In a murmur, he warned the crew above them that Gunther was on his way. He didn't bother telling Joe to keep low and quiet when he got there.

Up top, Joe cleared the darkened trapdoor on the roof and scuttled over to a makeshift tarpaulin tent that had been erected even with the low wall along the edge. Crouching inside, shielded from sight by the tent, Sammie Martens was manning a laptop computer whose unearthly glow lit her face. On its screen was a map, with the airport in its middle.

"Any sign of her?" Joe asked quietly.

"At the edge," Sam confirmed, tapping the image with her fingertip. "Looks like she's stationary near the corner of Gypsy Lane and Route 9, probably in a car."

They'd had Nancy Martin attach the GPS transmitter to her bra, between her breasts, where they knew it would be the most comfortable, and presumably the least visible.

"Wish we could tell if she's alone or not," he muttered, half to himself. They hadn't dared tell Ellis of this one small detail and had sworn Nancy to silence.

Sam made no comment.

Thirty feet away, low down and braced by the wall, isolated in all senses of the word, the police department's sniper sat alone, his eyes locked on the still darkness below them—a fitting symbol of the potential violence they were about to face.

"I can't wait for this to be over," Joe added.

Nancy shifted in her seat, taking advantage of the gesture to poke at the plastic module perched between her breasts. It wasn't really uncomfortable, but it did feel weird. And so huge, she was convinced all the world could see its bulge.

She also didn't like what it stood for. She felt like a snitch.

"You okay?" Ellis asked. Per agreement, she hadn't told him about the transmitter—she'd merely promised that tonight would put Mel where they'd been wishing him.

"Fine," she said shortly.

They were in his car, the one with the now nonradioactive trash in the trunk, parked along the edge of a narrow road leading to the airport a mile farther on.

"I wonder where Mel is," Ellis said.

Nancy didn't know, which bothered her more than she let on. She felt as if her head were about to explode, she was so nervous. Ever since her long afternoon with that cop, she'd been like a pressure cooker with the heat turned on, gradually building up steam to the blowing point. Her affair with Ellis already had her on edge. Tack on her having spilled her guts to the cops, for which she knew Mel would kill her. And now she had this . . . thing jammed between her boobs, making her feel like a radio beacon. She hadn't seen or heard from Mel since discovering his note at the trailer, and had grown steadily more convinced that the reason he'd disappeared was because he knew what she was up to.

Which, in a predictable vicious circle, only encouraged her own feelings of self-loathing. She felt like the Judas they'd all scorned of old—the unspeakable lifeform that could betray its own kind. The more she'd pondered it, the more she'd become disgusted with herself and, by extension, Ellis. Both of them had turned their backs on the rough-and-tumble life they'd chosen from puberty, but which had, nevertheless, rewarded them with friendship, camaraderie, love, and a true sense of belonging. It hadn't always been easy—the tolls of a nomad existence, the price that cigarettes, booze, drugs, and hard living had exacted, the daily violence she'd experienced, often at the hands of her own husband.

But somehow all of it—even Mel's growing craziness—began to seem less awful than what she'd just done to be free of it.

She felt cut down the middle by guilt.

The cell phone in her pocket burst into life, making her and Ellis both jump.

"Yeah—what?" she stammered into it.

Mel's voice sounded rich with self-satisfaction. "Where are you pussies? The fun's about to start."

"Mel?"

"Yeah, right. No, it's the fucking president, stupid. Get your asses up here."

"To the airport?"

She could almost taste the scorn as he answered, "God, you are a dumb bitch. Give me Ellis."

She handed the phone over, grateful for the exchange. She was doing the right thing.

"Yeah," Ellis said. He then listened a few seconds, muttered, "Right," and hung up.

He returned the phone, explaining, "We're just supposed to drive up and park in the lot. He'll find us. The place is deserted."

Nancy put the car into gear.

The drive up Airport Road and into the facility itself was eerie. There were no cars, no people, no signs of life at all the whole way.

"Creepy," Ellis said softly, craning slightly to see better out the windows as they pulled into the parking lot.

"It's late," Nancy said, mostly to comfort herself.

"Still," he said, adding, "You said the cops are here, right? Hidden somewhere?"

She started slightly, as if he'd pricked her with a pin. "Don't say that."

He looked at her. "Isn't that right? That this is how we're getting rid of Mel?"

"Yeah," she said with emphasis. Then, looking around at the emptiness, "I guess."

"You don't *know*?"

She stopped the car and turned on him angrily. "Ellis, fuck you, okay? Just shut the fuck up. I'm not some fucking cop. I *don't* know. I *think* so." She took her hand off the steering wheel and grabbed her forehead. "Leave me alone."

"He buggin' you, babe?" came a voice from outside, making them both shout in surprise. Mel's grinning face was hanging in the open frame of her side window.

"Mel—Jesus," she said.

Mel opened her door and stood back. "You people have got to chill. This is just another op."

Ellis got out from the other side. He was smiling, putting on a good front. "This is the mother of ops."

Mel laughed. "Okay, you got it." He looked back down at his wife. "Come on, Nance, heave your butt outta the car. We need to make like ghosts."

They both followed him across the lot to a rental van parked on the edge of the grass by the nearest taxiway. He patted its side. "My newest wheels—all nice and legal and anonymous."

He opened its rear double doors, reached inside, and pulled out the two M-16s, handing one to Ellis. "There you go, bucko. A little old-fashioned firepower. Got something else, too." He reached back a second time and pulled out two ballistic vests, again handing one to Ellis. "Just like the big boys."

Ellis was impressed. Nancy watched his eyes grow as round as a kid's. "Holy shit. You did good, Mel."

Mel had propped his gun against the van's side and was slipping the vest on over his head. "No point screwin' around, right?"

Nancy looked from one to the other. Mel misinterpreted her gesture. "You don't count," he told her. "You'll be behind the wheel, like always. By the time we get to you, the shooting'll all be over."

"There's going to be shooting?" she asked, remembering his assurances that the Niemiecs wouldn't be armed.

He laughed. "Not for sure. I don't want to wake up the neighborhood, but if we gotta, we gotta. You know that."

He brushed by her and slapped Ellis's shoulder as the latter was attaching his Velcro straps. "Come on. Let's get in place."

He looked back at his wife as they started off into the darkness between two of the buildings. "Just wait in the van, in the back, until after they get here. Stay out of sight till the last second, but be ready, okay? Don't fuck up."

"What about the car?"

"What about it? It's just a parked car, like all the others."

She nodded without comment and then cast her eyes over the entire scene—the few cars he'd mentioned, the darkened buildings, the starry sky overhead.

Where were the cops?

"The Turkeys have settled in," a quiet voice said over all their earphones. For no reason beyond playfulness, Mel and his duo had been code-named the Turkeys. The Niemiecs were, blandly, the Bad Guys. At the pre-op briefing, Willy had suggested calling the Secret Service for better labels. Nobody had gotten the joke.

Joe peered over Sam's shoulder. The dot representing Nancy's position had stopped moving at the edge of the parking lot. "Looks like we pinned the tail on the wrong turkey," he murmured.

"Turkeys One and Two are in motion," came the same voice. "Both armed with M-16s. Heading toward building B—previous location."

Each structure had been given a letter. B was the one nearest the easternmost taxiway, and the one they'd watched Mel check out a half hour earlier, when he'd arrived alone in the rental van. At the time, they'd had their first fright—he'd almost stepped on the hand of one of the hidden SWAT members while passing by.

Joe risked a peek over the roof's low wall to see the two shadowy figures of Mel and Ellis reach the corner of the hangar. Around him, half the cops had put on night vision goggles. The sniper, still alone in his far corner, was relying on his scope to give him the same advantage.

A new voice came over the radio. "This is Perimeter Four. Three cars just drove by, headed your way. Pretty sure they were the Bad Guys. Two black sedans—a Ford Fiesta and a Cutlass—and one Explorer SUV, color red."

Although nobody moved, Joe felt a distinct shift in the air. The last of the three groups had finally arrived. Something was going to happen after all.

The latecomers were the most casual of all, despite what they had at stake. They parked abreast, not far from the van where Nancy was hiding; eight young men got out, not four, as Mel had advertised, and assembled as if preparing to enter a sporting arena. They talked in normal voices; a couple were throwing fake punches. Joe could see several handguns tucked into waistbands here and there—another Mel goof-up.

The group, leaving two members by the vehicles, headed out between the buildings toward the landing strip. From the roof, one of them could distinctly be heard asking, "You sure nobody's here?"

"Nobody's ever here at night," came the answer. "That's the whole point."

Joe couldn't help wondering just how many people were in fact here—certainly enough that they were almost literally stepping on each other.

The group of six reached the grassy patch housing parked planes, halfway to the concrete runway, where, amazingly to the watching cops, three of them flopped down on the ground to wait, stretching out on their backs to gaze at the stars.

"Okay," came the soft, slightly amused voice in the earphones. "We wait."

It didn't take long. In the tradition of drug stakeouts, one standard was that everything ran late, the supposition being that neither dealers nor users were sticklers for time. But this scenario involved a pilot, so it turned out somebody had a watch and knew how to use it. At exactly 2:00 a.m. a faint humming became distinguishable in the sky, growing quickly into the thrum of an approaching aircraft.

The final effect, when it came, was startling if expected. Somehow, Joe had prepared himself for a darker version of what he'd seen at airports during the day—the sight of a plane, its wings wobbling slightly, the bounce and squeal of the tires hitting the concrete, maybe all accompanied by runway lights.

Instead, there was that distant sound, followed by a sudden and very brief stab of a light as the plane quickly pinned down the location of the strip, then more darkness and finally abrupt silence. Totally unseen, the small plane had landed as if large pieces from a film strip had been surgically removed from a movie—one moment it wasn't there; the next moment it was. But it never appeared on one of the taxiways. It stayed out on the runway, finalizing the accuracy of Mel's intelligence.

The six men roused themselves and jogged out toward the gloomy edge of the runway, almost vanishing from view.

The whole transaction took less than a minute, barely allowing the voice on the radio to ask, "You get the registration on that aircraft?" and get an affirmative answer. Then there was a sudden burst of noise as the engine coughed back to life, and the plane began receding back into the night.

In the meantime, the jubilant party of six, laden with

compact packages, still laughing and chatting, began stepping back out of the darkness.

"Okay," said the quiet voice. "Just as rehearsed. By the numbers."

Over his shoulder, Joe heard Sam whisper, "Boss, thought you'd like to know. Nancy's on the move."

She couldn't take it any longer. There was too much at stake, too many unknowns, too big a chance for everything to go wrong. Nancy eased herself out from behind the van's seat, where she'd been struggling in vain to see anything out of the windshield, and peered out the side windows for some sight of the two men by the cars.

She saw them to her right, loitering by the Explorer, smoking, their attention drawn by the sound of the airplane's engine. She took advantage of the diversion to silently open her door, slip out, and scuttle soundlessly toward the shadows cast by the nearby buildings. Once there, totally hidden, she jogged along the wall, aiming for where Mel had told them earlier that he planned to make his interception.

Her timing was good. As she reached the corner and faced the open aircraft parking area and the two taxiways, she saw not only the approaching band of drug dealers but, from the sides, the shadows of two rifle-toting dark figures emerging from separate corners to cut off the larger group.

Mel's loud voice pierced the night. "This is a robbery. Stop where you are and drop your weapons."

The group froze. Mel and Ellis continued forward, their M-16s becoming clear in the half-light. Surprisingly to Nancy, she noticed that they'd also donned black ski masks, adding a menacing aura to their sudden appearance.

"You can give it up or die. Real simple choice," Mel said, lifting his rifle to the firing position and adding, "These are fully automatic weapons."

The six men looked from one hooded gunman to the other in silence. Finally, one of them very slowly cleared a semiautomatic from his waistband, crouched slightly, and dropped it onto the ground.

"Everybody," Mel ordered. "Now."

The other five followed suit. As they did, Ellis faded back slightly, swung around, causing Nancy to duck out of sight, and shouted, "You two, keep coming with your hands up."

The men from the parking lot, attracted by the sound of voices, were caught unawares as they approached between the buildings. Transfixed by the change of events, they followed orders, passing Nancy without notice.

Mel waited until all eight were herded together and had deposited their guns on the ground.

"Take five steps back and drop the packages," he then ordered.

They complied as before, creating two piles of belongings.

"Take five more steps back, get down on your knees, cross your ankles, and put your hands behind your heads. Do it now, do it fast, or you will die."

Nancy crouched, transfixed, incredulous that Mel's plan was actually working. She watched as the group once more did as they were told.

Mel was now standing just ten feet in front of the eight kneeling men, his weapon still up and aimed.

"My partner," he explained, "will now come up behind you, from the back row to the front, and tie your hands together. Do not struggle, do not say a word, and lie down on your face when he's done. If you don't, I will shoot you and he will go on to the next man."

Ellis circled around behind them, slung his rifle over his shoulder, and extracted a bundle of white plastic zip ties from his pants pockets. One by one, he bound the men's wrists together and pushed them facedown on the grass. The entire operation went without a hitch, ending with Ellis standing at the head of a group of eight prone people, all utterly still.

For a split second, as if stunned by his own success, Mel didn't move, his rifle in place, now aimed vaguely at Ellis. They stood facing each other as if caught in a photograph.

And then everything changed.

The night vanished. With the flip of a switch, everything they could see, from the buildings to the runway, from the tethered planes to the dark spaces between the hangars—all of it became awash with blinding, painful, lightning-white light, supplied by over a dozen powerful roof-mounted halogen searchlights.

Simultaneously, a booming voice on a loudspeaker intoned, "This is the police. Do not move."

But Mel did move. With a ballet dancer's grace, he fired once into Ellis's chest, threw his rifle far to the side, and took three fast steps backward just as the SWAT sniper fired a single round where he'd just been standing.

Before anyone else could react, Mel was kneeling with his own hands on his head, shouting, "*Don't shoot. I'm unarmed.*"

As if magically, in the moment it took for all this to occur, he was surrounded by a circle of heavily armed, black-clad, helmeted police officers, all aiming their guns at him.

Ellis, for his part, was still slowly falling, a bright red string of blood working its way down the front of his ballistic vest.

Nancy, screaming, broke free from her hiding place and was instantly knocked down by a cop.

"*Hey, Ellis,*" Mel shouted, removing his ski mask while keeping his hands in sight. "Surprised?"

Ellis sat heavily on his heels. He was staring at his bloody hands, his rifle still dangling from his shoulder.

One officer seized Mel, pushed him hard to the ground, and pulled his hands up behind the small of his back.

Mel paid no attention. "You double-crossing fuck—takes one to know one, right?" he shouted at Ellis. "You think I didn't know you were screwing my wife? You may have squealed to the cops, but I fucked with your vest. Your bullets are dummies, too, asshole—just like you."

The cop frisking him finally yielded to temptation and mashed Mel's face into the grass, stifling him.

Joe stepped out of the building and freed a sobbing Nancy from the police officer pinning her to the ground. Holding her by the upper arm, he escorted her over to where two paramedics were trying to tend to Ellis, starting an IV and readying a defibrillator.

But it was clearly a lost cause. In the blinding new light, it was obvious he was dead, his naked chest, its clothing cut free, already touched with the lifeless pallor that comes like the counterpoint of a blush.

Nancy, all hope gone, collapsed by his side.

Chapter 22

The next time Joe visited Michelle Fisher's neighborhood outside Wilmington, there was already the tinge of winter's approach in the air. He still drove with the window down, but only because of the sun. Nights were beginning to declare the need to cover up.

He parked opposite Linda Rubinstein's ramshackle house and opened the car door to welcome her enormous dog, who this time was on patrol outside. The beast, a mix of perhaps a half-dozen large-headed canines, planted his snout in Joe's groin to get his ears scratched. Joe didn't argue with him. He couldn't exit from the car in any case.

"Bogey," a sharp command rang out.

The dog paid no attention.

Linda, still in slim jeans and a T-shirt, but with an open men's dress shirt over the top as well, appeared from around an outside corner of the house. She was carrying a basket with tomatoes in one dirt-stained hand.

"Bogey," she repeated. "Leave the poor man alone." She reached and yanked him back by the collar, adding, "I hope all your friends believe you when you tell them how your crotch got wet."

Joe laughed but couldn't resist checking. He was fine.

"How are you?" she inquired, leading the way to the sagging porch. "I didn't think I'd ever see you again."

"Really?" he asked. "I'll have to tell Doug Matthews that. He was hoping you and I would get something going."

This time she laughed, reaching the porch, putting the basket down, and waving him to his earlier perch on the railing. "If you weren't a cop, he might've been right. You want something to drink?"

"No, thanks. I'm fine. You don't like cops? I didn't get that when we met."

She settled into her chair. Bogey wandered off. "It's not a blind prejudice," she said. "Just something born of my time in the city."

"Things might be different up here," he told her.

She smiled. "Is that an invitation?"

He tilted his head and made a regretful face. "No. I'm afraid not. I'm here officially—at least sort of."

"Ah," she said, studying him.

He studied her in turn for a moment before commenting, "You haven't asked about the case."

She widened her eyes, but the look in them remained careful. "I figured you'd tell me if anything had happened. Has it?"

"In a way," he confessed. "But not how you might think."

"Really." She said it as a statement.

"Yeah. Every once in a blue moon, it ends up that what we had from the start was all we ever needed."

"Like when a car kills a pedestrian?"

He shook his head. "No. There we need to know if the driver was drunk. Or the pedestrian. Did they know each other beforehand? What was the lighting at the time? And on and on. Those actually get pretty complicated. I'm thinking more about a case like Michelle's. Before, that is," he added, "someone changes how everything looks."

She didn't respond, but he felt a stillness settle over her, as if she were waiting to hear a distant but telling mechanical click.

"Newell Morgan was pretty awful to her, wasn't he?" Joe asked.

She barely nodded. "I told you that."

"Yes, but you phrased it in terms of his being her landlord—wanting her out so he could sell the house. There was more to it."

"That's all I knew."

"You also said you'd never met him."

She hesitated. "Did I? I might have, once. I was over there a lot."

"So was he."

She didn't answer. She tried to swallow without revealing it to him.

"Newell Morgan was after Michelle sexually. He wanted to replace his son in her bed."

Joe could almost see Linda's brain analyzing what she should say next.

Finally, she went where he would have in her place. "Am I in trouble here?"

He sat forward and rested his elbows on his knees, so his eyes and hers were on a level. "I don't think so. But that's why I'm here. I do think you've done things you haven't told me about—things that normally would get you into hot water. But if I'm right, and if you confirm them, then I'm willing to let things rest as they are."

"So," she said, striving to sound natural, "what do you think I've done?"

He smiled and straightened. "That would be too easy. I've got to find out if the truth and my suspicions are one and the same. My telling you what I think would be a poor way of doing that."

She pressed her lips together for a moment. "I see what you mean. Puts me in a tough spot, though. If I say too much—more than you suspect—then I land myself in jail for no good reason. You're asking me to risk suicide."

He smiled. "Interesting choice of words."

She stared at him, and he could see at that moment an almost visible cloud lift from her brow.

"He almost pulled it off," she then said.

"Getting into Michelle's bed?"

"Yeah. He came by again and again, wearing her down. She started saying she could see maybe making an accommodation. He's just another guy, you know? Nothing a shower can't wash off, right? Things like that. But it was killing her."

"It did kill her," he suggested.

Linda's face saddened. "Well, yeah, in the long run. But at least he wasn't the primary reason anymore."

"Because of you," he stated.

She paused before finally nodding. "Yeah. I was there the last time he came by. I gave him hell. Told him that if he kept at it, he'd end up in prison, being put to the same use he was trying to put her to, only by a bunch of hairy guys. I also said I'd tell his wife and everybody else who gave a damn."

"And that did it?"

"He was a pig. He wasn't brave. Plus, he was going to get everything else he was after. Michelle didn't have a legal leg to stand on. The house was his, and she was going to end up on the street. All I did was spare her that last humiliation."

She sighed deeply and, staring at the floor, added, "At least I thought so."

"But she did commit suicide," Joe suggested quietly.

"Yeah," she admitted. "A while later. Not so much because of him, though. At least I can claim that. It was more the rest of it—Archie, the lack of money, her kids not wanting contact. In a way, it was even Adele and me doing what we could. Our offers of help just highlighted how badly off she was."

Linda looked up at him, her own burdens and struggle commingling with her sorrow. "Michelle died of a broken heart. She just turned on the gas to make it real."

"And that's where you came in."

She touched her upper lip with her fingertip and stared thoughtfully at the floor.

"You really have figured this out, haven't you?"

He nodded without saying a word.

"Yeah." She said the word slowly, dragging it out. "At the time, I was just so mad, you know? I had to blame somebody. And he was so easy. So deserving. I hated it that she would just be allowed to slip away, and that a bastard like him wouldn't suffer a single thing. It wasn't right."

Joe kept silent, letting her work through her story.

"It wasn't like I really pinned it on him," she said a little defensively. "Not that I wouldn't have tried if I'd known how. I would've put his fingerprints on her throat, the creep. But all I could do was muddy the waters a little. Turn off the gas, fiddle with the tank, crawl through from outside, open the windows . . . I did what

I could to draw your attention to there being someone else involved."

"You buried Georgia."

She'd gotten a little worked up admitting all this, and his comment brought her up short. Her face softened. "Poor Georgia. I doubt Michelle even thought about her. Such a sweet old cat. She didn't deserve being killed without a thought."

She stopped speaking for a while, simply staring off into space. Joe let her be.

But she gazed at him eventually and asked, "That's what tipped you off, wasn't it? Burying the cat."

He smiled at her, enjoying the way her brain worked. "It helped. Newell would've just thrown her in the woods or forgotten about her." He didn't mention how Mel—had he even been remotely involved—would have done the same.

Linda sighed again, shoving her hands between her thighs like a child. "God, what a life. So, what now? You lock me up?"

Joe rose instead and shook his head. "No. You actually did me a favor, pointed me places you knew nothing about. It didn't get Newell in trouble, but we put some bad people in jail along the way. Things have a funny way of working out."

She nodded, smiling sadly. "I guess they do sometimes, if not always according to plan."

About the Author

ARCHER MAYOR lives in Newfane, Vermont. He writes full-time and volunteers as a firefighter/EMT. He is also a death investigator for the state's medical examiner, and a part-time police officer for the Bellows Falls Police Department. Mayor has lived all over the U.S., Canada, and Europe, and has been variously employed as a scholarly editor, a researcher for TIME-LIFE Books, a political advance man, a theater photographer, a newspaper writer/editor, and a medical illustrator. In addition to his Joe Gunther series, he has written short stories, two books on American history, and many articles. You can learn more about Mayor at www.archermayor.com

A sensational new mystery
by master storyteller

Archer Mayor!

Please turn this page
for a preview of

CHAT

available in hardcover.

Chapter 1

"*Made it, Ma. Top o' the world,*" Leo quoted theatrically, his words shrouding his head in the cold night air. "What would you think if I went out like that?"

His mother twisted around in her wheelchair to look at him balefully. "I don't understand why such a wonderful dancer would do a movie like that."

Leo smiled down at her as he pushed her gently along a shoveled path across the broad courtyard before Dartmouth's Hopkins Center for the Arts, universally nicknamed The Hop. "I warned you, Ma. I told you it wasn't *Yankee Doodle Dandy.*"

"You said it was a gangster movie," she persisted, "not an ode to a deranged psychopath."

Leo burst out laughing. "Wow. You make it sound pretty deep. I just liked it when he shot the car trunk full of holes to let the guy inside breathe, or when he went nutso in the prison dining hall after finding out his mother died."

She faced forward again as they neared the curb. "How did I end up with such a disturbed child?" she asked meditatively.

"Hey," he told her. "You got one son who's a cop. Stands to reason the other should go to the dark side. It's nature's balance."

He went to pass by her on his way to unlocking the car when she grabbed his wrist in a quick-moving wiry hand.

This time, her expression was soft and appreciative. "I've been doubly blessed, Leo," she told him. "Both my boys are just right."

He leaned over and kissed her wrinkled cheek, warm in the evening's chilliness. "I love you, too, Ma. I hear they're playing Polanski's *Repulsion* next week."

She tapped the side of his head playfully as he moved away. "Oh, now *that* sounds like a comedy."

"You have no idea," he admitted.

She watched him bustling about, unlocking doors, starting the engine to get the heater going. It wasn't all that cold even though it had been dark for several hours. Dartmouth's trademark commons was coated with a new layer of snow, which shimmered under the glow of dozens of traditionally designed streetlamps. They, along with the formal brick buildings looming darkly beyond them and the enormous library's beautifully lighted steeple at the far end, lent the entire scene a timelessness, as if she might have been waiting for her son to hook up a horse and sleigh instead of starting a Subaru.

"All set," he said, stepping behind her once more and easing her chair off the sidewalk to where it nestled beside the car's open door.

She reached out and took hold of the two handles Leo had attached just inside the opening, one high and one low, and nimbly used them to assist herself inside. Her legs were too weak to support her, but they did move, which was a godsend in situations like this. She was already attaching her seat belt by the time Leo opened the car's rear door to slip in the folded wheelchair.

He joined her moments later, making the car rock as he half fell into his seat. An enthusiast by nature, he never did anything by half, including the most mundane of actions.

"You want to stop somewhere for ice cream or cocoa or something?" he asked.

Now she was looking at the façade of The Hop, from which they'd just come on their usual Friday night outing. Designed by the same architect who later did Lincoln Center in New York, it even looked like the kind of place that would offer a broad sampling of the arts—a little rebellious by one light, slightly worn by another. She and Leo came frequently, local beneficiaries of the college's mission to be a generous cultural neighbor.

"No," she answered him. "Not tonight. Drive me around the commons, though, will you? I love the buildings."

Leo backed out of their parking space and slipped into the sparse traffic, taking his first left to access the long eastern reach of the commons.

"Feeling touristy?" he asked.

She was watching the buildings go by, but also the students, huddled in their winter clothing, marching determinedly in small groups or singly, intent on their mysterious goals, which could as easily have been the next beer or a rendezvous as some scholarly pursuit. Although she'd been a local her entire life, even if from Vermont just across the river, she'd never had the envious, resentful view of the college so many other "townies" harbored, nor had she delighted in the depiction of the place supposedly made in the movie *Animal House*. She worshipped education, and while her sons had be-

come a police officer and a butcher, and hadn't bene-
fited from Dartmouth's offerings, she'd made sure
they'd developed an appreciation for music, literature,
and art and trained them to be analytical, appreciative,
attentive, and kind.

She knew college students could be self-indulgent,
narcissistic, and careless with the gift they'd been offered. Those were the clichés. But as Leo slowly circled
the commons, quietly allowing for her meditation, she
relished the fantasy she'd held forever, of places like this
being the incubators of the mind, where kids learned to
think, sometimes despite their best resistance.

"You should've gone here, Ma," Leo finally said.

She turned away from the buildings to look at him. "I
came close enough," she said after a thoughtful pause. "I
got access to that library and passed along what you and
Joe could bear. It would have been fun actually to sit in
class, but I can't complain—I've read what a lot of their
professors wrote."

Leo laughed again. "And you got to fall asleep in class.
We were always taking books off your lap after you
dozed off."

She whacked his shoulder. "Once in a blue moon, after
spending all day chasing you two around."

"You did good, Ma," he said after a pause.

It was a gentle taunt. He delighted in mangling English
around her, since she worked so hard not to do so herself.
But this time, instead of correcting him, she chuckled and
admitted, "I think I done good, too."

He smiled and turned on his right turn indicator at the
stoplight, preparing to go down North Wheelock and the
bridge into Vermont at the bottom of the hill. Of course,
much of what they'd just been talking about dated back a

few years. His mother had slowed down recently, reading less and watching more television. And since landing in the wheelchair, she'd ceased using that library card.

Their years together were numbered, clearly.

In the darkness of the car, his smile faded. As silly as it sometimes sounded when he admitted it out loud, he'd lived with his mother all his life, so far, and he was well into middle age. His older brother Joe had been the restless one, leaving home early to join the service, seeing combat halfway around the world, going to college for a few years in California. Even now, he lived in Brattleboro, near the Massachusetts border, sixty miles to the south.

But Leo had never seen the attraction. He and their mom lived in the farmhouse he'd been born in, and his room overlooked the fields his father had once tilled. When the old man died, so many years ago, leaving behind two boys and a young widow, the three survivors had looked to each other for their grounding. Joe had used that as a springboard to go forth into the world; Leo had seen it as all he really needed. He began working at the market in Thetford Center, just down the hill from the farm, and settled into a life of dating girls lacking in serious intentions, working in the barn on old cars from the sixties, becoming the most highly prized butcher for twenty miles around, and establishing an easy and permanent friendship with his mother.

Which he knew was closing in on a natural end.

"You're awfully quiet all of a sudden," she said softly.

They had just reached the bridge spanning the Connecticut River, a newly rebuilt structure which its designers had accessorized with a series of gigantic, evenly spaced concrete balls—a source of some humor in a school renowned for its testosterone.

"Just thinking about the movie."

She let it go. Whatever its virtues, *White Heat* didn't merit an excess of reflection. Leo had something private on his mind, and she had a pretty good idea what it was, or what she feared it might be. While grateful for a lifetime of Leo's company, she was not unaware of the peculiarity of a middle-aged son still living with his mother. The thought that she—or her circumstances, first as a widow, then as an invalid—had encouraged this situation only made her feel guilty. That having been said, she was also a pretty good observer of people, and her take on her younger son was that he was not only happy with the status quo but increasingly worried about what to do after she died.

She could sympathize. She'd been in much the same boat when their father had died. A good and decent man, much older than she, he'd had his greatest influence on them all only after his death, when they'd discovered the huge void he'd so quietly filled.

She suspected that Leo, less than Joe, would find the world an oddly empty place, at least for a while, once she followed her late husband into death.

She stole a glance at him as he turned left onto Route 5 on the Vermont side of the bridge and began heading north, parallel to the interstate, which he knew she didn't enjoy as much.

"Thank you, Leo," she said.

He looked at her quickly, both his hands on the wheel, a good and practiced driver. "What for? I thought you hated the movie."

"For taking me anyhow, for not choosing the interstate, for being a good son. I'm not sure I tell you enough how grateful I am for everything. You've given up a lot for me."

He laughed, if a little cautiously. His mother wasn't prone to such comments. "Totally selfish, Ma. Do you know how many times I've used you as an excuse to shake off some female with big plans? Unbelievable. There are women up and down this valley who think you're the worst thing since Cruella DeVille. You should be calling a libel lawyer instead of patting me on the back for being such a wonderful son."

She smiled and shook her head. She should have known better. Leo was her showman, quick to grab a joke when faced with a serious moment.

She decided to allow him his choice. "Really?" she therefore reacted. "No wonder I've been getting those strange looks. Good Lord. I always thought it was my breath, or maybe something horrible coming out of my nostrils."

They were surrounded by darkness now, moving quickly and alone along the smooth, twisting road, paradoxically comforted by the dark, semifrozen expanse of the large river to their right. New Englanders often felt at home while isolated in the cold. It was that aspect of their environment that most outsiders compared to their demeanor but which they themselves saw as simply encouraging strong character.

Leo was surprised. "Are you kidding about that?" he asked. "Have you really noticed . . . ?"

He suddenly stopped speaking, his hands tightening on the wheel. "Damn . . ."

Alarmed, she looked first at him, then out the window, expecting a deer to be standing in the middle of the road, an almost common experience. Instead, the road was beginning to shift away as they slid out of control on a slight curve.

"Shit," Leo said through clenched teeth. "Hang on . . ."

She was ahead of him there, clutching both the dashboard and the uppermost handle beside her. "Leo," she said, almost a whisper.

Ahead of them, the landscape changed from the comfort of the black macadam to a blizzard of white snow as they plowed through an embankment that exploded across their windshield. Beneath them, they could hear the tearing of metal against the remnants of a hidden guardrail, along with their own seemingly disconnected shouting. They were first jarred by several abrupt encounters with buried stumps or boulders, then became weightless as the car began to barrel roll, causing their heads to be surrounded by flying maps, CDs, lose change, and an assortment of now-lethal tools that Leo normally kept in the back.

In the sudden darkness following the loss of both headlights, Leo's mother focused solely on the sounds around her, muffled and ubiquitous, coming from all sides as they continued farther and farther downhill. She began thinking about the cold water that might be waiting at the bottom—if that's the way they were headed.

And then it was over. In one explosive flash, she felt a shocking blow to the side of her head, the sense of some metallic object, perhaps a lug wrench, passing before her face, then nothing.

Leo opened his eyes briefly before shutting them again with a wince, brought up short by a burst of pain in his left eye. He paused a moment, trying to remember, sorting through the throbbing at his temples to remember what had happened.

"Mom?" he asked suddenly, attempting to see again, ignoring the pain. He shifted in his seat, looking in her direction. The car was pitch-black and utterly silent. Carefully, he reached out and touched her, the tips of his cold fingers slipping on something wet on the side of her head.

"Oh, Jesus," he murmured. He made to turn toward her and shouted in agony, the entire left side of his chest suddenly spiking as if electrified. He sat back, panting, and coughed, feeling like his lungs were full of phlegm. He gingerly pushed through his overcoat at his ribs with his good hand and winced.

"Goddamn it," he said, mostly to hear his own voice. "Mom?" he repeated then, reaching out a second time, but lower, feeling for her shoulder, which appeared to be fine—maybe merely because it was there at all.

But she wasn't moving.

It was cold, and the other thing his fingers had felt was snow. Somewhere, there was a broken window. He had no idea how long they'd been there, had no clue if they were visible from the road. He didn't even know if they were both alive.

He followed her shoulder up to her neck and burrowed his index finger between her collar and the scarf she was wearing, probing for a pulse. He was a butcher, he thought ruefully. At least he knew his way around a body.

His fingers were too cold. If her heart was beating, he couldn't feel it, but he doubted he could have anyway. At least that's the comfort he gave himself.

"Okay, okay," he said softly. "Probably just as well. No pain, no struggling. She's got her coat on. Could be worse."

Still using his right hand, he touched the window next
to him. Intact. He didn't feel like they were on their side,
and he couldn't hear running water, which meant they
hadn't reached the river. So far, so good.

He felt down to the door latch and pulled it. Nothing.
Probably jammed. With even fewer expectations, he tried
the electric window toggle. He was rewarded with a
gentle whirring sound and a cool waft of air against his
cheek.

"No shit," he muttered, noticing how hard it was to
breathe, actually to move his lungs. The window had lowered all the way. He considered shouting, but with the
cold air had also come a wider silence, as from a chasm
without bottom. He knew this road—it either had traffic
or it was empty. There were no pedestrians and few
homes.

He had to get out.

He moved his feet and found his lower body uninjured.
That was good. But even at a hundred percent, struggling
out the side window of a small car wasn't easy. And he
knew by now he was far from a hundred percent. Just like
he knew that wasn't phlegm in his lungs.

"Ma?" he said, barely whispering by now. "Can you
hear me? I got to try to get help."

Nothing.

He sighed, gritted his teeth, took hold of the steering
wheel with his good hand, and pushed up with his feet,
hoping to launch himself at least partway out the window.

The pain was beyond imagination. It felt like lava, filling him with heat and blinding light, exploding inside his
head and making him gasp for air. Beyond that, he could
feel something fundamental shift within him, as if the
cellar of a house had suddenly vanished into the earth,

leaving everything above it precariously poised above a void. For a split second, he could almost see himself hovering in the air, somewhere between Heaven and oblivion, like a cartoon character that has just walked off a cliff but hasn't yet yielded to gravity.

And then he, too, collapsed into the blackness and the utter, all-encompassing quiet of a winter night.